MW01505006

PAYTON'S PURSUIT

The Winters Sisters

Book Two

By

JOANNE JAYTANIE

Copyright 2016 by Joanne Jaytanie.
All rights are reserved. No part of this book may be used or reproduced in any manner without written permission except in the case of brief quotations used in articles or reviews.

Payton's Pursuit is a work of fiction. Names, characters, places and incidents are products of the writer's imagination or have been used fictitiously and are not to be construed as real. Any resemblance to persons living or dead, actual events, places, incidents or organizations is coincidental.

ISBN: 978-0-9967001-7-7

Edited by Ruth Ross and Self-Publishing Services LLC (www.self-publishing-service.com)
Formatted by Self-Publishing Services LLC (www.self-publishing-service.com)

Dedication

To my sweet Doberman girl, Anya. Anya was my constant writing companion. Sadly, she has left this world behind. Yet, I still picture her on her bed next to my desk, lying on her back snoring softly, with her pink belly exposed. I miss you every day.

The Doberman on the cover was my girl: American, Canadian, International Champion Foxfire's Dream Voyager, OA, NAJ, ROM ~ 'KES' and dame of Anya

Thank you to all who have supported me. Especially to my husband, my soulmate, and my best friend, Ralph.

Table of Contents

Acknowledgments

Photographer of Kes, the Doberman on cover –
   Denise Caley Stringfellow, whose creative eye
   always captured the essence of her subject.
Author photograph by –
   Sarah Burlingame, thank you for your unending
   patience.

Chapter One

An explosion reverberated throughout the office. Payton snapped her head up, and clenched her jaw as she held tight to her chair. She looked around and expected to see her pristine office littered with fallen items, but not one thing was out of place—how very odd. Another shock wave of emotion rippled through her office, and this time it knocked her completely out of her chair.

"Okay, I've had enough!" She picked herself up off the floor, smoothed the creases from her royal blue linen pants, and headed for the door. Kes, Payton's little red Doberman, paced the length of her office and mirrored Payton's agitation.

Payton opened the door with Kes hot on her heels. The dog shot past her and flew down the stairs as she made a beeline for the back door.

"Not this time kitten," Payton said, as she jogged down the stairs behind Kes. She reached down and briefly scratched the top of her satiny head. "I have no idea what your Aunt Victory is up to, and the last thing I need is for you to get into the fray." Kes looked up and whimpered at her. "Don't worry, I'll be right back."

Payton gave her one last pat and closed the door behind her. She jumped into the electric cart and headed to the Winters Corporation research campus.

She followed the footpath down the hill and pushed a button on the dashboard of the cart, which opened the imposing wrought-iron gate connected to a twenty-foot tall security fence. The fence divided the Winters' home from the corporation. Both were discreetly situated amongst giant evergreen trees. The magnificent sight of the campus thrilled Payton every time she set eyes on it. Her parents would surely have been proud.

Another wave of emotion barreled over her and caused her to nearly roll the cart.

"Blast it all. What in the name of Pete is going on down there?" The steering wheel slipped through her sweaty hands. She slowed the vehicle, wiped her hands with the towel she always carried, threw it back on the seat next to her, and placed a death grip on the wheel. A trickle of sweat slid down her back. She shivered and stomped on the gas pedal.

She stopped the cart outside of a large two-story glass and brick building which housed Victory's labs. *What was her sister doing?* Payton jumped out of the cart and made her way into the building. As she walked down the hall in the direction of the labs, unbridled fury flowed through her. Without a conscious thought, her mind fought back with a surge of serenity.

She found the door to her sister's lab wide open. The lab looked as if a wrecking ball had torn through the room. Files covered the floor, chairs and tables were overturned, and broken glass littered the area. Tiny cracks ran the length of a large glass wall partition. It now looked as though the partition was covered with spider webs coated by morning dew.

Victory squatted down next to a bear of a man, and both of them tried to pick up the shards of glass. Payton pursed her lips flat and crossed her arms in front of her chest as she watched her sister joke with him.

"What in the love of Pete is going on here?" Payton yelled, as the adrenaline continued to sear through her entire body, making her practically vibrate.

Victory and the man jumped up, and nearly knocked heads, startled and confused by Payton's sudden presence.

"Payton, I didn't hear you come in," Victory said. "I wondered when you would finally get the opportunity to meet our newest guest. Payton, meet Collin McBain."

The time had arrived and Payton couldn't put off meeting Collin McBain any longer.

"I would be lying if I said it's nice to meet the man who kidnapped my sister and almost got her killed." Payton's breath hitched in her throat and a sharp pain stabbed at her temples.

Collin lifted his head and ever so slowly brought his gaze to Payton's. His ocean-blue eyes locked on to hers. The outer edges of her vision began to dim. The room started to spin and before she could comprehend what happened, her world faded to black.

"Payton, Payton, can you hear me?"

Payton heard Victory's voice as she tried to clear the fog from her mind. She opened her eyes a crack as she cautiously took in her surroundings. How did she get to Victory's office? Victory sat next to her. Concern etched her face.

"What happened? How did I end up here?" Payton asked.

"You fainted. Here, take a sip of water," Victory said. She tilted a glass to her lips.

"How did I get here?"

"We tried to wake you. When we couldn't, Collin picked you up and carried you into my office."

Payton took the glass and tried to sit up. Her head throbbed.

"Seems as though I scared Collin off," she said.

"No. When I couldn't get you to wake up, I sent Collin out to find Dr. Russell. They should be here any time."

"What? Why? I don't need the doctor. I just fainted."

"You didn't just faint, Payton. You were out cold for thirty minutes."

"Thirty minutes? Impossible." Payton looked down at her watch. Sure enough, over forty minutes had passed since she left her home office. She looked up at Victory in confusion. "Maybe I'm coming down with something. The flu is going around the campus."

"The flu doesn't make you faint. Dr. Russell needs to take a look at you."

As if on cue, a woman in a white doctor's coat, with her black hair wrapped tightly in a high bun, scurried into the room.

"You're awake. Good. Mr. McBain had me greatly concerned. He said you were out for a good ten minutes," Dr. Russell said.

"More like thirty minutes," Victory said.

Payton threw her sister a smoldering stare.

"Thirty. Then it's good I'm here. You need a full examination, little lady," Dr. Russell said.

"I'm fine, really," Payton protested. "I've been extremely busy. In fact, I think I forgot to have lunch. I got light-headed from not eating and my blood sugar dropped. No big deal."

"Payton, I've explained to you the importance of taking care of yourself. Do you still spend your nights working in your home office? Did you get any sleep last night? You look pale and at this rate you will run yourself into the ground. Then who do you suppose will manage the campus?" Dr. Russell asked.

Dr. Russell sounded more like her mother than a doctor. Her mother—how she missed her mom. The anniversary of her parents' death passed only a few weeks ago. Despair started to flood her body. Both her mom and dad were killed in an auto accident a little more than five years ago, but those years had passed so quickly. No, she could not think about her mom now. Payton pushed the thoughts of her parents from her mind.

"Payton? Did you hear what I said?" Dr. Russell asked.

"What? Yes, yes, I know. I'll try and take better care of myself. I don't have time for a full exam now. Our grand opening gala is only two days away. I have a list a mile long to get done."

Dr. Russell studied her as she took her pulse and listened to her heart. "I'll make a deal with you. Provided you don't experience any more blackouts and you promise to eat, drink plenty of water, and get the rest you need, I will let you go—but only if you agree to schedule a full examination, which is to include a complete blood panel next week, right after your gala."

"Ugh. Fine, I agree to your terms. As if I have a choice."

"Good. Sit here a bit longer. Drink another glass of water before you even think about getting up."

Dr. Russell closed her bag and nodded to Victory and Payton. "Ladies. I'll be on my way," she said, as she headed out the door. "My assistant will call you tomorrow to schedule an appointment, Payton, and I expect to see you before you head out for your dog shows," the doctor said, and she continued down the hall.

"Ugh," Payton repeated. "My fainting wasn't a big deal. Now look what you have done."

"Payton, what happened is serious. You've run yourself ragged. Between trying to get our campus fully up and functioning, along with organizing the huge grand opening gala, it's a wonder this is the first time you collapsed. You do realize you won't be any good to any of us if you get sick?" Victory asked.

Payton decided it would be better to keep the fact that she'd had a couple other blackouts to herself for the time being. *No sense in upsetting Victory any further.*

"I know, and I'm not the only who has run myself ragged. You haven't been to the house for dinner all week. Tristan will be upset if you let yourself get sick."

"Oh no, don't even attempt to turn this situation around. We are talking about you at the moment, not me," Victory said, as she poked her sister in the arm. "Fine. I'll be sure to be home for dinner, if you promise to join me."

"It's a deal. Now, I've drunk my two glasses of water. I need to get back up to the house. I have a phone conference in twenty minutes." Payton sat up and swung her legs to the floor; so far so good. She stood up and felt steady enough, except for a blasted headache that came from the percussion section gigging in her head.

"Here," Victory handed her two pills. "Dr. Russell said to take these for your headache. And before you ask, the pain shows all over your face."

Payton left the building and walked back to her cart. She started to feel a slight spinning again. "Dammit, not now," she muttered to herself.

She had the vivid sensation of being watched. She looked up and scanned the grounds. Way off to her right, up by the tree line, she saw him. Collin sat under the trees and watched her. She could swear she felt the heat of those devastating light-blue eyes. The spinning in her head threatened to make her sick or black out again. What in heaven's name could be wrong with her? She broke her gaze from Collin, turned her back to him, and got in the cart. She needed to get out of here, now. To be safe, she decided to take the long way back to the house. It would cut the time close for her meeting, but it would keep her from going in Collin's direction. She stomped on the gas pedal.

* * * *

Collin sat motionless and watched Payton's every move. *What the hell happened back there?* One minute he experienced another of his uncontrollable fits of rage, and the next moment a blanket of calm and serenity wrapped around him. Amazing feeling after so long. Those hazel eyes were gorgeous, but women never made him feel serene, no matter how pretty. All three of the sisters were something, but Payton was the pick of the litter. As breathtaking as Payton was in her designer blue suit with her shimmering wavy cinnamon hair falling past her shoulders, she still couldn't be the source of the calm that enveloped him.

"Get a grip, McBain," Collin scolded himself. She didn't even notice him. Hell, she hit the floor, out cold the second he looked up at her. Collin didn't even get a chance to properly introduce himself—not that she would care. He got the distinct feeling Payton would never forgive him for kidnapping her sister. *What does it matter?* Not like he would spend much time around her anyway.

Like Victory said, he wasn't in his right mind when he kidnapped her last year. Victory forgave him. If Payton were petty enough to hold a grudge, he'd do his best to avoid her. *Who am I trying to kid? She will make my life miserable the entire time I live on her campus.*

Collin watched Payton turn her back to him and get into the cart. Yep, she hated him. She intended to avoid him and take the long way back to her house. He was here to stay. He would be living and working on her campus for who knew how long, but that didn't mean he needed her blessing.

Ten bungalows were built on the outskirts of the campus and Victory insisted both Morgan and he have their own private bungalows. Victory would always support and remain loyal to Collin, but sadly he could tell her sister Payton didn't feel the same. He couldn't blame her really. Up to now he'd done nothing to win her loyalty. *Thank God I work with the more mature sister.*

Hell, Victory continued to do everything in her power to find a way to help him cope with his current situation, which never ceased to surprise him. To be fair, Victory insisted there was no "cure," which meant the changes made to his DNA could not be undone. Nonetheless, she continued to search for a way to help him deal with his condition and get some control over these bouts of rage, blackouts, and lapses in time. The sooner Victory discovered a solution, the better it would be, and not only for his sake. Collin's blackouts and rage were trouble for everyone, and he was terrified he'd hurt someone again.

He stood up, stretched his six-foot three-inch muscular frame, and jogged back down to the lab. He shouldn't leave Victory to clean up his latest mess.

Collin entered the lab and found two men removing the remains of the glass partition and Victory fully engrossed in something on her computer.

"Sorry about the mess," he said to Victory and the men.

Victory looked up and smiled. "Don't give it another thought. Where did you go? I was beginning to worry about you."

"Figured I needed to make myself scarce. Don't think your sister thinks much of me," Collin said.

Victory stopped and focused her full attention on him. "What makes you say such a thing?"

"What is there to like? First, I kidnapped you and nearly got you killed, and now, I've destroyed your brand new lab."

"Collin, none of us hold your past or present actions against you. From the instant you were injected with the wolf DNA, all bets were off. You and Morgan are the first humans ever injected with foreign DNA. No one has any idea what changes to expect, and as we already witnessed, the DNA affects each of you differently."

"A nice way to put it," Collin snorted. "Morgan's abilities are an asset to him. Me, I'm evolving into some angry wild animal, with no sense of right or wrong."

"Tell me you don't really see yourself that way, Collin? You, my friend, are totally off base. True, Morgan's naturally heightened abilities have helped him adapt more easily. We will find a way to deal with your bouts of rage. In no way does it qualify you as an animal," Victory insisted.

"Whatever you say, doc," Collin said. He tried to act nonchalant. Sometimes he could kick himself. He knew Victory felt responsible for the genetic tampering he had suffered on the island, and he had a way of needling her with her fears constantly. "Dumb jackass," he murmured under his breath.

"I heard you," Victory said.

"Dimrod." How many times would it take him to remember the woman's keen sense of hearing? It shouldn't be difficult to recall since they shared the same trait.

"If anyone had done to Emma what I have done to you, they wouldn't live to see tomorrow. All in all, I suppose I have to give her credit. I guess Payton is handling this better than I would. She has every right to not want to spend one minute in my presence."

"You have totally misconstrued the entire situation, Collin. Payton pushes herself way too hard. Our facility sprung up in only eight months and we have tripled the number of our employees. Payton is the CEO and oversees every aspect of what happens on this campus. She's extremely hands-on. Don't take her reaction personally. She is tired and overworked."

Well, wasn't he a dumb ass? Go ahead; make her sister look like a cold-hearted bitch. Now I will win some brownie points for sure, he thought. "It looks like the situation is pretty well under control here. If you don't need me anymore, I think I'll go hunt down Morgan and take a run," he said.

When Collin first arrived at the campus, Victory insisted that he must always be accompanied when doing PT. She had established that stress and adrenaline were his triggers when he lost control. However, until she could define which types of stressors and adrenaline, he needed a constant chaperone for all activities involving any situation that might cause a reaction. Morgan had to escort him even while doing exercise, which in the normal person would reduce stress. However, his whacked-out system now reacted differently. Since Victory couldn't be certain of the outcome, Morgan was quickly becoming Collin's shadow.

"Sounds like a good idea. Try to stay focused and on task. When your mind wanders and your senses become more acute, you know you run the risk of triggering your wolf DNA." Victory looked at the clock on her desk. "I promised Payton I would join her for dinner. I should probably head out of here in an hour. Collin, can I ask you a personal question?"

"Why not? You already know all the dirt on me," Collin said.

"Who's Emma?"

"My baby sister."

"Oh, I know Morgan has a sister, but I wasn't aware you do. You've never mentioned her before."

"One more thing Morgan and I have in common; we're both big brothers."

"Seriously? How wonderful, Collin. Is Emma here in Washington? We should arrange a time when she can come and visit you."

"Emma lived here until just recently. Like all the other aspects of my life, the timing sucks. I called to speak to her when I first arrived back in Washington, right before Morgan and I left for the assignment at Braxton's facility. She's no longer in Washington State. She's now in San Francisco at some fancy boarding school. Damn it all to hell, she is only twelve years old and her mother has already shipped her off. The woman never was any kind of a parent. Emma might as well be in China."

"Oh Collin, I'm sorry. Hopefully you can catch up with her when she comes home for the holidays," Victory said.

"Maybe." He didn't want to think or talk about Emma any more. "I don't want to keep you, doc. I'll see you in the morning."

* * * *

Would this day never end? Payton wondered as she headed back down to the campus. There was a problem with the bungalows and the builder needed her on-site before she could call it done. As she reached the first bungalow, she experienced a searing hot stab to her temple. She rubbed a hand across it to try and ease the pain. "Now what?" she muttered.

She parked the cart and started to the area where the builders worked.

"Collin, knock it off," a booming male voice sounded.

She looked to her right and saw the lights in Morgan's bungalow flash on and off. Payton headed for the disruption. She would not have these men destroy the bungalow before it was even a month old. She stormed up to the door and knocked, and was rewarded with a crash.

"Collin, I'm serious man. If you don't pull yourself together, you are really going to piss me off," Morgan said.

Payton stepped inside. Before she could confront the two men, a hockey skate whizzed past, missed her head by scant inches, and crashed through the bay window. Morgan ducked and bobbed to stay out of the trajectory of flying objects. Collin stood in the middle of the room, sweat pouring down his body and danger and destruction radiating off him. Payton's mouth fell open as she struggled to process the scene. She yelped and ducked as the twin to the first hockey skate hurtled straight toward her, causing the banging inside her skull to rise to a fevered pitch.

Both men turned in the direction of the sound. The remainder of the objects in play dropped to the floor. Collin, wild-eyed and panting, glared at her for a heartbeat and then turned and propelled himself out of the broken bay window. Morgan rushed over to Payton and scooped her up from the floor. Using his foot, he kicked a chair right side up and gently placed her down. He hurried to the kitchen and grabbed a towel and glass. He filled the glass with water and soaked the towel. He returned to Payton and placed the towel across her forehead as he handed her the glass.

"Are you okay?" Morgan asked. "You weren't hit, were you?"

She struggled to regain her equilibrium and sit upright. "I'm fine—really," Payton said. "What in the world were you two fighting about?"

"We weren't fighting. Collin had a bad day and was telling me about it. I was distracted, trying to get myself ready to go running, and I guess I didn't realize he was getting upset. Something triggered and he flipped out. Regrettably, you walked in on him almost in full wolf mode."

"Almost—" Payton said.

"Believe me, it gets a lot worse. If you are really okay, I should head out to find him. Victory will have a cow if she finds out Collin is running amuck." Morgan rubbed absently at his eyebrow. "You aren't going to tell her, are you?"

"No, but I think she will figure it out when she sees this place."

Payton caught the worry as it flashed across Morgan's face.

"Don't worry, Morgan. Go and find Collin. I'll get the builders to replace the windows tonight. I expect the two of you to clean this place up and behave yourselves for the rest of the evening."

"You have my word," Morgan said as he started for the door. "As soon as I can locate him, I'll drag his sorry ass back here."

Chapter Two

"You have the attendance list finalized and the security is tight?" Payton asked Noah for the umpteenth time.

"Don't worry, Payton. We have security under control. Your only job tonight is to be the perfect host," Noah reassured her.

"I'm sorry, Noah. It's just that the Secretary of the Department of Homeland Security will be in attendance tonight. I simply can't believe the secretary is coming to our little town," Payton said.

"He is not coming to see the town. The secretary is here to get a look at the awesome state-of-the-art facility you and your sisters built," Noah said.

"With help from the government." Payton always felt uncomfortable in the limelight. "We never would have been able to build our facility here if they weren't willing to sell us the state land, and don't forget about the contract we have with them."

"Maybe so, but you, Victory, and Willow are the ones who have made this all happen. Enjoy tonight. There aren't many people able to say they hosted a party the Secretary of Homeland Security attended. Our team will handle all the heavy work," Noah said, with a cocky smile. "Tonight's mission is the kind of mission we live for, a walk in the park. Tonight will be a flyby for the secretary. He's only scheduled to be here for an hour, tops. You take him on a tour and he gets his photo ops. Everyone is happy."

"Are you sure we have control of all the photographers? Lawrence Braxton, from Biotec can't discover that Collin or Morgan are here."

"Don't worry. It's covered. Morgan and Collin will be out of sight before a single camera comes out, and because of the high security, all phones will be collected at the main gate. I will not allow that man a chance to reacquire Morgan, and the longer he believes Collin is dead, the better. Really Payton, we are pros at this. I would never compromise the anonymity of my team. Please, just enjoy your gala," Noah said.

Payton wished she could take Noah's cue and remain calm. All the same, in less than two hours, their facility would be filled with senators, mayors, and specialists in every field imaginable, along with all the 'who's who' of the scientific community. She wished Wyatt could be here to oversee his team. Unfortunately, Wyatt got called away to Washington, D.C., where he needed to report to his boss, General Roberts. The timing couldn't have been worse. Thank goodness Tristan remained behind.

"Where's Tristan?"

"He went to oversee security; Homeland Security isn't good enough in his mind. He doesn't trust anyone else to organize it."

They continued walking through the building.

"You did an awesome job with the transformation of the ballroom," Noah said.

"I have to say, I'm in awe of how my decorations came together."

Payton took in the entire room for the first time. Tonight's event was in the main ballroom, a room that could house three basketball courts. The building was appropriately named, "The Meeting Place." The sisters wanted a name easily remembered, and it was their hope this building would be used by their community for events year-round.

The room sparkled tonight, with its warm red mahogany floor. Payton had selected oversized crystal chandeliers to be hung throughout the ballroom. She'd decided on intimate round tables that seated eight each, covered with crisp white linens. Fine china trimmed with silver and Waterford crystal wine and water glasses shone on each table. There were eye-catching crystal hurricane candleholders as centerpieces on each table; each holder housed a tall white pillar candle and was immersed in fresh cut flowers. Magnificent works of art created by local artists decorated the walls, and massive vases of flowers dotted the outskirts of the room.

Noah sniffed the air. "I'd say you outdid yourself, Payton. Not only is the ballroom beautiful, it smells like we're in a flower garden."

"The room smells divine." She took one last look around and said, "I guess I need to get back to the house and get ready for tonight. I'll return in an hour. Give me a call if you need me."

"Take your time, Payton," Noah said.

She flashed him a quick smile. "And might I say you look handsome in your dress blues."

"Why thank-you, ma'am," he replied with a slight bow. "It's one of those times we all have to look our best. Logan will arrive at your door with the limo to escort you and your sisters back down here when you're ready."

Payton said her goodbyes and left the building. She stepped out the door and stopped to appreciate the campus. She marveled at the transformation of her and her sisters' property and their lives. Nine short months ago she lived alone with her Dobermans in the family home on a sprawling fifty-acres right outside Poulsbo, Washington. She managed her parents' company, the Winters Corporation, which at the time stood at the other end of town. Today, she shared the family home with her sisters, Victory and Willow, along with Victory's husband, Tristan. While Payton loved the idea of the house once again full of family, the rest of the changes in her life required some getting used to.

The Winters Corporation had outgrown their original site and the sisters had chosen to build a new campus on the far side of their personal property. They purchased the adjacent twenty-five acres of state forest from the government, and with a sizeable bank loan, built a brand new state-of-the-art research facility. Payton felt relieved they had decided to forgo the offer of a government grant. The Winters sisters were financially overtaxed at the present, yet they weren't concerned. With Payton's expertise, they would be back in the black in no time. Thanks to the local bank, the Winters Corporation belonged to no one except the family—and of course the bank.

* * * *

Mayor Franklin volunteered to be the announcer for the evening's event. She had also promised to keep the gala flowing. Franklin watched as the Winters sisters entered the ballroom and paused to absorb their surroundings. The room fell silent with anticipation. All eyes turned toward them. All three sisters wore full-length gowns. Willow's was a crimson one-shouldered gown that hugged her and flared out at the floor. Her blonde hair was pulled up with a few select curls to frame her face. Victory wore a royal blue gown, which fell straight down from her shoulders and was slit a third of the way up her right leg. Her caramel-colored hair was a riot of loose curls. Payton wore a strapless violet blue gown that spilled over her curves like water. Her cinnamon-colored hair looked kissed with gold and was pulled loosely back in a twist that flowed down her back.

The room erupted in applause. "May I introduce the hosts of tonight's wonderful gala," the mayor said.

* * * *

Victory, Willow, and Payton smiled and gave slight curtsies. Jack, Logan, and Noah walked up to the sisters and offered their arms to escort them into the ballroom.

"You women sure know how to make an entrance," Noah joked.

"Thank you, I think," Payton said. The activity in the ballroom had increased tenfold since she left an hour earlier, and the energy resonated through her. "Are Morgan and Collin well-hidden?"

"They are. What better way for them to blend in than to be dressed in civilian clothes? They are just two more guys in tuxes. No big deal," Noah said. "Morgan is assigned to casually walk the perimeter of the back of the building, and Collin is manning the security cameras. He is holed up in the security room with one of your regular guards, totally out of the line of fire."

"I really don't see how we are going to pull this off. I mean, for goodness sakes, Collin was in the hospital, with doctors, and nurses, and staff," Payton said.

"Don't worry, Payton. We have a lid on the situation. Yes, Collin spent time in the hospital, the difference being the hospital was a high-security facility. He was admitted under a false identity, and there are only two top-security medical personnel who know his true identity," Noah reassured her. "Biotec and Braxton know nothing, except that Collin fell off a cliff and died."

"Yes, but it's the Secretary of Homeland Security we want to keep the information from," Payton said.

"Believe me, this isn't the first time, and it won't be the last time he is kept out of the loop. The president, General Roberts, and Victory all believe it is imperative to keep Collin's survival a secret, and it's in everyone's best interest. The secretary is in attendance merely to see that the government's money will be put to good use. Tonight, everyone is here to see your extraordinary facility. Tomorrow, everyone will return to their lives, all warm and fuzzy. Collin and Morgan will remain ghosts and return to their private lives, such as they are."

"I'm sorry for my obsessive concern, Noah. I know you're right."

"Don't take this wrong, but why don't you and Willow have escorts tonight? I assume there are a couple of lucky guys you two date," Noah said.

"Willow is extremely busy between hiring new employees to get our campus up and running, and flying back and forth to England to help with the transition there. She hasn't had any time for a relationship," Payton said.

"What about you?" Noah asked.

"I have too much on my plate right now. I couldn't even think about starting a relationship. Besides, I'm terrible when it comes to picking the right guy."

"I don't believe you for a second," Noah said.

"It's true. The last guy I had a serious relationship with was when I attended graduate school. I thought I was in love and he was the one. Right. He always asked about our company, how things were going, and what projects the corporation was working on. I chalked it up to his interest in me." She made a puffing sound. "I realized how off-base my judgment was after my parents were killed. He didn't love me; he loved our company. He actually had the nerve to inform me he would be the best person to manage the corporation."

"Ow, that had to sting," Noah said. "Don't let one idiot taint your life and keep you from finding Mr. Right. Believe me Payton, there are tons of egotistical jerks out there. There are also tons of really great guys and you deserve one of them."

"Maybe one day. Not now, though. The campus demands my full attention." She tilted her head up to look into his face and smiled. "Thank you, sir, for the kind escort. I should take my leave of you and join my sisters."

As Payton started across the ballroom, a tremor cascaded down her spine. She continued her pace and scanned the vicinity to locate the source. She saw nothing and no one that should cause such a reaction. She slowed her pace to take another look around and caught a movement out of her peripheral vision. In one of the corners halfway up the wall, she noticed the security camera tracked her movement. She stopped and stared at the camera, and observed that it also stopped. She tore her gaze away and proceeded toward her sisters. A slight throb started in her temple.

"Dammit, not now," she mumbled to herself, as she stroked the side of her head. If she made it through the night, she only had one more week until the dog shows. She loved to pack up her motor home, load her dogs, and head for the shows; it gave her time to unwind, fully appreciate her dogs, and spend time with her friends. She planned to stop along the way and enjoy a day or two alone at a campsite where she could clear her mind of all the demands of the company. She swore she would take the entire two weeks off to relax and enjoy time alone with her dogs.

Payton caught up to her sisters, who were being introduced to the secretary.

"And here she is," Victory said. "Mr. Secretary, this is our sister, Payton. Without her there would be no campus."

"Pleased to meet you, Payton," the secretary said, as he reached out to take her hand. "I was just telling Victory and Willow that your research campus is very important to the country. We have high hopes for the future and I want you to know that any and all of my resources are at your disposal."

"Thank you, Mr. Secretary. Victory is our head of research, and as such that will be her call. I have complete faith in my sister's abilities," Payton said.

"As do I. But, please do not hesitate to call on me, if need be. I'm sure you all understand the military implications of Braxton's experimentation. In conjunction with the contract comes my promise of additional scientists and labs, and money to pay these people, when you so chose. From what I know of Braxton, he is a madman. He has killed at least one of our military men, Collin McBain, and that in my eyes is one too many."

"Let's begin our tour of the campus," Payton said. She dropped her gaze and blushed.

* * * *

Collin needed to be kept out of the line of fire during the gala, due to his unstable outbursts and because he was supposed to be dead. As a result, he was assigned to the security room, where he and the guard stared at the bank of screens before them and kept an eye out for anyone or anything that looked suspicious.

He understood the "all hands on deck," for their team had a limited number of men, and every man had a job. He also figured Tristan wanted him somewhere where an eye could be kept on him. He appreciated the effort, but unfortunately it didn't make a damn bit of difference. He felt hemmed in and uncomfortable. True, there was only one other person in the room, yet still he felt inundated by people, even if they were only images on a screen. Consequently, it took every bit of focus for him to keep himself together.

The last thing the sisters needed was for him to spiral into a fit of rage in the middle of their important event, ruining the gala and giving Payton one more reason to despise him. *Why did it matter what she thought?* From what he could see, Payton Winters was just one more spoiled rich girl, totally focused on business and making a profit, and he was their newest asset.

Try as he might, Collin found it more and more difficult to stay in control while being immersed in people and their thoughts. Their emotions rolled off them and saturated his mind. At this rate, he would have to burrow himself into some deep dark hole or go insane.

He felt more and more agitated, as though his own skin suffocated him. The blackness of rage began to consume him, and he knew he would have to escape soon before he totally lost his grip on sanity and howled like a wolf.

Using the controls on one of the cameras, he surveyed the room to locate Noah or Logan. Yes, he had an earpiece, but he didn't want to risk being overheard by the guard. He saw her then. She looked like a Greek goddess, and his breath caught in his throat. She wore a ravishing strapless purplish blue gown that looked as if it were made especially for her. The gown hugged her every lush curve. She glided across the ballroom floor, her red hair shimmering and flowing down her back. Simultaneously, he noticed the beast within him start to quiet. Coincidence? It had to be—it better be—and yet he couldn't deny this happened to be the second time that seeing Payton Winters brought a sensation of peace and quieted his beast.

As if she sensed his stare, she turned to the camera, stopped, and stared directly into the lens. It felt as though they locked eyes. For a heartbeat, he saw a look of pain flash across her beautiful face. Collin braced himself, but his reaction to her rejection was muted. He expected anger to overwhelm him. He waited. Nothing. *How could that be?* He wondered. What spell did Payton hold over him? Did she do it on purpose? Was she even aware of the effect she had on him? Could it possibly be he'd found something or someone to anchor him, to bring him some sanity? Why her? Why not someone he enjoyed being around. She would definitely become a top priority to him; he needed to figure out their connection. Although, there did remain one slight problem—she despised him.

Chapter Three

"I can't tell you how sorry I am," Collin mumbled through gritted teeth, as he found himself picking up shards of glass off of the lab floor—again. His emotions got the better of him and he managed to shatter the glass partition for the second time in less than a week.

"It's not your fault, Collin. It's still all new. It will take some time to get total control over your emotions," Victory said.

"Yeah, well at the rate I'm breaking things, Payton is going to start taking the cost of these partitions out of my hide." *And probably enjoy doing it.*

"Don't worry about the partitions. Maybe we should use something stronger. What concerns me is the length of time it takes you to recover from these issues. You stormed out of here over two hours ago. I have to say, I was worried sick until Morgan found you. I know the gala proved difficult for you. Is it still a source of discomfort twenty-four hours later? Collin, I am concerned for your well-being. If only I could discover one tiny lead to point me in the right direction."

Should he tell her? Victory would probably think he was totally insane. But each day he lost his battle a little more, and now instead of a blackout for an hour or two, the blackouts were stretching to six hours or longer. The past weekend he'd lost an entire day. He knew if he told her the truth it would certainly upset her.

"Maybe I know something," Collin said cautiously.

"Really? What? Collin, if you have any information you need to share it with me," Victory said.

"You're gonna think I'm crazy."

"No, I won't. At this point, any information could help with your issues."

"Issues," Collin snorted. "Only you would call my psycho behavior an *issue*. It's Payton."

"What about her? I told you not to take it personally. I promise you, she doesn't hate you."

"No, that's not what I mean. When Payton is around me, she seems to calm me. I feel like she pulls me back from the edge of insanity. Don't say it. I know it's crazy."

Victory stared at him.

Collin could see the wheels turn in Victory's head. She got a faraway look when she started to process new information.

"Victory—did you hear what I said?"

Victory shook her head.

"Yes, I heard you, and no, I don't think you're crazy. I noticed your change in demeanor last week when Payton came down to see what happened the first time you broke the partition. I wondered at the time what brought her down here. Your melt down wasn't loud enough for her to hear you all the way up at the house. Even with my ultra-keen hearing, I'm not sure I would've heard your outburst from the house. You recovered quickly once she arrived, although at the time I didn't put the two together," Victory said.

"Yeah, and I've noticed she hasn't shown her face since, at least not when I'm around."

"She has locked herself up in her home office, trying to see her way clear to take off for the dog shows this weekend. If what you are saying is true, this could be the big break I've been searching for and quite beneficial for you, Collin," Victory said.

"You think? I don't think Payton will see this breakthrough in the same way," Collin said.

"She'll be fine. Don't worry about her. At least you have given me something to go on. I feel I have spun my wheels for months and I was beginning to wonder if I took on more than I am capable of. A prime example of why I had hoped Claremont would team up with us. The ability to work alongside them would've provided additional experts to bounce ideas off."

"Claremont?"

"Yes, they were the company I worked for when Braxton kidnapped me. Regrettably the Claremont board decided they didn't want to be involved in a government contract."

"Victory, you are the leading expert in your field. You're amazing. You don't need Claremont and I assume the government bigwigs felt the same way," Collin said.

She studied him for a moment. A smile spread across her face.

"Thank you, Collin. I'm honored you have so much faith in me." She looked at the antique clock on her desk; it was five on the dot. "Collin, let's call it a night.

I need to have a talk with my sisters and come up with a plan for you, which must include Payton."

"Good luck with that. I wouldn't want to be you when you fill Payton in on your bit of news."

* * * *

"What's important enough I had to leave my personnel reports unfinished?" Willow asked. She held the back door open for her petite black Doberman, Asia, and followed her into the house. "Have I mentioned how much I love the fact I am able to work at home and take Asia to work with me every day? Thankfully I have definitely found the perfect spot for her overstuffed chair, right next to my desk. She is wonderful with all the employees. She has become my official greeter. By putting people at ease, she makes my job easier—especially during intense conversations. Since we increased our personnel by two hundred people, Asia is my lifesaver."

"Asia's just in time for dinner," Victory said. "Asia, go lay down." She walked to the other side of the kitchen and plopped down next to Dax, Parker, and Kes. Victory placed the last bowl on the dog table and turned to the anxiously awaiting brood. "Okay, come over here and sit." All four Dobermans did as they were told. They sat directly in front of their own bowls and never took their eyes off of them, drool spilling from their mouths. "Good dogs. Okay." Before the last word completely left her mouth, they dove into their meals.

Payton giggled as she continued to chop vegetables for their salad. "Well, at least the dogs like your cooking."

"Hey, watch it. Back me up, Willow," Victory said, and frowned at her sister.

"I have to go with Payton on this one. Your cooking skills leave a lot to be desired," Willow said. "Thank goodness you live with us. I bet Tristan doesn't even know you can't cook, let alone boil water."

"I can too." Victory glowered at her two sisters, who shook their heads in unison. "Okay, maybe you're right." She folded her arms over her chest and thought. "Teach me. Teaching me to cook will give us a good reason to spend some quality time together."

"Under one condition," Payton said. "We all stay around to clean up afterward, and I don't want to hear any excuses like, 'I have to be someplace' in order to get out of clean up."

"Boy, you drive a hard bargain," Willow said. "All right; I'm in. I wouldn't want Tristan to starve to death if you and I are ever out of town at the same time."

"Very funny," Victory said, as she handed Willow a glass of wine. "At least I can pour a mean glass of wine."

All three of the sisters broke out in laughter.

"Speaking of Tristan…where is he?" Willow asked.

"He needed to work late again tonight. With Wyatt out of the office, Tristan is doing both of their jobs. He can't wait until his brother gets back in town. We hardly ever see each other; he is stuck in the office constantly—and he's not the office type."

"Let's get the salad and pasta on the table. We can sit down for dinner and hear what has Victory all atwitter," Payton said.

Victory waited to broach the subject of Collin until after they finished their meal. She refilled each of their wine glasses while she contemplated the best way to start.

"Come on, sis. We both know you too well. Just start at the beginning," Willow said.

"There lies the problem. I'm not really sure where the beginning is. Okay," she took in a deep breath and started. "Last summer when I took a few weeks' vacation here at the house and we helped Payton with some of the remodel, remember how we finally decided the time had come to move on with our lives? Losing Mom and Dad almost destroyed us. Four years in mourning is a long time to grieve and not move forward."

"I know," Payton said. "I couldn't find the inner strength. I realize now the fault lay on my shoulders, for keeping the house like a time capsule. I guess I thought if I didn't change anything, I could pretend their deaths never happened. It was stupid."

"It wasn't stupid, Payton," Willow reassured her. "How unbearably difficult for you to stay behind and never leave the house. Victory and I chose to ignore their deaths, too. We did it by never coming home. Nevertheless, in the end we came together and moved forward, and that is what counts."

"Payton, you have it all wrong. I'm not chastising you for how you handled your grief," Victory said. "I want to talk to you about Mom's office. The one room you refused to change. Willow and I convinced you to make the space your own. I wanted you to have Mom's desk, and that's why I took on the project of refinishing it."

"And I'm genuinely thankful you did. I love Mom's—my office. I find peace and inspiration when I'm in there. I never said thank you," Payton said.

"Knowing how you love the space is all the thanks I need," Victory said. She reached out to give Payton's hand a squeeze. "Anyway, while I prepared to strip down the desk, I noticed a bottom trim piece had come loose. I pulled on the trim and the piece opened like a tiny door. I was attempting to glue the piece securely back into place when my fingers skimmed across a strange bump—something taped to the back of the trim. I pulled on the tape and found a USB drive."

"What?" Payton asked.

"Why didn't you tell us?" Willow asked.

"It took us an extremely long time to get to where we were. I couldn't inflict any more pain and concern on the two of you," Victory said.

Payton and Willow stared at Victory. Silence rang through the room for what seemed like an eternity.

Willow broke the silence first. "You have always felt you needed to shield us. We're all grown women now, Victory."

"I know, and I'm sorry. The information I found on the drive shocked me, and I guess if I'm being honest with myself, I needed time to digest what I discovered," Victory said.

"What did you find?" Payton whispered softly.

"Mom's personal diary—or at least part of her diary. We all know the stories about how Mom had a tough time conceiving. That it took her until the age of thirty-four to get pregnant with us."

Both Payton and Willow nodded, not uttering a word.

"In her diary I found a brief mention of her work on the fertility drug she used. I assumed she fine-tuned the drug to her specific DNA for maximum benefit," Victory said.

"Her fine-tuning the drug would make sense, since she was a brilliant geneticist and molecular biologist," Payton said.

"True, except what if they did more extensive changes?" Victory asked.

"You mean *she*, what if she did more extensive changes," Payton said.

"No, I mean *they*, as in Mom and Dr. Ryker," Victory said. "In her diary, Mom reveals how she couldn't get pregnant. She went to her colleague, Dr. Ryker, and explained her problem. She asked him if he would be willing to work with her and help her fine-tune the formula she invented. But what if they did more than just fine-tune?"

"What are you trying to get at?" Willow asked.

"I'm not sure yet, but I can tell you that Mom invented a drug and she used it to help get pregnant with us. Mom mentions Dr. Ryker and talks about them testing the drug together. Unfortunately, we have no way to verify any information from him. When Dr. Ryker went on vacation to England fifteen years ago he disappeared. No one has heard from or seen him since," Victory said.

"That's crazy. I thought he moved to England," Willow said. "I'm positive his personnel file claims he moved to England. It didn't mention a word about him disappearing. Okay, so what you are saying is, Dr. Ryker disappeared and Mom manipulated her fertility drugs. That's what you couldn't tell us? What's done is done. It's not the end of the world and like you said, we need to move on."

"It's not the whole story," said Victory. She took another deep breath and attempted to center her thoughts.

"Victory," Tristan's voice popped into her head.

"I'm fine, sweetheart. Sorry I interrupted your work. I'm in the middle of explaining everything to my sisters," Victory said to him.

She felt wrapped in the warmth of his embrace as he faded from her mind.

"Victory, are you okay?" Payton asked.

She smiled reassuringly at them and refocused on the task at hand. "Yes, I'm fine. I'll explain about that too."

Her sisters stared at her in absolute confusion.

"You know I have always been able to understand what animals are feeling, and you have both teased me about my hearing ability," Victory said.

"Actually you're kind of creepy about your hearing ability. As far as being able to understand animals' basic feelings, I think that is what makes you such an outstanding vet—your empathy," Payton said.

"But your hearing ability has sure come in handy over the years," Willow said.

"You have no idea," Victory said. "My hearing isn't only keen, it's unnaturally so, like a dog. I can hear up to twice the frequency range of human ability."

"That's not possible," Payton said.

"I knew my keen hearing would freak you two out, so I never told you," Victory said. "While I was held captive at the Biotec facility, Tristan discovered I have another special trait. I can amplify others' telepathic abilities. I became able to speak to Tristan telepathically, and he to me, although I still need to work on making out all of his words. His feelings and emotions are always crystal clear, except the words don't always come through. Tristan on the other hand, never experienced a single problem in understanding every word I said telepathically to him. Never, since the first time I started using my ability. Most likely because he and his brother, Wyatt, have possessed a telepathic connection since birth, his mind tended to be open to someone else's thoughts."

"This is crazy," Payton said. She was always the last to be convinced of new things, especially if she were asked to believe in something she could not actually see.

"Are you telling us you can understand when anyone communicates telepathically?" Willow asked.

"No, I can't understand them. I provide power to their connections. When we were held captive on Braxton's island, we were surrounded with an advanced security system. Somehow the system blocked all telepathic powers. I have continually worked on figuring out how that was done.

"Anyway, Tristan was supposed to keep his brother, Wyatt, updated telepathically, except he couldn't boost enough power to break the force field. One night he watched over me as I slept. While I slept my guard dropped, giving Tristan and Wyatt the extra power they needed to break through and contact each other."

"You're saying, Wyatt and Tristan are telepathic?" Payton asked. "Can you talk to Wyatt?"

"No, I can only communicate with Tristan," Victory said. "If I'm in the same room Tristan is in when he makes a connection with Wyatt, I feel a slight buzz in my head. For a brief time on the island I could communicate with Morgan. Our connection happened early on, when I first started to tap into my powers. I think the combination of the psychic security system locking in all the powers, and the fact I was just beginning to learn the ability, gave me the temporary link to Morgan. As my focus improved and my connection with Tristan became stronger, I lost my connection with Morgan."

"Wait a minute. Are you trying to tell us you think whatever Mom and Dr. Ryker did to her fertility drugs caused these changes in you?" Willow asked.

"Not only me. All three of us," Victory said.

"I don't have any special abilities," Willow said.

"I believe you do. You have yet to open yourself up to them," Victory said. "Or like me, you have always used them and never thought anything about these abilities. It is something normal to you."

"I don't have any special abilities either," Payton insisted.

"Explain what brought you to my lab last week, when you first met Collin?" Victory asked.

"Absolutely not a thing to do with having any special abilities. Didn't you feel the wave—" Payton stopped cold as she recalled the moment she realized not a single thing in her office was out of place after she felt the disruption.

"You did feel a wave, Payton. You felt a wave of energy, generated from heightened emotions," Victory said.

"What on Earth are you talking about? I don't feel others' emotions," Payton said.

"Yes, you do. You appear to get dizzy and have headaches every time you get close to Collin. Collin is extremely unstable right now, and it takes every ounce of his ability to try to keep a grip on his sanity. I think his negative energy engulfs the area, and your sensitivity to this energy causes your headaches," Victory said.

"Great. If what you say is true, I will have to avoid him and anyone else who radiates intense emotions," Payton said.

"Payton has a good point," Willow said. "If she feels energy the way you think she does, then why doesn't she pick up on your energy?"

"I don't claim to have all the answers—yet. My thoughts are it is somehow related to us being triplets. She doesn't feel my energy because it has been a part of her since before she was born," Victory said. "She may not possess my energy, but she is familiar with it, so my energy does not affect her. It's normal to her and to you."

"If what you say is true about Payton's ability to feel others' energy that could be a real issue, considering our primary research for the next six years. Also, as the CEO of our company, she can't exactly stay away from the campus and do her job at the same time," Willow said.

"Don't panic. Payton can work through her newfound abilities. I did, and I can help her. We need to find a way for her to shield herself in extreme situations," Victory said.

"How long do you think it might take you to find some answers?" Payton asked.

"I'm not sure. Everyone is different. However, there is one positive effect of your ability," Victory said.

"Really? Please tell me because I don't see anything positive from where I sit," Payton said.

"You seem to be a grounder for the person with the extreme emotions. Collin noticed that you have an effect on his emotions. He confided in me that your presence has the ability to calm him no matter how upset he gets."

"Really? I'm glad for him, sincerely. Regrettably, it's at those times I feel like I'm being drained. If I am going to function around him and any others, I need your help—now," Payton said.

Chapter Four

Tristan walked into the Situation Room. It was the first time his new SOCOM team had gathered together. Jack, Logan, and Noah were his original team and played a pivotal role in Victory's rescue from Braxton. Tristan would lay down his life for them and knew they'd do the same for him.

Morgan and Collin were new to the group. Tristan spent time working with both of these military men, who had also been Braxton's guinea pigs, while they were all held captive on the island. Tristan trusted Morgan, but he was still holding out a verdict on Collin. Yes, Collin saved Victory's life when he threw himself at Max, one of Braxton's minions, and tried to wrestle a gun from him. On the flip side, Collin kidnapped Victory from the island and put her in danger in the first place.

Collin's mood swings since being injected with the wolf DNA made him unpredictable in Tristan's eyes. Granted, Morgan also got injected with foreign DNA, but so far he appeared to be adapting to it more easily. According to Tristan's brilliant wife, Victory, this was because Morgan had a predisposed heightened ability, whereas Collin did not. The foreign DNA seemed to want to magnify the host's natural abilities. When there were no natural abilities, the DNA burrowed its own path, wreaking havoc throughout the host's system. Hence the problem Victory currently worked on, discovering where the foreign DNA wanted to gravitate to in Collin's system.

"Okay guys, I want to get home to my wife at a decent hour tonight. Everyone grab their coffee and sit your asses in a chair. We only have two minutes until our meeting starts," Tristan said.

"Geez, used to be you would want to spend all night here, every night. Throw a wife into the picture and all bets are off," Noah joked.

"Cut the guy a break, Noah. They are still newlyweds. Give him another six months and he'll be singing another song," Logan said.

"You guys are hilarious. You should take your show on the road," Tristan said, as he too grabbed his coffee and sat down. He didn't even want to know how many cups he'd drunk that day.

Jack worked his magic on the computer. "I have General Roberts and Captain Wyatt."

The room fell silent as the main screen on the far wall lit up.

All six men jumped to their feet, coming to attention as the general came into view.

"Evening, men, as you were," said Roberts. "Glad to see Tristan could wrangle you all together on such short notice. Morgan and Collin, welcome to the team."

"Thank you, sir," the two men said in unison.

"And thank you for allowing us the opportunity to be stationed here. We realize circumstances played a great deal in your decision. We won't let you down," Morgan said.

"I won't lie to you. Your unwilling participation in Braxton's experiments played a contributing factor. Nevertheless, you two have been on my short list for a while now. The complications you are now experiencing simply accelerated the process. Okay, let's get down to business. Jack, I understand you have finished deciphering the files the team took off Braxton's computer during their extraction of Victory."

"In a manner of speaking, sir. Braxton proved to be extremely paranoid, as we all know, and he took his paranoia to new heights. He implemented a worm in his files—something I have never seen before—and that in itself, speaks volumes. As soon as I started to decrypt the files, the worm triggered. I detected absolutely no forewarning. The virus moved astonishingly fast. I didn't even realize there was a problem or that the files were corrupted until I reopened them. It took me and my tech team weeks to get the blasted thing open. We took all the precautions," Jack said.

"So, what you are saying is there isn't anything new gleaned from the USB drive," Roberts concluded.

"Pretty much, sir. I managed to catch a tidbit here and there, nothing very substantial. Picked up the term 'second wave' a time or two and 'Kaleidoscope Group,' but no more than those two items. I'm sorry, sir."

"No need to be sorry, son. You did the best you could. This development tends to reconfirm our previous thought that Braxton is not working alone. The Kaleidoscope Group is still out there and viable—all things we already knew. Even spending the majority of our time on this, we have not identified a single player involved in his group. All we are certain of at this point is the Kaleidoscope Group is a highly clandestine corporation which has stayed under the wire. Based on what Tristan discovered while he and Victory were on the island, Kaleidoscope Group is owned by a cartel of ultra-rich business tycoons throughout the country and possibly throughout the world. Jack's research uncovered the information that the group has a network extending throughout a number of countries," Roberts said.

"If I were a betting man, I would say Braxton, even with all his power, is a mere pawn in the whole picture. As far as the new term Jack retrieved, my gut tells me 'second wave' is not a good thing," Roberts said.

"What's our next move, sir?" Wyatt asked.

"We tighten our ranks and keep digging. We all know Biotec and Braxton are only just the tip of the iceberg. Make sure security around the Winters Corporation is buttoned up. We don't want a repeat performance for Braxton to have an opportunity to snatch any of the sisters. No one gets in or out of the campus without passing all the checkpoints, and I mean *no* exceptions. The sisters are never to leave the campus without an escort," Roberts said.

"You do realize your demand will cause Tristan grief?" Wyatt asked, as he read his brother's mind.

"They won't like being followed around or limited in their movements," Tristan said.

"Explain the situation to the sisters. Use your persuasive charm to make them understand. They know firsthand what these people are capable of. All three sisters made the decision to become involved when they took on the government contract. When the

Kaleidoscope Group makes their next move, you can bet they will aim for one, or all, of them," Roberts said. "Any questions?"

"No, sir," replied the team.

"Good. You are all dismissed, except for Tristan," Roberts said.

As soon as the door closed behind the last man, Tristan asked, "What about Payton? She plans to take a short vacation and head off for her dog shows in three days. She needs the break, sir."

"Unless something changes, she can go. I realize they have their own lives to live, and I want to allow them as much freedom as possible, within my guidelines. I want a two-man team on her around the clock. The first man will be Collin. He is to travel as a long-time friend with Payton."

Tristan's jaw tightened slightly.

"What the hell? Doesn't the old man know Collin and Payton can barely stand to be in the same room with each other?" Tristan asked Wyatt telepathically.

"Hear him out, Tristan," Wyatt said.

"No, I'm not crazy," Roberts said. "Don't worry; I have yet to master the art of reading thoughts, but it doesn't take a mind reader to know you asked your brother if I was crazy."

"Sorry sir, no disrespect. So you do know Payton and Collin aren't exactly friends?" Tristan asked.

"I'm well aware of the situation. I get daily reports from Victory. She informed me only today that Collin seemed to be having a more difficult time with his focus. With Collin's input, she also discovered that Payton might ground him and calm his nerves. We have to work that angle before we lose Collin. I'm not saying she's the solution, but we need to explore the possibility."

Tristan let his mental shield slip when he heard Victory kept Roberts updated and not him. Yes, they talked about her research, but he hadn't heard this about Collin. He would need to discuss the matter with her when he got home. He understood top secret—hell, he lived with top secret every day of his life—but she was his wife, and there should be no secrets between them.

"Calm yourself, little brother. Victory did exactly what Roberts asked of her. You can't condemn her for doing what your commander requests. Do you tell her everything?" Wyatt asked.

"I didn't ask for your opinion and don't call me 'little brother.' You are all of ninety minutes older than me." Tristan reminded Wyatt.

"General Roberts, would you like me to inform Payton? And may I inquire as to when we might expect Captain Wyatt to return?" Tristan asked.

"Yes, tell her. I need him here for three more days, after which he is all yours," Roberts said. "If there is nothing else, I say we call it a night, gentlemen. Don't you have a new wife waiting for you at home?"

"Yes, sir, I do. Thank you, sir," Tristan said.

"And thanks for leaving me to deal with Payton," Tristan said to his brother.

The last image Tristan saw on the oversized screen was the slight smirk on his brother's face.

* * * *

"Sweetheart, I need to speak with you and your sisters," Tristan pushed into Victory's mind.

"Hurry home and you can join us for dessert," Victory answered without hesitation.

"I'm impressed. Your skills are improving."

"Huh, I didn't give it a second thought. Drive carefully, my love."

"Tristan will be here shortly and he would like to speak with all of us," Victory said, as she continued to pour coffee for them.

"Wow. I have to say, that is super creepy. It will take me some time to get used to your mode of conversation," Payton said.

An instant later all four Dobermans lifted their heads from their resting places and charged to the back door. A baritone laugh broke out from the kitchen.

"Yes, I'm glad to see you all too. Stay down now," Tristan said.

Tristan walked into the dining room while all the dogs circled around him and still managed to give him the space to walk.

"Good evening, ladies. I hear you saved me dessert."

Victory jumped up and sprang into his arms as she lavished kisses all over his face. He kissed her thoroughly. After he came up for air, he said, "Boy, I was only gone for twenty-four hours. I can't wait to see how you greet me after I'm gone for a few days." He smiled down at her and placed her feet gingerly back on the floor.

"We can. Please do us a favor and keep that behind closed doors." Payton giggled.

"I can't make you any promises," Victory said. She went into the kitchen and grabbed dessert and a glass of milk for Tristan. She knew her husband, and she guessed he'd drunk coffee nonstop all day. She set the plate and glass down in front of him.

"Milk?" he whined like a teenager.

"If you can honestly tell me how many cups of coffee you drank in the last twenty-four hours, I will get you a cup."

"Fine, I'll drink the milk," he said. "So, Payton, are you still planning on going to the dog shows?"

"Yes, I need some downtime. My plan is to head out in three days. Why?" She scowled at him. "Don't you even think about telling me I can't go."

"I wouldn't dare," he said, waving his open palms in surrender. "You do understand you all continue to be in danger. Roberts wants two men assigned to go with you."

"What?" Payton asked.

"We can't become lax. Braxton and Kaleidoscope Group are waiting for that moment, the perfect opportunity to grab one of you. There is no problem with you going; you just can't go alone," Tristan said.

"So what? You intend to have two men follow along behind me everywhere I go? Yeah, they certainly won't draw any attention," Payton said.

"No. We have a better plan worked out." Tristan assured her. "One man will be with you the whole trip. He will be an old friend and will travel in your motor home. The other will not be seen. Even so, he will keep close tabs on you."

Payton stared at him in disbelief. "You want me to take one of your men with me and act like he is a long-lost friend?"

"Something along those lines," Tristan said.

"Really? You're serious?"

"Very."

"And what if I refuse?"

"You stay on the campus. Those are your choices. It's up to you."

"Payton, it's for your own good," Willow said. "We couldn't live through another kidnapping or worse." Willow's eyes began to tear up.

Everyone sat quietly and waited for Payton's response.

"Fine. I know you're right. We were both basket cases when Victory got kidnapped. I certainly wouldn't want to purposefully put my family through that pain again. At any rate, I want it on the record; I'm not happy about the whole situation." Payton glared at Tristan across the table.

"Duly noted," Tristan replied.

"When do I meet this long-lost friend?"

"You already have," Tristan said. "Collin."

"What? No. Out of all the guys General Roberts could choose? Collin is not going to work. I'm sure Victory has told you about my problem with him."

"No. Actually, General Roberts did." He glanced at Victory, who gave him a worried smile.

"Sweetheart, I'm sorry I didn't tell you. General Roberts made me swear I wouldn't say anything until he had a chance to speak with you."

"I understand. I'm not happy about it, but I understand," Tristan said. "Back to the point, we will lose Collin. If you leave and Collin stays here, we have no idea how long he will be able to hold on to his sanity. We could possibly lose him forever."

"Yeah, Victory explained that. What about me? What about my sanity?" Payton asked.

"Payton, I can help you. We won't let you go without the tools you will need to function," Victory said. "This won't be forever, Payton. I'm working on a number of things and with luck I will find some way to stabilize Collin. For now, you are his only hope. I'm truly sorry, but Tristan is correct. Collin could lose his grip on sanity if you leave him behind."

"No pressure. I'm heading to bed. Something tells me the next three days will be long and difficult," Payton said.

Chapter Five

"Try again," Victory prompted.

"Ugh. I can't do it," Payton said.

"Yes, you can. You need to learn to focus. Stop thinking about every other little thing you should be doing and zero in on your mental barriers."

Payton eyed her warily. "I thought you said you can't read minds?"

"Believe me. It doesn't take a mind reader to know you are not concentrating on the task at hand," Victory said. "We have spent the last day working on total concentration and you still cannot master the simple skill. If you can't even train yourself to fully concentrate on one thing, we will never be able to move forward. We are both getting impatient. I think the time has come for a new approach. You are going to start practicing yoga today. This will teach you how to breathe, focus, and clear your mind. It's a wonder you don't have a total meltdown with the way your mind wanders."

"Wait one minute. I can concentrate and I'm good at my job." Payton started to get defensive. "If I didn't know any better, I would think you're calling me an airhead."

"No, you are brilliant. And yes, you are great at your job. You are required to solve a multitude of problems and issues at any one time, and your mind has the ability to deal with all those problems at the same time. What you have a difficult time with is quieting your mind and centering all of your attention on only one thing. This has proved to be even more of a challenge than I first thought. If you can't make some kind of breakthrough today, there will be no way you and Collin can travel together," Victory said.

"Well, I don't have time to find a yoga class," Payton said.

"Who said anything about finding a class? I have already arranged for an instructor to come to you."

A knock sounded on the door of Victory's office.

"Come on in, Marsha," Victory said.

The door opened and a tall, lean woman who wore black yoga pants and a zippered sweatshirt walked in. She smiled at the two women. "Am I early?" Marsha asked, as she entered the room.

"No, not at all. Marsha, I would like to introduce you to my sister, Payton."

Marsha crossed the office and held her hand out to shake Payton's.

"Nice to meet you, Payton," Marsha said.

"Nice to meet you too," Payton said, as she eyed Victory.

"Marsha has come three times a week to work with Collin and Morgan since they arrived on campus. She has made some real progress with them," Victory said. "In fact, Willow and I offered her a permanent, position with the company and have decided to hire her on full-time. She has agreed to manage the campus fitness program. Marsha, Willow told me today your office will be ready for you tomorrow."

"Wonderful. I can't tell you how much I look forward to working here. Your place is great, and I have a lot of ideas, although those can wait for a few days. Victory told me today and tomorrow you will be my priority, Payton," Marsha said.

"Great, and welcome aboard," Payton said, and smiled at Marsha.

"If you're ready, we should get started. It's such a fabulous day out; I thought we could start down by the lake. When do you need her back?"

Victory looked over at her clock, which read five minutes after ten.

"Let's all meet at the café at one," Victory said.

"Sounds great. We'll see you at one," Marsha said. She turned to leave the office.

Payton remained glued to her spot for a second longer as she looked over at her sister.

"Gee, thanks, sis. Not only am I the last to know about our new hires, now I'm being sent to yoga boot camp," she mumbled under her breath.

* * * *

Immersed in trying to solve Payton's problem all morning, Victory was starting to feel drained. She looked at the little antique clock on her desk made of sterling silver and in the shape of an old Victorian picture frame. The clock was a treasure of her mom's, bought on her eighteenth birthday on her first trip to

England. Her mom told Victory she found the clock in an antique shop in London. For as long as Victory could remember visiting her mother at the office, the clock sat proudly displayed on her desk.

She brought herself back to the present and realized she still had thirty minutes before Payton and Marsha would be meeting her for lunch. All the same, she was ready for some fresh air and decided a stroll to the café would be in order.

* * * *

"I think this is a good spot to quit," Marsha said. "You've worked hard all morning; let's head for the café."

"Sounds like a plan to me. Doing yoga has worked up my appetite," Payton said.

They left the lake and headed back to the heart of the campus.

"I really am honored to work here. Besides the great opportunity and the wonderful people I have met, this campus is astonishing. I have never seen anything like it. I love to look out in the distance and see the inlet and the town marina," Marsha said.

"Thank you. I'm extremely proud of what my sisters and I have accomplished. We didn't want a run-of-the-mill office complex, especially since the campus sits adjacent to our home. We've created an actual community and we hope our employees feel like they are part of the family. All the buildings are constructed out of brick or stone."

"Yes, they're all beautiful and look warm and inviting. Every time I enter the campus, I get the sensation of stepping back in time into a cozy village."

"The ambience of an intimate village happened to be exactly what we were going for. What makes it even better is that the inner workings of every building are a polar opposite of the building's external appearance. Each building houses the most cutting-edge, high-tech equipment money can buy," Payton said.

"That I believe. I got almost giddy when I saw the equipment in the wellness facility. Most of the equipment I have only seen in pictures, and I can't wait to start experimenting with it," Marsha said.

"Great and please let one of us know if there is any additional equipment you would like to add," Payton said.

They approached the campus café, one of Payton's favorite buildings. The sisters modeled the café after an English cottage. The building was made of large stones. Oversized windows trimmed in white flanked three sides. The back of the café had wall-to-wall French doors that slid open to let in the summer breeze or the ebb and flow of spring showers. As they approached the café, Payton caught the scents of the array of flowers that blanketed the yard in front of the building. There were delphiniums, snapdragons, lavender, and honeysuckle, along with a variety of ornamental shrubs and trees. The entire entry was awash with color and fragrance.

Payton greeted several people as she and Marsha made their way through the café and out to the patio. The theme continued there with enormous pieces of slate, which lined the ground. Tiny stones filled the cracks in between the pieces of slate. Raised flower boxes ran the entire length of the outer edges of the patio and overflowed with flowers in every color nature offered. Victory was already seated at a corner table.

"I hope you didn't wait on us for long," Marsha said. She sat down across from Victory.

"Not at all. I needed a break and left the office a few minutes early," Victory said. "How did yoga practice go? You look slightly less stressed."

"The first hour and a half I loved. All I did was sleep," Payton said. "I could really get into yoga."

"Yoga Nidra," Marsha chuckled. "We still have a great deal of work to do on meditation. She went out like a light."

"What? You told me to relax," Payton said. "I did enjoy the poses."

Victory giggled. "That's our Payton. Zero to one hundred with nothing in between. Do you think you can help her by tomorrow?"

"Victory, you know firsthand this takes time. It's a practice, not a destination. I'm sure I can start her in the right direction; I can teach her the basic poses. She's a quick study," Marsha said. "But as far as having her ready in a few days...that's impossible."

"She needs to have a base. Do you have any ideas on how you can support her for the coming two weeks?" Victory asked.

"I can burn a disc for her to take on her trip. Or what if we scheduled a Skype session every morning?" Marsha asked.

"Good idea. I warn you though, most of my days start awfully early," Payton said.

"I will make it work. After you come home we need to set up a regular schedule and no excuses," Marsha said.

"Okay, it's a promise. Hopefully, taking yoga regularly will get Dr. Russell off my back," Payton said. "She's always on me about the need to relax and not work such long days. I'm sure my days won't shorten anytime soon, and if I break them up with yoga, she can't complain—much."

"Great. Let's order some lunch and discuss how the next day and a half will be scheduled," Victory said.

"Are you ready for a test run?" Victory asked Payton.

They worked all afternoon. Marsha taught Payton to focus and create a mental shield.

"It's after seven, Victory. We've been at it all day. I'm tired," Payton whined.

"We only have one more day to get this right. We need to know how you will handle yourself around Collin. One short test and we can end for the day."

"Fine, let's get the test over. I can't tell you how much I look forward to getting dizzy and going home with a headache," Payton said.

"Concentrate. Payton, I know you can do this if you'll only practice what you have learned." Victory picked up the interoffice phone and buzzed Collin, who answered on the first ring.

"Hi doc, what's up?" Collin asked.

"Collin, I need you to come to my office, please."

"On my way," he said.

Payton started to pace the office floor.

"I sure hope we have made enough headway. The last thing I want is to cancel my trip. I really need some time away, even if it means I have to take Collin with me."

"Stop pacing, Payton. Sit down, work on your breathing, and focus. You need to create a mental picture of your barrier. Start working on finding your picture and calm yourself," Victory said.

Payton settled herself in a chair, closed her eyes, and started her breathing exercises. A few moments later, Collin stood in the doorway of Victory's office. Victory placed a finger to her lips, which informed him to enter the room quietly. He did as instructed and sat in a chair across the room from Payton. Seconds passed, minutes, eventually melting into an hour. Payton remained sitting, eyes closed, breathing evenly in and out.

"How long does it take that man to get here?" she finally asked as she opened her eyes.

Payton found herself staring into the abyss of ocean-blue eyes and a breathtaking sculptured face, framed with short, light-brown hair. Collin didn't flinch a single muscle.

"What? How long—" Her words stopped when the room began to spin and unconsciously she reached for the arms of her chair.

"He arrived over an hour ago, Payton. Clearly you can focus on a single thing. Focus and put your barriers back up," Victory said.

Payton tried and tried, but she continued to be distracted and a nauseated feeling started to override her system.

"I can't," she said, irritated at herself because she was falling apart once again in front of Collin.

"Thank you, Collin. We will continue where we left off tomorrow," Victory said.

"No problem." He looked back at Payton one last time. "Sorry," he said. "I feel a little guilty since I am feeling more centered and peaceful than I have all day." Collin left the office, his comment hanging heavy in the air.

"Great. Now I'm sick to my stomach and I look like an idiot to him yet again," Payton said. "The entire thing is hopeless."

"No it's not. You were doing great until you realized he was in the room. Only then did you lose your focus. We'll return to it in the morning. Let's go pick up Willow and head up to the house. It's my turn to cook."

"And I thought this day couldn't get any worse," Payton moaned.

Chapter Six

"What's the verdict?" Payton asked Victory.

It was early evening, and she'd worked nonstop all day, going from Victory, to yoga, and back to Victory.

"I spoke with Tristan and Collin," Victory said. "They left the decision up to me."

"Why Tristan?" Payton asked with a confused look. "I mean, I realize he is Collin's commanding officer; nonetheless, how does he know if Collin can mentally handle being around me for a week or not?"

"Tristan worked with Collin for the past week. He has taught Collin the same techniques I have taught you, with one difference. Tristan is trying to make Collin aware of his overpowering emotions, and teach him how to rein his emotions in. You need to push your powers out and keep your barrier up," Victory said.

"There is quite a big difference between the two of us, wouldn't you say? He can mentally drain me, and what can I do to him? Bring him peacefulness? This is not fair," Payton said.

"I understand your feelings and hesitation. Maybe you should stay home," Victory said.

"No, I've been looking forward to my trip for months."

"I don't think you *or* Collin are ready. If we had another few weeks, or even a month, I would feel better about sending him with you."

"Well, I can't leave him here. You've made it utterly clear that he could totally lose his mind."

"There could be one possible aid for you. I have finished up a project I started when I first got back from the island."

Victory opened her desk drawer and pulled out a bracelet. The bracelet was a silver band with a dime-sized circle in the middle. She handed it to Payton.

"Put this on."

"What is it?" Payton took the bracelet and slipped it on her wrist.

"It's your safety net. You push the circle down and it emits a jamming signal that will disrupt the psychic wave Collin gives off. It's got a limited range and you have to be within ten feet of him."

"Wow. Why didn't we just start with this and forget all the other stuff?"

"Because both of you need to learn to control your abilities. You'll be around others who give off extreme emotions and you need your abilities to become second nature. Use this only as a last resort. I don't know how or if it will affect you if you use it too often. Collin could become immune to it, or even worse, you could develop side effects."

"I'll be careful."

"Okay then. Morgan will keep a close eye on the two of you. If at any time he thinks there is a problem, he has full authority to pull Collin out, no questions."

"I feel much better about the trip between this bracelet and Morgan. Oh no—" Payton said, as a thought popped into her head. "We have missed a highly important aspect of the whole trip, Parker and Kes. They have no relationship with Collin, and if they feel any type of threat from him the situation could go bad—fast."

"Come with me," Victory said. She waved her hand and beckoned for Payton to follow.

Payton followed Victory out of the building.

"Look," Victory said, as she pointed down to the lake.

Far off in the distance they saw two men and two Dobermans jogging around the lake.

"Who are those men?" Payton asked.

"That is Tristan, Collin, Parker, and Kes."

"What?"

"You heard me. Tristan and Collin have a daily routine of taking the dogs out to jog. They have taken the dogs with them every afternoon for the past week."

"Really," Payton said, as she crossed her arms and tapped her foot. "So now they're all best buddies, I guess."

"Don't you want them to have a relationship?" Victory asked.

"Of course I do. I simply think it might have been nice if someone thought to tell me," Payton said.

"Come on, sis. This is a good thing. Don't you still have loads of packing to do? Are you sure you want to leave tomorrow? Your first show isn't for three days."

"This is supposed to be my vacation. I would like to take my time. If I don't finish packing tonight, I will do it tomorrow, and we will leave when I'm ready," Payton said.

"Kes, Parker, let's go," Payton said, her arms full of what she hoped would be the last of her packing.

The dogs were enjoying the sun while at the same time keeping a close eye on Payton. Both dogs jumped up and headed for the motor home.

"No pushing. One at a time."

The two skidded to a halt as they reached the stairs of the vehicle. Being gentlemanly, Parker stopped and allowed Kes to climb the stairs as he followed along behind her. They both headed for the overstuffed chairs.

"You know the drill. In your crates while we travel."

They hung their heads and slowly climbed into their respective crates.

"Oh, don't give me your woeful looks," Payton giggled, and she latched the crate doors. "You guys have nice cozy beds. Stop being such babies."

"Knock, knock," Collin's deep voice sounded from the doorway. "Permission to come aboard?"

Payton steeled herself as she reached for the bracelet. She closed her eyes and took in a cleansing breath as she focused on erecting her mental barriers. It worked. She almost let out a squeal of joy. Maybe the trip wouldn't be as terrible as she had previously imagined.

"This isn't a boat," she said.

"Could've fooled me," Collin said. "Have you looked at the size of this thing? I've seen freighters smaller than your motor home."

"Ha, ha," Payton said. *Could this man really have a sense of humor? That would be a total shock*, she thought. She saw Collin as always serious and moody. "You are welcome to enter. I hope you brought all your stuff with you. I'm ready to hit the road."

"I got all I need right here," Collin said, as he climbed the stairs and lifted a large bag.

"All you have is one oversized duffle bag? This isn't a military trip, Collin. You are allowed to bring along whatever you want."

"This is not a duffle bag, this is a rucksack," he said, as he pointed at the bag. "I've traveled this way for the past twelve years. Habit I guess."

"I'll wait if you would like to bring anything else," Payton said. She thought it sad he could fit all of his needs into one olive-green duffle bag.

"Nope, I'm good. Where should I stow it?"

"The guestroom is the door on the left," she said, as she nodded in the direction of the hall. "Is Morgan ready to go?"

"He's ready and waiting."

"Where is he? He will be riding with us, right?" Payton asked.

"Nope. From the second we pull out of the driveway he will be our shadow, on our six."

"Pardon?" she asked.

"Sorry," he said. "He will be right behind us the whole time, but you won't see him."

"Kind of creepy, don't you think?"

"Don't worry; you'll get used to it. Do you want me to drive?"

"No, thanks. I prefer to drive, although I'll keep your offer in mind."

Payton took one last tour through the motor home; she made sure she had secured any loose items before they started their journey. She double-checked the locks on the crates and went to the refrigerator.

"Would you like anything to drink?"

"I'll have whatever you're having," Collin said.

Payton pulled out two bottles of green tea and tossed one to Collin.

"Okay, let's start our adventure." As she headed up to the driver's seat, she noticed Collin hesitate. "Problem?"

"I'm not sure where you want me to sit. Would you prefer I stay back here?" Collin asked.

She looked at him quizzically. "Why would you think such a thing? Come up here and sit in the passenger seat."

"I don't want to crowd you any more than necessary. I understand you still need to really focus on your barriers."

"True, so the more focused and calm *you* remain, the better it will be for the both of us."

"I can see we are going to have a rough time," he said.

"Only if you decide to throw things and break up my motor home."

"I'll try to control myself."

"I should hope so. But if it gets really bad, I have this." She lifted the arm that had the bracelet and pointed to it with her other hand.

"What? A fashion statement?"

"Not even close. This is a failsafe created by Victory. A jamming device: if I press this button, your emotions will be blocked."

"Great. Then I don't have to worry."

"We still have to work to control our emotions. This is only to be used if your emotions get too overwhelming for me to deal with. So far, it does feel as though your work with Tristan has tempered your mental pull on me."

He smiled and dropped down into the passenger's seat. Payton felt a twinge, seeing his face light up for the first time. *Don't be an idiot. We can hardly stay in the same room together.*

"Glad to hear it. I've worked really hard to tone down my emotional outbursts," he said. "Understanding how I affect you is enlightening. I have to say, this is the most I have felt in control for over…months. I'll try to keep my emotions reined in, but you might have to remind me every now and then."

"Don't worry; when you see me fall flat on my face, you will know you went too far," she said.

"I'll try not to let that happen," he chuckled. "I know I'm not your favorite person and most likely the last one you wanted to come on the trip with you. Since we have been thrown together in our current situation, I hope we can make the best of it, and maybe one day even become friends."

"With time, anything can happen. Let's take this one step at a time. Buckle up."

Payton snapped her seatbelt and started the engine.

An hour went by without a single word spoken between them. Payton started to feel fidgety and uncomfortable with the silence.

"So, tell me about yourself. How in the world did you end up in Braxton's facility?" she asked.

He looked at her in bewilderment. "I thought your sister filled you in."

"She only told us what happened on the Hawaiian island, nothing about how you came to be there. Did you work for Braxton before?"

"No," he snorted. "If I had, I would have realized what kind of a sadistic asshole he really was, and I would have put him out of his misery."

"I wish you would have. And if you ever tell anyone I agreed with you, I'll shoot you."

He smiled at her.

"I wanted to be home for a while. I saw it as a chance to spend some time with my baby sister. I hadn't seen her since our grandfather died. When we were informed of an assignment here in Washington, Morgan and I volunteered. We were told the assignment would be a short and simple job. Lawrence Braxton requested two military personnel to spend a week at his San Juan Island facility, doing strength and endurance testing. The mission was only supposed to be one short week, after which our commanding officer promised us leave. I should have known the mission was too good to be true. We got to the facility in time for dinner. Being the perfect host, Braxton had our meals brought to our suite. He drugged us. Neither one of us remember any details after dinner. We were there to help him; who knew he was crazy enough to mess with military volunteers?"

Payton briefly took her eyes off the road and scowled at Collin.

"You better not be beating yourself up over what happened. It's not like you were out on a dangerous mission or in some foreign country. You thought you were there to help the man with a military-related contract, and you were sent in by your commanding officer. How could you possibly suspect you were in danger?"

"I guess. When we woke up, we were no longer in a posh suite. We were lying on cots in a largely bare-bones room. Made our barracks look like the Hilton. We were locked in, and there were guards on us twenty-four-seven. I'm sure you know the rest. We were injected with wolf DNA, tortured, tracked, and drugged. End of story," Collin said.

She was dismayed that he made the major turning point in his life sound so clinical.

"No, not end of story. It is the beginning of life as you now know it. You can't simply ignore what happened to you, Collin. These events are what turned you into the man you are today."

"Lucky me," he growled. "You can't even stand to be around me, and I can't blame you if you hate me. Shit, I kidnapped your sister and practically got her killed."

"My feelings about you have nothing to do with hate, and no, I don't hate you. How could I? I hardly know you. It's all about how you make me feel. I get sudden splitting headaches when you're around and sick to my stomach, and my body is like lead being drawn into the ground."

"What a cheery image. You don't feel like lead now, right? As long as we keep up our work on tempering my emotions and erecting your barriers, you should be fine," he said.

"I hope so. You kidnapped Victory off the island during one of your blackouts, correct?"

"That's what they tell me. The entire event is all a murky haze. The first thing I actually remember is being at my cabin. Max, one of Braxton's minions, caught up to us. Fortunately Tristan's team got to the cabin first. My primary concern was to keep Victory safe. We snuck out of the cabin and thought we were in the clear, but no such luck. Max, damn him, was hot on our trail and the last thing I remember, I struggled for Max's gun, and he and I rolled off the cliff."

"You must have been terrified." Payton gasped.

"No, not really. I had no time to think. I did what the military trained me to do and reacted to the threat."

"And you never tried to kill Victory. You kidnapped her because you saw her as the solution to your problem. When she was threatened, you protected her," she said.

She couldn't believe she was justifying Collin's actions with regards to Victory's kidnapping. Only two short weeks ago she didn't want to be near the man who kidnapped Victory. Now, hearing his side of the story gave her second thoughts.

Parker let out a whine and scratched at his crate door.

"I hear you, Parker. We will stop in a few minutes, buddy," Payton said.

"Does he need to go?"

"Yes, and it's almost their dinner time. Their internal clocks are amazing."

"We've been on the road four hours. You look tired," Collin said.

"I have to say, this constant practice with regard to my mental barrier tires me. Victory said eventually I

74

would put up my barriers without even realizing it, but 'eventually' hasn't happened yet."

"I think we should stop for the night and take it easy."

"I'm way ahead of you. There is an RV park approximately ten miles down the road. I've made reservations to spend the night."

"Sounds like a plan."

Payton easily maneuvered the enormous motor home in the tight confines of the state park. She backed the motor home into her assigned spot, leveled the vehicle, and hooked up the electricity, water, and sewer in a matter of minutes.

"I have to say, I'm in awe at your skill with this beast of a vehicle. You are quite the one-man, I mean, one-woman team. How can I help? I don't want to get in your way. But I need to pull my weight."

"The next thing we need to do is take Parker and Kes for a walk, after which I will feed them. While I fix dog dinners, you could pull the folding chairs out of the back storage, along with the barbecue grill," she said.

"I'd say we worked together pretty well," Collin said, and sipped on his wine.

"We made it through the evening without any major catastrophes," Payton said.

She lay on the sofa with her legs tucked up to one side. Kes crawled up and wedged herself behind Payton's leg and rested her head on Payton's hip. Parker remained on the floor next to Collin's chair, his head across Collin's feet.

"Seems you've made a friend," she said, as she nodded in Parker's direction.

"I hope so. I really enjoy being around your Dobermans. I never knew they were such wonderful companion dogs. I think I might have to get one of my own when this is all over."

"Okay, Payton, my turn. Tell me a little about yourself?"

"What you see is pretty much my life." She swept her hand through the air, drawing attention to the inside of the motor home.

"You enjoy going to dog shows, manage the family business, and spend time with your sisters. Are you trying to tell me there is nothing more? What about a boyfriend?"

"No time."

"Ever?"

"I did have a boyfriend in college, and I thought he was the one." She shrugged.

"He wasn't? What happened?"

"I guess I should have seen the signs early on. He always asked about the company. I chalked his constant questions up to conversation and his interest in my family. I ultimately saw the light right after my parents were killed. He didn't ask how I was handling their deaths, or even try to comfort me. The only thing he wanted to know was who would run the company. It was then that I realized his only real interest was in the family business, not me," Payton said.

"Sorry to hear. He was a jerk, but there are lots of great guys out there. Do you mean to say you have never gotten involved with anyone since him?" Collin asked. *More likely, she chased guys away with her ice princess demeanor.*

"No one serious. The company takes a great deal of work and I haven't the time or interest to invest in another relationship." Payton squirmed. "Tell me the rest of your story, Collin."

"There's really nothing exciting left to tell. My granddad raised me, and I joined the military a day after my eighteenth birthday."

"What happened to your parents?" she asked.

"My mom died of breast cancer when I was nine. My dad tried to take care of me, but his attempt at fatherhood left a lot to be desired."

"What do you mean? You were his son. He should have made it work."

"Yeah well, no surprise to me. He wasn't around much before Mom died. He didn't even have a clue how to be a parent, which I find difficult to believe because his father did a great job of raising me. One day Dad took me to my granddad's and told us he had returned to active duty. He said he would come back and get me after his tour."

"And what? He never returned? You were just a little boy. Your mom had died and now you were losing both your parents, and worse, being abandoned by your father. No one should have to grow up like that."

"As far as I know, Granddad never heard from him again. Nine years later, he came back to Washington State with a new wife. He married her while he served in Scotland. Dad and his new wife brought their four-year-old daughter back. His wife also had a sixteen-year-old daughter from a previous marriage."

"Did he welcome you back?" Payton asked.

"No. His wife didn't want me. Besides, I'd just joined the Army. Thanks to the guidance of my granddad, I made something of myself. I got into the pilot program. Somehow I managed to score in the top five percent of my class and got into Delta Force," Collin said.

"I'm glad you had your granddad. He sounds like a wonderful man."

"He was extraordinary. He started with nothing, and built his own business from the ground up. It kind of reminds me of you and your two sisters."

Payton smiled, flattered at the comparison; she knew how he loved and respected his granddad.

"And there was Emma," Collin said.

"Emma? Is she your girlfriend?"

"No, Emma is my baby sister—well, half-sister, but I never think of her in those terms. She was the four-year-old daughter of Dad and his second wife. Emma and I have a great relationship. I've really missed her over the past year."

"You said your dad and his wife lived in Washington. Did they stay?" she asked.

"His wife did. Dad got killed over four years ago on his last mission. Let's put it this way: The official story is he's dead. Unofficially, he is MIA, Missing in Action."

"How terrible," Payton said.

"It is what it is." Collin shrugged and leaned back into his chair. "You take the risk when you serve your country."

"What happened to the sixteen-year-old girl? The second wife's daughter and Emma's half-sister. You never mentioned her name."

Payton felt the start of a tingle in her head that quickly picked up speed and turned painful.

"Collin, what's the matter?" she asked as she put her hands up to her temples.

"The name—I can't remember her damn name." He did not realize he had allowed his emotions to break free.

"Calm down, Collin. It's not a big deal. I forget names all the time," she said.

Collin tried to pull himself from the edge of anger. He could feel the darkness; it threatened to invade his mind.

"Collin, please—"

Before Payton could finish her sentence, Parker cautiously lifted his head, backed away from Collin and sat in front of Payton. He placed his body between her and a possible threat, a low, guttural growl emanating from deep within him.

"Collin, you have upset the dogs. You need to focus. Use the new skills Tristan taught you," Payton insisted.

Collin looked into Payton's face and saw the agony in her eyes. The realization he'd caused her pain snapped him back into the present.

"I'm sorry, Payton. I didn't mean to hurt you." He fought for control and centered himself on his breathing.

Parker stopped growling but remained sitting squarely in front of Payton.

"I think it's a good time to call it a night," Payton said. She rubbed once more at her temples. "Why don't you head to bed? I'll take the dogs out."

"I'm fine now, really. I can help you."

As Collin stood, Parker and Kes stiffened, both stayed glued to their spots.

"No. I'll do it. You've taken a couple of steps backward, as far as they're concerned. It will take some time until you re-establish their trust again."

"I'm such a jackass! I'm really sorry Payton. I never meant to cause you pain or for Parker and Kes to feel they have to defend you around me. I'll try harder. I have so many holes in my memory and what is there makes no sense. Even so, I can't let you go out alone. I'll keep my distance from you and the dogs, but I need to be out there with you. Anyone could be lurking around, just waiting for their chance to grab you."

"I'll have two Dobermans with me. They would have to be pretty stupid to approach me."

"Not if they're carrying a gun. And I know you don't want to put your dogs in danger."

"I suppose you're right. Make sure you keep a good distance away. And don't worry about the gaps in your memory. Victory will find an answer. She won't stop until she does."

Chapter Seven

"We set up in record time," Payton said, as she opened the door to the motor home and allowed Parker and Kes access to the exercise pen enclosure. The enclosed space worked out to be ten feet wide and ran the entire length of the motor home.

"This is your idea of a vacation?" Collin asked. He stretched out in one of the lounge chairs with an iced tea in his hand. "Seems like a lot of work when you are all by yourself."

"Not too bad. I have my routine, and it usually takes me about ninety minutes to get to this point. I don't get enough physical activity in my everyday life. I jog and exercise; nonetheless, my actual workday is all mental. I love the break."

"It's sure beautiful here. Of all the places I have travelled and the stuff I've seen, I can honestly say this is the first time I've been to Montana. Do you come here often?" he asked.

"I try and make the show every year, mostly because of the scenery. I think Montana is quite awe-inspiring. I'm going to take my bike out and give these guys some exercise." Payton said.

"I can't let you go alone, you are still in danger."

"Fine, I'll stay here in the overnight parking and ride between the rows. I can't be gone long anyway, I still have to bathe and groom Kes."

"Stay where I can see you."

"Will you be okay here?"

"Don't worry. I won't fall apart or turn into a raving maniac—at least I hope I won't," he said, with a quirk of his lip.

"Can you cook?" Payton asked, when she and the dogs returned.

"Yes. I taught myself at a young age. I only had three choices as a kid. Learn to cook, eat Granddad's sandwiches, or go out to dinner every night. Personally, I'd rather have dinner at home."

"Me too," she said. "The galley is yours, Chef McBain; I need to bathe Kes."

Collin sat in his chair and sipped on his glass of red wine as he watched Payton bathe Kes. The love she had for her dogs surprised him. He couldn't even recall the last time he felt this at ease. Certainly not since the injections and, for that matter, nothing came to mind before the blasted things. Could one person really be this important to his well-being? He hoped for his sake, and for Payton's too, that Victory could find an answer for him—and quickly.

His cell beeped, and he looked at the screen to find a text from Victory. These sisters were a little unnerving. It made him wonder if they could read his mind. Victory wanted him to go inside and open Payton's computer. He got up and went into the motor home. As he flipped up the computer screen, it began to play, "Lean on Me." He chuckled and hit the dialog box; it brought Skype on-line.

"Hi Collin," Victory said. "I see you guys made it okay."

"How did—" he started.

"Magic," she said. "Take it easy. We aren't that good—yet. I spoke with Payton."

Collin blew his breath out and relaxed. His face felt flush as the blood run back into it.

"Damn, you really had me going, doc."

"Sorry," she said. She tried to stop from laughing. "How is everything going?"

"The place is unbelievable. Like a small town sprung up in less than a couple of hours. There are rows and rows of motor homes, trailers, and even some tents. The variety of dog breeds I have seen is unreal."

"Wait until the show starts. You will see twice as many. Tons of people stay in local hotels and come to the show site during the day," she said.

"Payton seems to really enjoy the whole adventure." He automatically glanced up to be sure he could still see her.

"Payton's Shangri-la. Win or lose, she is in total bliss while at the dog shows. She even enjoys all the backbreaking work. Tell me about you, Collin? Payton filled me in on last night. Are you feeling any ill effects?"

"You mean besides the fact I caused Payton pain and created doubt in Parker and Kes?" he said, his mood sobering.

"Don't be hard on yourself, Collin. Payton told me she talked you through it, and you got hold of yourself before things went bad. Parker and Kes will come around. They know you, and believe it or not, they trust you. Simply be yourself, and they will be by your side in no time."

"If you say so, doc," he said, none too sure she wasn't feeding him a line of bull. "I'm feeling good today. This is the most relaxed I've felt since before this whole nightmare started."

"Glad to hear it. Keep up the work on your exercises, and we will talk again tomorrow. You better figure out what you are going to make for dinner. My sister says if you can cook the way you claim, she might keep you on as her chef. Good night, Collin," Victory said, a smile lighting up her face.

"See you tomorrow, doc."

He sat at the table for a few minutes longer and watched Payton. She was toweling Kes dry chatting away to the dog. He hated to go out and impose on their time together. He shook his head, got up and headed into the galley to start dinner.

"Wow, smells divine. What did you make?" Payton asked, as she opened the door and the two dogs charged up the steps.

"Pasta primavera. Get washed up; dinner is ready," he said.

"I didn't think my kitchen held anything so elaborate."

"You would be amazed at what I can create." Collin smiled and wiggled his eyebrows.

"Really delicious, Collin." She dabbed at her mouth with her napkin. "The first gourmet meal ever prepared in my little galley. If you ever decide to get out of the military, you would make one heck of a chef." She stopped abruptly. "How insensitive of me. As if you have a choice right now. I'm sorry; I wasn't thinking."

"Don't worry about it. I know what you meant. You can't guard every word you say to me. If you do, our situation will be even worse. I can leave in a year when I come up for re-enlistment, but then I won't have the research support I have now," he said.

"Well on that note, I met up with a group of my friends while I was out. I told them I brought along a college friend. They want to get together tomorrow night and have a potluck. We do potlucks almost every night while we're at the shows. How about we really amaze them and you whip something up?"

"You're on," Collin said.

The next morning they got up early and headed for the show. Collin watched Payton and Kes move around the ring; they reminded him of dancers. The pair glided flawlessly. Kes showed in all her glory, a stunning bitch, striking her poses with natural grace. Apparently the judge agreed with Collin, and the crowd around the ring erupted as he pointed to Kes as Best of Breed. Winning Breed made for an extremely long day, since Kes needed to go back to show late in the afternoon to participate in the Working Dog Group.

"You don't have to come back to the ring with us. You can stay and hang out with Parker, if you prefer," Payton said.

"Are you kidding? I get to see the whole deal today, and I find the dog show fascinating."

Collin didn't want to miss a minute of seeing Payton's face light up as she worked with Kes. He was surprised to see such a simple thing as working with her dog brought her such joy. He could tell today was her perfect day. Maybe he'd misjudged her, and she wasn't all about the "bottom line."

"You still have to make something for tonight. Are you sure you won't be too tired?" she asked.

"I'm sure," he said. "Come on; it's getting late." He picked up her grooming bag and held the door open.

* * * *

"Where's Katie?" Payton asked, as she hugged Dannie, another of her friends. "I stopped by the Toller ring earlier, but I didn't see her."

"She said something came up at the last minute. She sent me a text and said she would meet up with us in Oregon," Dannie said.

"Too bad; I hope nothing is wrong," Payton said.

"She told us not to worry. Best guess, her blasted boss came up with another project before she could slip out the door, damn man," Dannie said. "So, this is your college friend?" Dannie smiled over Payton's shoulder at Collin, who stood a few steps behind her.

"Oh, yes, sorry. Dannie, meet Collin," Payton said.

"Hi Collin. Oh, and he can cook too," Dannie said, as she looked at the dishes Collin held in his hands and gave him a wink.

"Down girl," Payton said. "Don't scare him away. Collin is a great cook."

"Looks like. Come on, Collin. I'll show you where you can set your dishes down, and I'll introduce you to the gang," Dannie said, and she batted her eyelashes at him and threaded her arm though his.

Payton could swear she noticed a bead of sweat trickle down Collin's neck. She snickered to herself. She would watch him squirm for a bit under Dannie's flirtation; it would be great entertainment.

It was well past eleven by the time the party broke up. By the looks of things, they were the last people still moving about in the camp area. There wasn't a person in sight as they headed back to the motor home.

"We should have left earlier. I show first thing in the morning. I hated to leave; it's been a long time since I have seen everyone. I still have to take the dogs out for the night," she said.

"I'll take them out," Collin said. "You are beat, and I wouldn't mind a walk before I went to bed."

"Are you sure?"

"My pleasure."

Collin, Kes, and Parker had walked to the far side of the parking area when Collin caught a movement out of the corner of his eye. Both dogs popped their heads up and sniffed the air, and Collin did the same.

"We know that stench, don't we, guys?"

Their stubs wagged wildly.

"Ha, ha, you're a riot, McBain," Morgan's voice floated out of the darkness.

"I wondered when you were going to check in. You had me worried; I started to think you were falling down on the job," Collin said.

"You haven't exactly presented the opportunity. How's everything going?" Morgan asked. He reached down and scratched Kes on the head.

"Not bad. I kind of enjoy the clean mountain air and all the dogs. You?"

"Not a hair out of place on my end. We thought for sure Braxton would have someone on you two. I haven't seen anyone lurking around. You guys pack up and head out tomorrow, right?" Morgan asked.

"Far as I know," Collin said.

"I'll stay out of sight as long as I don't see anyone suspicious. We'll touch base again after we get to Oregon," Morgan said.

"Roger, see you in Oregon."

* * * *

"Katie," Payton squealed as she ran up to a girl blow-drying the toller she had on a grooming table. Katie put her toller on the ground and ran to hug Payton. "It's good to see you. It's been what, four months? We all missed you in Montana. I'm glad you made it to Oregon."

"Me too; I've missed you," Katie said. "I hear everyone is going out to a Mexican restaurant tonight. How about you join me for dinner in my motor home?"

"Sounds wonderful, as long as you don't mind if I bring somebody? He's an old college friend." Payton looked around and didn't see Collin anywhere.

"No, I'd love it. In fact I have a friend travelling with me I want you to meet. How about around six?" Katie asked.

"It's a date; we'll see you at six," Payton said. She hugged Katie, and then turned to head to her ring.

* * * *

Kes was done showing for the day, so before they returned to the motor home, Payton took her on a relaxing walk. As they headed back, Payton caught a whiff of something that smelled heavenly.

"Umm," Payton sighed, as she opened the door to the motor home. "What delicious treat did you whip up for tonight?"

"I made minestrone soup and chocolate cake," Collin said.

"You are going to make some woman an awfully happy wife. Are you ready to go?" Payton picked up the other leash and snapped it on Parker.

"They're going with us?" Collin asked.

"Sure are. They love Katie's tollers. Kes and I have travelled to many a show with her and her tollers. Wait until you see them all play."

"Tollers?"

"Nova Scotia duck tolling retriever—tollers, for short. Here, you take Parker and I'll grab the cake."

"Let me help you," Katie said, as Payton and Collin came into view. She opened the exercise pen and took the cake from Payton. "Wow, your cake looks divine. I didn't know you baked, Payton."

"I don't. Collin made the cake—from scratch, I might add," Payton said.

"Well, we might have to forgo dinner and have cake," Katie said with a laugh.

"Nothing doing," Collin said. "We missed lunch, and I'm starved."

The two women looked at one another and broke out in laughter.

"Katie, meet Collin," Payton said.

"Hi, Collin. Come on in. I opened a bottle of wine. I also have beer, if you prefer. I want you to meet my friend," Katie said.

Payton unhooked the leashes from the dogs as two tollers flew out of the motor home.

"Wow. They look like small golden retrievers with the tips of their tails, paws, and lower part of their chests all dipped in white paint," Collin said.

"That's a common assumption. They are the smallest of the retrievers and are often mistaken for a small golden," Katie said.

Payton and Collin followed Katie into the motor home and left the door open for the dogs to move freely in and out. A woman stood at the stove, her back to everyone. Her flaming red hair was pulled back into a ponytail. She put down the spoon she held and turned to greet everyone.

"Sarah?" Collin asked.

Payton stood dumbfounded as she looked from Sarah, to Collin, to Katie. *How could Collin possibly know a friend of Katie's?* She wondered.

"You know her, Collin?" Payton asked.

"One way of putting it," he said. He looked as bewildered as Payton felt. "Sarah is Emma's half-sister. What in the hell are you doing here?"

"Oh my gosh, Collin, I thought you were dead," Sarah said. "This is more than I could have hoped for. It's been such a long time."

"Why don't I get us some wine and we can all sit down while Sarah explains what's going on?" Katie said.

"Katie, how do you know Sarah?" Payton asked, as she took the glass of wine Katie handed her and sat in a chair.

"We went to high school together. I knew your father too, Collin," Katie said.

"I suppose Katie told you I would be here," Payton said.

"I didn't," Katie said.

"I have a friend who went to your gala last week. She mentioned she spoke briefly to you about your dogs and you mentioned you would be attending these shows, Payton," Sarah explained. "I only hoped to meet you and see if you, or Victory, could help me. Collin, you being alive and well surely saves me time, which I am currently running extremely short on. "

"So what's this all about?" Collin asked, as he eyed her suspiciously.

Payton could feel the uneasiness in Collin. A ripple of emotion ran over her and made goose bumps rise on her arms and her hair stand on end. She crossed her arms and rubbed her hands up and down them in an attempt to rid herself of the sensation.

"I think I might be in trouble and if I make the wrong decision, Emma could be in trouble too," Sarah said.

Hearing Emma's name mentioned piqued Collin's interest. His eyes turned turbulent as he focused his entire attention on Sarah. "What does Emma have to do with anything?"

Payton could feel the threat edge his voice.

"If you will sit down, I will tell you the whole story," Sarah said.

Collin studied Sarah. Payton held her breath and waited.

"Fine. I want to hear about whatever this is and how Emma is involved. And Sarah, you better tell me the whole story."

Sarah picked up the bottle of wine that sat on the counter and filled her glass. She walked across the room, set the bottle and glass on a side table, and sat in the chair across from Collin and Payton.

"Five years ago, I got offered the position of a lifetime, but everything changed three weeks ago."

Chapter Eight

"When I graduated from college, I was the youngest in my class and had managed to finish my four-year degree in only two years," Sarah said. "I received numerous job offers, except I hadn't decided what I really wanted to do. One day my Uncle Dave stopped by the house and offered me a job with the company he worked for. His position in the company is Vice President, and I figured working for his company would give me a great foot in the door."

"Wait. Uncle Dave?" Collin questioned her. "You and your mom came from Scotland. I wasn't aware you had any relatives in the States."

"We don't. He's not my real uncle, but he has been part of the family for as long as I can remember, and I have always called him uncle. Uncle Dave is a good friend of Mom and your dad's. He always spent time at the house, although now that I think about it, he seemed to be there more often when your dad got called away on a mission. Thinking back, I believe Mom and Uncle Dave engaged in a relationship while your dad was still alive," Sarah said.

"So, they were screwing around," Collin growled.

"I'm pretty sure. Although, Uncle Dave hasn't been around much the last couple of years. Mom has moved on to another guy—men and their money are her favorite pastime. Anyway, I jumped at the offer to work for Uncle Dave's company—especially when he told me I would be the administrative assistant to the CEO and owner," Sarah said.

"Congratulations, but what does this have to do with you and Emma being in trouble?" Payton asked.

"My uncle is Dave Anderson and I work for Biotec, as Mr. Braxton's assistant," Sarah blurted out.

"What?" Collin yelled. He jumped up from his seat at the same time as Payton.

"Do Anderson and Braxton know you are here?" he asked.

"More importantly, do they know Collin is alive?" Payton asked.

"The answer to both questions is no. Like I said, Dave hasn't been around. I've only seen him at work for the last year. If you would both sit back down, I will explain." Sarah waited while they took their seats and continued. "Three weeks ago all hell broke loose at the main office. Mr. Braxton made it a habit to disappear for long periods of time. This last time he has been gone for almost a year. At first I didn't think a thing of it. Uncle Dave has often handled the running of the company in Mr. Braxton's absence."

"Don't call him 'uncle,'" Collin snapped. "He's not, thank God, because if he was your uncle, he would be Emma's too."

"I understand. Anyway, over the last few weeks I started to hear rumors. Someone said the main site where I work, on San Juan Island, would soon close down for good and all the employees would be transferred to other sites abroad. I couldn't get any real information though, so I started to do my own investigation," Sarah said.

"I decided to stay on the island for a couple days. As I often did when I worked long days, no one thought any different of it. I have my own room there. I waited until everyone left for the day, went back to the offices, and got into Mr. Braxton's office. I started to access his computer when I heard the door unlock. I shut down the computer and ran behind the bar and prayed to God whoever entered the office wouldn't look back there. The door swung open and uncle—sorry, I mean, Dave entered and talked on the phone to Mr. Braxton. I got really nervous when he plopped himself down in a chair," Sarah said.

"What did he say, Sarah?" Collin prompted her.

"I didn't understand everything at the time. Dave said he had commenced with the reorganization of the departments one at a time. He'd offered transfers to the employees picked by Braxton and was tying up loose ends where needed. Dave said he placed Emma in the school Braxton wanted her in, and would use her school as a way to keep me in line, if need be."

"That slimy bastard," Collin hissed.

"Collin, he said you were dead." Tears trickled down Sarah's cheeks. "After he picked up the file he had come in for, he started for the door. On his way out I heard him say something about the facility being ready for use in two months. I don't understand? Why would they move everyone off the island if they still intended on using it?"

Collin glanced at Payton.

"Anyway," Sarah continued. "I waited in the darkness for over an hour and then ran back to my room. The next day, Dave came to see me and offered me a transfer. I told him I wasn't sure I wanted to be shipped abroad, because I wanted to stay close to my sister. He told me to take some time off and think about it. He implied my decision to take the job abroad would be in Emma's best interest. He said as long as I did what I was told, Emma would be given the best possible education, and if I didn't, he couldn't guarantee anything."

"Douchebag," Collin hissed again. "If he touches one hair on Emma's head, I will tear him apart slowly limb from limb."

"I didn't know what to do. I needed someone to help me. Before my friend told me she saw you, I started to think about contacting Victory. I met her last year when she spent some time on the island while she interviewed with Mr. Braxton about a possible project. I thought she might have enough influence to help me," Sarah said.

"An interview?" Payton snorted. "If you call being forced into something you don't want to do because your family is being threatened an *interview*."

"What?" Sarah asked, horror etched in her face. "No, that can't be right. Mr. Braxton is a prominent businessman."

"Why are you here, Sarah?" Collin asked.

Sarah took in a deep breath and let it out slowly.

"You're right. I am dearly sorry for any way I might have unknowingly added to your family's grief, Payton. Please believe me when I say I truly believed Victory had an interview. He brought people there all the time for the same thing." She paused for a moment. "I really don't think Dave will hurt Emma. He has known her from the age of five; he wouldn't do anything to her. The worst he would do is to pull her out of the school. Which would be bad enough I guess, I don't think I could afford to keep her in a private school."

"He could and he would hurt Emma. If he really cared for your mom like you say, he would make her death look like an accident and be there to pick up the pieces when she fell apart," Collin said.

"How could he? He loves her." Sarah put the back of her hand up to her mouth in an attempt to stifle her sobs.

* * * *

Payton remained quiet and she concentrated on her barriers as wave after wave of fury rolled off of Collin. She knew she needed to bring him back from going down his dark path before he went too far. She felt as if she were in the eye of the storm and needed to stop his wayward emotions now. She reached for the bracelet. It wasn't there. Then she remembered she had removed it to take a quick shower earlier in the afternoon. She was on her own.

"Collin. I understand that you are upset, but you need to get a grip. You will be of no use to Emma or Sarah or yourself, if you don't calm down and focus. You stay here. I'm going to go outside to make a call," Payton said.

Collin nodded that he understood but his gaze never left Sarah.

A few minutes later, Payton returned with her laptop and the bracelet on her wrist.

"Katie, I know I am asking a lot, but would you mind going outside for a while?" Payton asked.

Katie looked at the group. "I understand, Payton. I think I will take my dogs for a walk." She left the motor home.

"I called Morgan," Payton explained to Collin. "He will contact headquarters and wants us to wait here. He will join us as soon as he reaches them."

There was a knock on the door. Collin went to answer it and found Morgan.

"They will be Skyping us shortly," Morgan said. He took the laptop from Payton and placed it on the kitchen table. The four of them gathered around, and in seconds Payton's computer played, "Lean on Me." She touched the screen and Tristan, Wyatt, and Victory came into view.

Sarah looked totally confused. "Mr. Grant?" she asked.

"Mr. Farraday," Tristan corrected. "I work for the government and was sent in under cover as Victory's lab assistant to keep her safe. Collin and I met on the island."

"Collin...Collin wasn't on the island," Sarah said, and shook her head.

"Yes, Sarah, I was. I will fill you in later. For now, we need to deal with Braxton," Collin said.

The three repeated the story Sarah told them.

When they were finished, Wyatt spoke. "Sarah, I want to believe you are a pawn in all of this. On the other hand, we have no real way to verify what you have told us. How long did Dave give you to decide if you wanted to be transferred?"

"He told me to have all my arrangements made within six weeks and to return to the office after such time," Sarah said.

"Does your mother know where you are now?" Wyatt asked.

"Yes, out on a show circuit with Katie, something I do quite often. I told Mom I would be gone for the entire circuit. No one expects me back in town for the next two weeks. Besides, Mom is out of town with her latest fling. I truly think she is thrilled to be rid of both Emma and me."

The room went silent as everyone absorbed the unfolding events.

"I've told you the truth," Sarah said, tears threatening to spill from her eyes. "I know in my heart Emma is in trouble."

"No one has said we don't believe you. We need to discuss the issue privately. Is there a place she can go and wait?" Wyatt asked.

"Sarah, go back into your bedroom. We will come get you when we are done," Payton said.

"Will you help me?" Sarah asked.

"Yes, Sarah. Now do as Payton asked," Wyatt said.

"I'm going after the son of a bitch," Collin said. "I will find Emma and bring her home, and I'm going after Braxton. I won't stop until I find him."

"Stand down, soldier," Wyatt said. "I know you are upset; you have every right to be. But you are not running off half-cocked. You still work for me."

"Upset?" Collin snarled. "I'm more than upset."

"I understand. However, you are under my command and until things change, you will take orders from me. Do I make myself clear, soldier?" Wyatt asked.

"Crystal, sir," Collin said.

"Good; let's work on our plan."

"I don't know if I trust what Sarah has told us," Victory said. "I find it difficult to believe she knew absolutely nothing about the goings-on in her own office."

"This is exactly why we need to bring her back here and debrief her. We need to find any loopholes in her story. If she did tell the truth, she could be our first break," Tristan said.

"How are you holding up, Payton?" Victory asked.

"A challenge at times, but I'm dealing with it," Payton said. She and Collin had just started to get into a groove. She might even go as far as admitting that she enjoyed being with him—almost.

"Good," Wyatt said. "I understand Collin's need to be the one who goes after his sister. Sadly, at the current time, he is unable to function rationally for any length of time without you. Are you open-minded to the idea of going with him?"

She looked up at Collin. He didn't make a single sound, simply stared at her. She felt a tiny vibration, something all together different from anything she ever felt from him before—a plea for help. Desperation showed in his eyes and determination resonated throughout his body. She could not allow him to lose his baby sister. Emma meant everything to him, for she alone represented all he had left of his entire family.

Payton silently thanked the universe for her family; how truly sad it was for Collin to have only Emma.

"Yes," she said.

"Good. Morgan will join you two. I sent Logan and Noah on ahead. They will come in by helicopter a few miles from you. We have no time to waste. We need the four of you back here immediately. You will all get on the helicopter as soon as humanly possible and return back to campus. Noah will drive your motor home back, Payton. He said he will take care to bring your dogs home safely," Wyatt said.

"That will work; all four of our Dobermans have gotten to know your entire team and react to them as friends. You are the only one who hasn't spent much time with them," she said.

"They should be there any minute," Wyatt said.

"Captain, Logan is on the phone," Jack said, in the background.

"Hold on," Wyatt said, as he took the phone. "What's up, Logan?" He listened. "What? Shit. I'll tell them." He disconnected the call and looked at Payton. "Tell me you didn't leave Parker and Kes at your motor home?" he asked.

"No, they came with us. Why?" Payton asked.

They all heard him let out an audible breath.

"Because the guys arrived at your motor home, and found the door standing wide open. I'm sorry, Payton. The place looks like a hurricane ripped a path right through the entire vehicle," Wyatt said.

"How could someone destroy the motor home that quickly? I just left there not twenty minutes ago," she said.

"Seems you have been followed," Wyatt said. "My guess is that with all of you away from the motor home, your shadow took advantage of the first opportunity presented to see what could be found."

"No, sir," Morgan said. "They were not followed. I made sure I had the place buttoned down since before Payton and Collin pulled in. My guess is these jokers arrived today, or they might even be part of the dog show."

"Well, either way, you have to be highly careful. We no longer know if Braxton is aware Collin is alive. The last thing we need is for Braxton's crew to get hold of either or both of you again," Wyatt said.

"Yes, sir," Collin and Morgan said.

"See you all shortly," Wyatt said, as he disconnected the call.

"Payton, you and Morgan take the dogs back to the motor home. I'll get Sarah and explain what I can to Katie," Collin said.

Payton stepped into her once-perfect oasis and found chaos. Every piece of furniture had been ripped up. Drawers and cabinet doors were torn from their places, and food was scattered throughout the main salon. Her office looked as if a five-year-old threw a tantrum and tossed everything into the air. She couldn't even tell if anything might be missing. Payton felt relieved she'd decided to take Parker and Kes with them to dinner.

Her knees buckled. Morgan caught her, and Logan turned a chair right side up to place her in it. She knew things could be replaced, but still, her beautiful home was destroyed.

"I'm sorry, Payton," Logan said. "We will make sure your motor home looks brand new after it's repaired."

Logan picked up shards of glass from the floor. "Let's at least get this glass picked up, Morgan. I don't want the dogs to cut their pads."

Payton attempted a smile. "Thanks, Logan. Things can always be fixed. I'm grateful we took the dogs with us; they can't be replaced."

Collin and Sarah walked in. Sarah sucked in her breath as she surveyed the destruction around her.

"Holy hell," Collin muttered. "I'm sorry, Payton. Whoever did this will pay."

"I understand you are upset for me, Collin, however can you tone it down? I can't deal with all the destruction and your extreme emotions at the same time," Payton said.

Sarah looked from Collin to Payton with puzzlement on her face.

Chapter Nine

Wyatt decided the Winters campus would be the securest place for Sarah, and the sisters agreed. He, the SOCOM team, Sarah, Victory, and Payton all gathered in the conference room across from Payton's office.

"Thank you for putting me up, Victory. The bungalow is beautiful," Sarah said.

"It wasn't only me. My two sisters and I made the decision together," Victory said.

"Thank you all," she said. "When can I get my cell phone back? It's got all my pictures of Emma on it. And if she calls, I need to talk to her."

"You won't get it back for a while," Wyatt said. "I'll make sure you get some print copies of your pictures. In the meantime, Jack is still working on the phone. We need to make sure there is no tracker attached to it. If you were to use or turn on your phone now, Dave would most likely be able to locate you; he would figure out which cell towers the cell phone pinged off. We will put in a blocker on the phone to mask your GPS location."

"Then I will get it back?" Sarah asked.

"Eventually. Now tell us about your duties at Biotec," Wyatt said.

"Basic administrative stuff really. I screened calls, wrote reports, and kept Mr. Braxton on schedule," she said.

"You knew everything he was involved with?" Tristan asked.

"No, not everything. Only the routine day-to-day activities. All Mr. Braxton's confidential stuff got handled by Dave. But I saw some of the reports and will tell you what I know," Sarah said.

"We will need a complete list of everyone Braxton ever met or worked with," Wyatt said.

"I can recreate a list, but it will take me some time," Sarah said.

"Have you ever heard the term, Kaleidoscope Group?"

Sarah stared into space, as if she tried to access her mental files. "I don't recall ever having heard or read about the Kaleidoscope Group. Although, one day while I was in Mr. Braxton's office to retrieve a file he requested, a slip of paper fell out of the file and I picked it up off the desk. I remember being confused at the contents of the note. It read, 'emergency meeting with KG scheduled for Tuesday.' I didn't know a KG and wasn't aware of any meeting. The idea there was a meeting scheduled I didn't know about bothered me for a bit, but I quickly forgot. Is it possible the note referenced the Kaleidoscope Group?"

"Most likely, otherwise, it would be too coincidental. How long ago did this happen?" Wyatt asked.

"Hmm…maybe a month before the last time I actually saw Mr. Braxton."

"Okay, Sarah; this is what we need for you to do. We have provided you with a computer at your bungalow. We need you to take as much time as you need and list anything and everything you can remember that was out of the ordinary, not in your daily routine or Braxton's. Even the smallest, most insignificant thing could make a world of difference; don't leave anything out, even if you think it's not important. We also need a list of every business and personal associate you can recall; basically anyone who came into contact with Braxton. There's a man outside the door who will escort you back to your bungalow and stay with you. You are free to come and go as you please within the confines of the campus. You will not have any connection to the outside world, and that includes Internet," Wyatt said.

"It sounds a little as though I am a prisoner," Sarah said.

"Not a prisoner, Sarah. We are trying to keep you safe. Remember, you came to us. Now you have to play by our rules, if you want both Emma and yourself to get out of this whole mess unscathed," Wyatt said.

"I understand. I want my sister out of the academy and with me."

"For now she is safe. We will go in and retrieve her as soon as we know the playing field," Wyatt said.

Sarah nodded, got up from her chair, and left the room without so much as another word.

"You think she told the truth?" Morgan asked Collin.

"I don't know. I never really got to know Sarah too well. The last time we saw each other was over three years ago, and only for a day. I think Emma is important to her and I know she loves her. Other than that, your guess is as good as mine," Collin said.

"We won't know for sure until everything plays out," Wyatt said. "Ladies, would you mind giving us the room?"

"No problem," Payton said. "I have a ton of things to take care of before Collin and I head out...which will be?" She looked at the men.

"Best guess is you only have a day or two tops," Wyatt said.

"I better get started," Payton said. She and Victory left, closing the door behind them.

"Okay, Jack, what have you discovered about the school? I could tell by the way you were fidgeting that you were dying to tell us what you had found," Wyatt said.

"Sorry, sir," Jack said. "Guess I need to work on not fidgeting. I dug through Internet files on the school for the last couple hours. They have created a great smoke screen. Braxton is on the board of directors at the Wright Academy."

"Figures," Collin said.

"It gets better. All the students at the academy are considered geniuses. Collin, your little sister must be brilliant," Jack said.

Morgan snickered.

"Not one word," Collin said. He cut him off before a snide comment could slip from his lips.

"Most of the students accepted into this academy are financially unable to pay for any private education.

The students graduate from the school and go on to a couple different colleges. I wouldn't be surprised if Braxton wasn't somehow financially involved with the colleges. If I have more time, I can find out."

"No need to now, but keep the information filed away," Wyatt said.

"Yes, sir. After the students graduate from college, the majority of them go to work for Braxton to pay back their loans," Jack said.

"Have you been able to track down any graduates?" Tristan asked.

"That's where it really gets tricky. There are no driver's licenses, credit ratings, mortgages, or bank accounts, nothing for any of the names I have found. It's as if they never existed."

"What is Braxton doing with all these students?" Wyatt asked. "You said he is on the board. Is he the owner of the academy?"

"No, sir. The Kaleidoscope Group is listed as the legal owner."

"Son of a bitch," Collin said. "They are creating their own little work force at best, and their own army, at worst."

"Would be my guess," Jack confirmed.

The room fell into complete stillness. Finally, Collin broke through the silence.

"I'll be damned if they are going to add Emma to whatever experiments they are up to."

"Take it easy, Collin. We'll get her out," Wyatt said.

* * * *

"When can I expect to see Sarah?" Braxton's demanding voice boomed through the phone.

"She's a little apprehensive," Dave Anderson answered. Dave sat at Braxton's desk; he double-checked that he had delivered all the information Braxton requested.

"What do you mean, apprehensive?" Braxton yelled.

"She doesn't want to leave her sister. I gave her some time off to think about her decision. With Sarah away, I have time to get organized without her looking over my shoulder and asking questions."

"She's not suspicious about our other activities is she?" Braxton asked.

"No, sir."

"This is not the time for you to hire someone new. You get her on board. Convince her that the move will be good for her career. Offer her a salary increase, more responsibility. Hell, threaten her if you have to; whatever it takes, get her here."

"I'm sure she will come around, sir. She always does."

"When will she be back in the office?"

"In two weeks," Dave said.

"And have you kept tabs on her?"

"Yes, sir. She took off with her friend and went to the dog shows. Same as she always does on vacation, when she's not spending time with Emma. We do have one small matter."

"And what matter might that be?"

Dave could hear the agitation in his boss's voice, never a good sign.

"Payton Winters is at the same show, which again, is not unusual. When I found out, I sent a local in to check her out. I instructed him to search her motor home for any bit of information we might be able to use, like her laptop," Dave said.

"What did he find?" Braxton asked.

"Nothing; the place was clean. She didn't bring her computer. Merely on vacation," Dave said.

"The two women don't know one another, and weren't together?" Braxton asked.

"No, sir." Dave only hoped he spoke the truth. "Actually, due to the mess my guy made, Payton has turned around and headed home."

"And Sarah?" Braxton asked.

"The tracker on her cell shows she is still at the dog show."

"Good. Keep me updated with any changes."

"Yes, sir. Sir, what do you want me to do, if I can't convince Sarah to transfer?" Dave asked.

"You better hope you can. Sadly, if not, I don't want any loose ends. Do I make myself clear?"

"Yes, sir," Dave said.

"Given your history with the family, that won't be a problem for you, will it?"

"No, sir. I have no history. I did my job."

An audible click sounded and the line went dead, which indicated Braxton ended the phone call. Dave knew his boss wasn't happy about his latest update. Sarah better agree to the transfer, for both of their sakes.

* * * *

"Any questions?" Wyatt asked, in-between mouthfuls of food. The men had been shut in the conference room for so long, Payton had sent dinner in.

"Sir, if we are done for the night, do you mind if I head back to my bungalow?" Collin asked. Because of their training, the team could keep their emotions in check. Even so, the endless hours Collin had spent with all of them in a closed room started to wear on him.

"Are you doing okay?" Morgan asked.

"Better than I would have done a week ago, except as I get tired, everyone's emotions start to magnify. I need to clear my head, and the only way is to be alone," Collin said.

"Yes, we have covered about all we can for tonight," Wyatt said. "And you're looking kinda pale. Get out of here. We can finish up tomorrow morning, before you head out."

"Thank you, sir," Collin said.

"Morgan, you should go too. You have had a long week," Wyatt said.

"Yes, sir." Morgan rose from his chair and followed Collin out the door.

As Collin entered the hall, the weight of his team's emotions evaporated, but he could still feel one source. Payton had stayed late in her office. He was stunned he could actually feel her presence.

"Payton is still here," he murmured to himself. He walked down the hall and knocked on the closed door.

"Come in," Payton's muffled voice answered.

He opened the door and expected to see her at her desk, but her chair was empty. He stepped into the room and looked around. He must be hearing things now.

"Collin, do you need me?" Her voice floated in from the open French doors.

He walked through the open doors and found Payton. She sat cross-legged on a blanket on the floor of her patio. She had scattered a few candles about on small tables.

"You're here late," he said.

"I wanted to stay around in case you needed my assistance."

"You were worried I would flip out from being enclosed for such a long period of time," he said with a smile.

"The thought crossed my mind," she smiled back at him.

"I'm fine, just tired. Thanks for sticking around, but it's late and you should get back up to the house," Collin said.

"I'll leave within the hour."

"You can't go home alone; it's dark out."

"I'll be fine. I go up to the house after dark quite often."

"Collin's right," Morgan said, as he stepped out on to the patio. "You stay right here. I'll make sure Collin goes straight to his bungalow, and I'll come back and escort you to your house."

"No, I don't want to put you through any trouble," Payton said.

"No trouble, really Payton. Besides, if I don't escort you, I'll never hear the end of it from Victory or my captain."

"Fine, I'll wait here. See you in the morning, Collin," Payton said.

"Night, Payton." He walked off the patio into the night.

* * * *

"It's such a gorgeous night out," Payton said. She and Morgan walked the path up to her house. "Thanks again for walking me home, Morgan."

"No problem. Like you said, it's a gorgeous night."

Payton stumbled and put her hands out in front of her in an effort to shield herself as she fell. Morgan grabbed her arm as she headed for the ground.

"Are you okay?" he asked.

"It's Collin. His emotions shot right through me; I feel like I have been hit by a strong wind. We need to head back and see if he is all right," she said.

"He's fine. He's totally beat and is having a difficult time with his focus. He went back to his bungalow, and he promised me he would go to bed."

Payton gaped at him. "You can feel him too?"

"Not in the same way you do, but yes, I can," he said.

"What do you mean? You can't help ground him?"

"No. I've always possessed a natural ability to sense people's energy. Since I was injected with the wolf DNA, my abilities have magnified. Especially when relating to people I am emotionally attached to," Morgan said.

"Like your long-time partner," Payton said.

"Exactly. Can you stand?" he asked, as he let go of her arm.

"Yes. I'm fine."

When Payton and Morgan arrived at the kitchen door, they found Victory waiting for them.

"We were concerned." She opened the door and motioned for them to both come in.

"I should get back," Morgan said.

"Please come in and have a glass of wine with us. I have an idea I need to discuss with the two of you," Victory said.

The three went into the living room where Willow sat on the loveseat, with Asia tucked up behind her legs. Parker and Dax were sprawled out on the carpet and Kes held Payton's seat. Payton walked over to the overstuffed chair Kes occupied and snuggled in beside her. Morgan and Victory claimed the last two chairs.

"Payton you look exhausted," Willow said.

"It's been a rough day," Payton said.

"You are worn out, Payton, and that is the reason why I asked you all here," Victory said. "I'm extremely concerned about you leaving tomorrow to accompany Collin on his mission."

"I can handle it. I did fine with him the past week. I think I have started to get the hang of my barriers. I'll be okay," Payton said. "I didn't even have to use the bracelet, but I will take it with me as a backup."

"I don't doubt your resolve, Payton. Nonetheless, last week you were in a familiar situation with people you knew, and there was no threat to you or Collin. But this mission it will be a totally different situation. Both of you will be under stress, and in unfamiliar territory. I'm not certain the bracelet will be strong enough if you need to engage it."

"Victory has an extremely valid point," Morgan said.

"Well, what do you suggest I do? Collin can't function without me for any long period of time, right?" Payton asked.

"Very true. His outburst during our walk here proved the point," Morgan said.

"I believe it's time to give my genetic buffer a try. I've created a serum that I can administer via an injection directly into Collin's bloodstream," Victory said.

"How do you know the serum will work?" Payton asked. "What are the side effects? Are you sure your genetic buffer is safe?"

"I'm fairly certain the serum will work, or at least slow down the DNA that invades his system. I have researched the coupling of foreign, or canine DNA, and human for a number of years, and I have tried to create a linked pathway between the two, to allow both to coexist in one host. As far as side effects, I don't know for sure, and side effects will vary from person to person. I have tested the serum over the past year, and the results have been positive. I'm eighty percent sure my serum will help him," Victory said.

"Eighty percent? There is still a twenty percent chance he could continue to get worse," Payton said.

"Yes. There's always a chance when we deal with human DNA. What I can tell you is I have worked on my buffer serum for more than four years. This isn't something I dreamed up overnight. And if we don't try my buffer soon, we will be unable to help Collin."

"What if you try the serum on me first?" Morgan asked.

"I know you want to protect Collin, Morgan. However, your body has dealt with the change in a totally different way than Collin's. Therefore, your reaction to the serum will be significantly different. There will come a time when we will have to introduce a buffer into your system, but the time is not yet here. You are not in a crucial period, and I plan to use every second I have before I introduce a serum into your system," Victory said.

"Great. What you are saying is Collin is the guinea pig." Payton felt more and more protective of Collin.

"Payton, you're not being fair," Willow said.

"I understand how you feel, Payton, and yes, Collin is the guinea pig, thanks to that bastard, Braxton. All I can do now is try to help him," Victory said.

Payton looked down at the glass of wine in her hands. She knew she unfairly blamed her sister for Collin's predicament. If it weren't for Victory, Collin would not have a chance of surviving the injustice forced upon him.

"I'm sorry, sis," Payton said. "I know none of what happened to Collin and Morgan is your fault. You are their only real hope. It's just all so damn scary."

"I know. Tomorrow morning I'll explain everything to Collin. I would like you to be there too, Morgan, since this involves both of you," Victory said.

"I'll be there, doc," Morgan said, as he stood up from his chair. "It's been a long day, and I still have to pack. I will bid all you ladies good night."

"There's one more thing we have to discuss," Willow said, after Morgan left.

"What else could possibly have happened?" Payton asked.

"I have to leave tomorrow and go back to our offices in London."

"Why now? You left Angie in charge and she is more than capable," Payton said.

"Yes, Angie is excellent. Sadly, last night on her way to her car in the company's parking garage, she got mugged."

"What?" Payton and Victory asked.

"Oh my God, is she all right?" Victory asked. "Sounds like déjà vu all over again; remember my colleague, Lisa Evans?"

"You think this is the same thing?" Payton asked.

"Who?" Willow asked.

"I forgot, you were in London when the whole Lisa situation took place," Victory said. "Lisa was the employee found dead in the Claremont Research parking garage. The police classified her death as a mugging gone wrong."

"Come to find out, Lisa was murdered by one of Braxton's henchmen, Detective Howard," Payton said.

"You two think Braxton was involved with Angie's mugging? Possible, I suppose. Fortunately, the doctors believe she will make a full recovery. She sustained a broken leg and a couple broken ribs and will be out of commission for at least four months according to her doctor. I need to get out there and see what's happening in the office and find a temporary replacement for her," Willow said.

"I don't like this one bit," Payton said. "What if Braxton is somehow behind Angie's accident? What if he orchestrated the entire mishap to get you to go to England alone?"

"Don't worry. I won't be alone. I explained the situation to Wyatt. He is sending the whole Beta

SOCOM team with me. Come to find out, Wyatt has two teams under his command."

"Well, I feel much better about you going with a full team as your chaperone," Victory said. "Still, I don't like the idea that both of you will be off the campus. It gives Braxton multiple opportunities to reach one of you."

"We will both be careful, sis, and we have lots of protection. I should only be gone for a week or so as long as everything goes okay," Willow said.

"Can you hold down the fort without us?" Payton asked.

"I should be fine. I can Skype either of you when I have a problem," Victory said.

"Well, remember you are now in charge of the entire campus. Translation, you can't hide yourself in your lab twenty-four seven," Payton said.

Chapter Ten

"Payton," Victory called, as she knocked on her sister's door for the third time. She tried the knob and found it unlocked. She found Payton, wedged between Kes and Parker, with a pillow over her head. Both dogs lifted their heads as Victory opened the door, yet neither one budged a muscle. "Payton, honey, it's time to get up." She gently shook Payton's shoulder.

"It can't be time to get up already. I just fell asleep," Payton moaned her voice still heavy with sleep.

Parker rolled over on his back and stretched, the length of his body nearly covering the entire length of the bed. Kes extended her back legs straight out behind her. Her stub wagged nonstop, and she licked Payton on the cheek. Payton giggled as she scratched both of the dogs.

"It's ten in the morning. The guys are getting itchy. Logan wants to get you guys down to San Francisco."

"It's ten o'clock? I never sleep late; are you sure?"

"You had an exceptionally tough couple of days. I convinced the guys to let you sleep a little longer. How do you feel?"

"Like I have a hangover."

"That's a side effect of your emotions on constant overdrive. They aren't meant to work nonstop and at full capacity. I've made breakfast for you. Take your shower and dress, and I'll have fresh coffee for you."

"Wait. You made breakfast?" Payton looked skeptically at her sister as she headed for the bathroom.

"Yes, pancakes and bacon. Even I can make pancakes," Victory said, as she threw a pillow at Payton. "I'll see you downstairs. Come on, guys, it's time for your breakfast, too."

The two dogs hopped off the bed and trotted out the door behind Victory.

"I'm impressed," Payton said, as she took a last sip of coffee. "Did Willow run down to the campus?"

"No, her plane took off about two hours ago. She told me to wish you luck and to give you a hug. She didn't want to wake you up. She said she would wait to hear from you after you reach California," Victory said.

"And Collin?"

"We got together first thing this morning, and I explained the entire situation to him. He insisted on the injection immediately. If you ask me, I think he agreed on the serum more for your sake than his. I introduced the serum into his system three hours ago, and so far he hasn't noticed any changes. You and Morgan are tasked with watching for any variances. Your main priority is to keep tabs on him. I need all three of you to journal every day. You are my eyes and ears and an extremely important part of my research."

"Gee, no pressure," Payton said.

"I'm sorry, Payton; you must understand that tracking each and every minute for any change in Collin is terribly important."

"I know. We are talking about Collin's life; his entire existence depends on a positive outcome from the new serum. It's just that you have placed an extreme amount of pressure on us to record every nuance; after all, we aren't scientists like you."

"You don't need to have my background. You and Morgan know Collin well, and I have faith you will take notice of any change in him. Send me a text with any and all changes; that's all I need," Victory said.

"I'm packed. I guess I should head to the helipad," Payton said.

"I'll drive you there. Let's take the cart."

"You two be good," Payton said. She hugged her two dogs and gave them each a kiss on the top of their heads. She also said goodbye to Asia and Dax, picked up her bags, and headed for the cart.

Collin and Morgan met them at the edge of the helipad as they pulled up.

"Let's get this show on the road," Morgan said, as he grabbed Payton's bags. "Logan is cranky." He loaded her gear into the helicopter.

Victory got out of the cart and walked over to give her sister one last hug. "Promise me you will be extremely vigilant. You are walking into the belly of the dragon. Braxton is a cold-hearted bastard and he will stop at nothing to get what he wants."

"I'll be careful sis, I promise." Payton hugged her back. "You need to stay put here on the campus while we are gone. Make sure you review all my incoming emails. I'll check my emails whenever I can. I know your research is your first priority. Still, don't forget you are the only one left to run our company, and management of the entire campus is important too. You're in charge; don't forget."

"I know. I'll stay on top of things. Thank goodness our home is only a mile away. I foresee some excessively long days on my horizon."

Payton smiled at her one last time and turned to the waiting men and helicopter. Morgan jumped up into the aircraft and slid to the far side as she approached. He eyed Noah, who sat in the passenger seat next to Logan.

"You gonna hold his hand on the trip down?" Morgan joked.

"Nope, I've been instructed to hold your leashes during the mission," Noah shot back.

"Since when? Are you saying Wyatt doesn't trust us?"

"He trusts you; it's the string of wolf DNA he's not completely comfortable with," Noah said.

"What do you mean? Does he think we will scrub the mission and bay at the moon?" Morgan snorted.

"Deal with it, dog boy. Until we know how you and Collin will function in mission conditions with your new genetic makeup, you will have a full-time leash holder."

* * * *

Collin waited at the open door. When Payton got close to him, he held out his hand to help her up into the aircraft. She hesitated and stiffened as she realized that until now, she and Collin never actually made physical contact, at least not when she was fully conscious. The last thing she needed today would be a screaming headache to start the trip, or worse yet, to fall face first on to the concrete as she blacked out.

"I won't bite," Collin said.

"You biting never crossed my mind. What I am worried about is being inundated with your emotions," she said.

"I've got them under control. You need to trust me Payton, if we are to see our mission through." His hand remained outstretched.

She rubbed her wrist with her opposite hand to confirm she had put on the bracelet. She steeled herself against the inevitable onslaught of sensations, and she lightly placed her hand into his palm and waited.

What she felt totally caught her off-guard. Instead of a myriad of animosities that threatened to consume her, she became immersed in a deluge of warmth. The heat sizzled up her arm and spread straight up her spine. Color instantly stained her cheeks. She glanced up into his electric-blue eyes and caught his twinkle of satisfaction. Hastily, she stepped up into the helicopter and pulled her hand free from his. The abrupt release left her feeling cold and alone.

Collin waved at Victory and then jumped in beside Payton.

"Let's go," Collin said to Logan as he rapped on the back of the pilot seat and turned back to slide the door closed.

* * * *

"Who owns this house?" Payton asked, as she waited for Morgan to unlock the door.

Collin stayed close to Payton, and Noah brought up the rear, keeping a keen eye on everything that happened around the quartet.

"It's one of our safe houses. We have them scattered throughout the country and abroad," Noah said.

"Well, how convenient. I assume there is no room service?" Payton asked. She smiled at the three men. "I'm glad we brought you, Collin; at least we will have wonderful meals."

"Oh, Collin can cook? I'm in heaven. At last, a mission where I won't have to eat MREs," Noah said.

"MREs?" Payton asked.

"Meals, Ready to Eat. Precooked and prepackaged meals, and I do loosely use the term, 'meals,'" Noah said.

"Yuck," she said, and wrinkled her nose.

"Yup, that about sums them up," Noah chuckled.

Morgan opened the door and motioned for the others to enter. The interior of the house actually surprised Payton; it was clean and conservatively decorated in a traditional décor.

"Wow. Not what I expected. I thought it would be the kind of safe house you see in all the cop shows," she said, with a giggle.

"Please, we are much more civilized than cop shows," Noah said. "We even have a manager who takes care of the place."

"A stranger takes care of your place when you are not here? Are you sure that's safe?" she asked.

"Totally. All of our people are thoroughly vetted," Noah said. "Our staff has no idea who we really are. To them, we are businessmen who are on constant travel.

The cleaning staff schedule is in the kitchen. If we have a conflict, we need to call the manager. Okay, there are five bedrooms upstairs; the lady gets first choice. There should be a few drinks in the refrigerator, but we will need to stock up on food. Collin, since you will be our chef while we are here, I need you to make a list of the ingredients you need, and I'll go to the store."

She heard Morgan snicker.

"What are you laughing about? I'm lead on this mission, which makes you assigned to washing the dishes," Noah said.

"Wait one minute—" Morgan said.

Payton giggled again. She enjoyed listening to grown men act like a bunch of kids. They got along like brothers.

"You guys work out the details. I'll do whatever jobs you assign to me. I will be upstairs; I need to unpack."

* * * *

"Damn. Man, you really can cook," Noah said. He rubbed his belly as they sat around the kitchen table and finished up dessert. "I'm going to request you on all my missions."

"Would you mind explaining to me what our next step is?" Payton asked the men.

"We are on a recon mission, nothing else," Noah said, and looked directly at Collin.

"Wait a God damn minute. Wyatt said we would get Emma out," Collin said.

"You know the drill. We will get her out after we have the lay of the land and all the players involved.

125

Until such time, Emma stays put. She is safe for now, and I'm sure you want her to remain safe, don't you?" Noah asked.

"What happens tomorrow?" Payton asked, as she attempted to defuse the situation.

"Tomorrow I'll get a look at the school. Morgan, you will be my wingman. You and Collin will stay put. No one on Braxton's crew has ever seen me, and I'm going in posed as a parent looking for a school for my child."

Payton looked over at Collin and she tried to get a read on him. He appeared pale and tired.

"Collin, are you okay?" she asked.

"Yeah, all of a sudden I feel wiped out. If we are finished for the night, I think I will call it a day," Collin said.

* * * *

"How's it going?" Victory asked.

Payton sat on the bed, laptop open, Skyping her sister.

"As good as can be expected, I guess."

"Did something happen?" Victory asked.

"Collin seemed pretty stable for most of the day. Either I've gotten better able to keep up my barriers, or your serum concoction really helps," Payton said.

"Tell me what happened," Victory said.

Payton relayed the events of the day, blow-by-blow to her sister.

"It's not alarming that he looked tired at the end of the day. I saturated his system with the buffer. He became over-stimulated. Eventually, as the serum works into his body, his moods and energy should start to level out. At least that is my goal. He started out on a high today; by the end of the day, he burned out. Don't worry too much. It is highly likely his days could get even rougher before they get better," Victory said.

"Okay, I'll try not to worry—much. Did you know Noah got assigned to accompany us?"

"Yes, Tristan told me last night, and I believe Noah's attendance is a good decision. Even though I personally like both Collin and Morgan, we have no idea what the ultimate result will be from the foreign DNA. With Noah there it lessens my worry. Your safety is his number one priority."

"Well sis, I'm really beat and tomorrow will be a long and trying day. We will talk again tomorrow night, unless you have any problems at work."

"Don't worry about work. I have everything under control. Good night, Payton."

Payton woke to the wonderful smell of breakfast cooking. She got out of bed, showered, and dressed in record time.

"What is that fabulous aroma?" she asked, as she entered the kitchen.

"Only my famous crab and artichoke quiche," Collin said. "Grab a chair and I'll fix you a plate."

"You look better," Payton said, as she sat.

"Yeah, it's amazing what a good night's sleep will do. Last night was the best I have slept in months."

He handed her a steaming mug of coffee. As she took the mug, their fingers brushed against each other.

Sparks flew between them, and the hairs on her arm actually stood on end.

"Have the guys left?" she sputtered as she pulled the mug to her mouth.

"They took off about an hour ago. Now comes the hard part."

"And what, might I ask, is the hard part?"

"Waiting. If there is one thing I hate, it's waiting."

"Well, let's think of an activity to do after breakfast to take your mind off the wait."

"Such as?"

"Can we go for a walk?"

"Sorry. I have strict orders to stay inside," he said.

"Okay, there must be some board games here, or we can download a game."

Collin gave a lighthearted laugh. The sound enveloped her in warmth and made her feel safe. She blinked her eyes. If she wasn't careful, this man could wrap his infectious smile around her heart. All the same, she had to keep a constant vigil in his presence. In the next instant he might inadvertently cause her such severe pain it could drop her to her knees.

"Why are you laughing at me?" she asked.

"Because only you would suggest we play a board game in our current situation."

Collin's satellite phone rang.

"Go," he said. "Roger." He disconnected the call. "Morgan said Noah is inside the school. Nothing out of the ordinary has happened. Morgan is taking pictures and will canvas the area. We probably won't hear from them again until they get back, unless they run into a snag."

"Now we wait," Payton said, as she picked up her plate and headed for the sink. "Well, since we might be waiting awhile, I challenge you to a game of whatever."

"You're on," he said.

Chapter Eleven

Morgan, Noah, Collin, and Payton gathered around the computer as Noah reported on the day's events to Wyatt and the rest of the team.

"There are definitely some deep pockets involved in this school. The students who attend the academy are from all over the globe. From the sound of it, the majority are there on scholarships provided by the board," Noah said, and confirmed Jack's prior information.

"And does the Kaleidoscope Group own the school?" Wyatt asked. He feared he already knew the answer, as Jack was rarely, if ever—wrong.

"Jack's intel is spot on. Except they are going by KG International," Noah said.

"Isn't that sneaky? At least we have verified the information Sarah gave us. Did you get any more information with regard to KG International?" Wyatt asked.

"I asked a couple of questions but got shut down and I decided not to push it. The administrator informed me if I thought of any further questions, I could speak to the chancellor of the academy."

"Who is?" Wyatt asked.

"Chancellor Braxton," Noah said.

"Did they happen to tell you when he might be around?"

"No, sir, only that he is currently out of the country on a goodwill mission. And if you believe their story, I have a bridge I'd like to sell you."

Everyone laughed; it helped to relieve some of the tension.

"Collin, did you get a chance to review the pictures Morgan sent us?" Wyatt asked, once again all business.

"Yes, sir. Sorry to say, Emma did not appear in any of the pictures," Collin said.

"I see. Morgan, tell us about the security."

"Four-man security team. Electronic locks on all the doors, number pads, nothing fancy. The entire academy is enclosed by a twelve-foot wrought-iron fence. No motion detectors on the outside, pretty basic," Morgan said.

"Inside is about the same, keypads, no motion detectors. Only two guards inside, it gives the appearance they are not too concerned with security," Noah said.

"Okay. I'll have Jack identify every student you got pictures of and any teachers or other employees you might have taken. You guys all sit tight until we see what we have and relax for the night. We will connect with you again tomorrow at zero seven hundred," Wyatt said.

"What's for dinner, chef?" Noah asked, and slapped Collin on the back.

"Nothing fancy: Salad, fresh veggies, and I'll grill us some steaks," Collin said.

"Man, my mouth is watering just at the thought. Since we're off for the night, how about I go and pick us up some beer and wine?" Noah asked.

"Do you mind if I tag along with you?" Morgan asked. "I need to pick up a couple items. I'll wear a baseball cap and sunglasses."

"Yeah, sure. Might as well make it worth the trip. Payton, Collin, make me a list."

The two guys took off, prepped with "must haves," and left Collin and Payton to start the dinner.

"What can I do to help?" Payton asked. "I've felt the ebbs and flows in your energy all day. I'm sure the serum must be excessively taxing to your system, coupled with being confined in the house and having to deal with all our emotions. I don't want you to overdo it. We both know if you get rundown, things could be really bad for both of our sakes."

"Afraid I will blackout and begin howling?" he asked in a half-teasing tone. "You're right. I guess I have started to experience the first of those 'bad days' Victory warned me about. I could use some help chopping veggies, and you could put the salad together. If you'll do that, I could work on a dessert."

"You don't have to ask me twice. If my help means you make one of your phenomenal desserts, let me at them, coach."

Collin smiled at her.

"What?"

"I find our situation totally amazing. A month ago you couldn't stand to be in the same room with me.

Now it's almost as though we have become friends. The world is an interesting place."

"We *are* friends, Collin. At least I feel you are my friend. I guess I can't speak for you," Payton said.

* * * *

Collin studied her as she moved around the kitchen. What about this woman held his brain together? And why her? Never in his life had he relied on anyone, until this perfect stranger walked into his chaotic life with the power to bring clarity and serenity. This little slip of a woman held his life in her hands; it was an extremely terrifying situation.

Payton's auburn hair hung loose and free today. As her hair caught the sun that flooded in the windows, he could swear he saw gold sparkle through it. Her tan shorts and light purple tank top accentuated every curve. *What happened earlier today?* He wondered. His fingers barely grazed Payton's, and he could swear he felt sparks. *And hell, what about the other day?* He only took her hand to help her get in the helicopter and fireworks erupted through him. *Shit, it was better than sex*, although he hadn't actually experienced sex with Payton. *Get a grip, McBain. She is only here out of necessity, not by choice.*

She abruptly stopped humming and turned, locking gazes with him. Her eyes appeared a dark emerald green.

"Collin, have you started to feel worse?"

"Hmm? No, taking a short rest and trying to decide what kind of dessert to make."

He knew she didn't believe him by the slight frown on her face.

"I got a sudden jolt of emotion, not the standard start-of-a-headache kind, but a jolt all the same. Are you thinking about Emma? I'm sure she will be fine; try not to worry."

Collin realized he could almost predict her train of thought now. It was typical for Payton to be worried about him—*or could it be more? Could she somehow have tapped into his psyche and actually read his thoughts? Not only ground his emotions and feel the impact, but also genuinely understand what he felt? Don't be a dumb ass. We've spent a great deal of time together, it's just woman's intuition.* He brushed the thought aside, and thought of a plausible answer to her question.

"I'm sure you are right. Emma will be fine until we can get her out. How are you doing over there?" he asked, as he rose from his chair.

Everyone raved about dinner. Collin was simply glad it was over. He needed to get to his bedroom before his legs completely gave out.

"I think I'm going to call it a night," he said.

"Do you still feel ill? Your color is pasty again," Payton said.

"I'm tired is all, and I still need to report in to Victory," Collin said.

When he got to his room he closed the door, grabbed the laptop, and settled into his bed. He closed his eyes; he needed some time to compose himself. *Might as well get this over with.*

"How are you holding up, Collin?" Victory asked. "You don't look well. Maybe we should pull you from the mission."

"No, I'll be fine. I felt good for most of the day. I just get drained by early evening."

"You need to take it easy and rest. It will take time for your system to process the serum. Don't push yourself. I mean it," she said.

"Yes, ma'am," Collin said. "I'll take it easy. It's not as though I've been doing excessive work. Making dinner is the highlight of my day."

"Exactly my point. When it starts to heat up, I don't want you to fall apart," Victory said. "Remember, it isn't only your sanity we are talking about. Payton is tied to you, whether the two of you want to admit the truth or not."

"I understand, Victory. I would never consciously put Payton in danger."

"I know you wouldn't. It's the unconscious part I worry about. Please, rest. We'll talk again tomorrow. Good night, Collin."

* * * *

The next day seemed to drag on with everyone confined to the house. Morgan and Noah spent the day preparing for their next recon. Collin tried convincing Wyatt to agree to let him go with the two men, but his efforts fell on deaf ears. After he spent the entire day cooped up with everyone, his body once again began to feel like lead. He could better appreciate how Payton felt, the first few times she found herself in his presence.

"You ready to go?" Noah asked Morgan. He looked out the window. Dusk had finally fallen.

"Been ready," Morgan said.

"Okay, let's lock and load."

The two men slipped out the back door and melted into the night.

"Guess there's no more to be done now. I think I will go up to take a nap. Holy Hell, I feel like an old man," Collin said.

As he stood, the room around him began to tilt. He started to fall, and felt as if he were taking in the scene from a distance. Two arms wrapped around him and broke his fall. Then they dragged him to the sofa. *Damn, that woman is strong*, was the last thought that played though his conscious mind.

"Welcome back," Payton said. She sat on the edge of the sofa and held a cool cloth on his forehead. "How do you feel?"

"Guess I'm overtired. I should go to bed."

She pushed him back as he tried to get up.

"You are to stay right where you are, mister. You're lucky I caught you the first time. I'll go and get you some water. You look like you could use some aspirin. Don't move," she warned. She emphasized her warning with a shake of her index finger.

"Yes, ma'am. I got a little dizzy is all; I'm fine now," he said.

"Oh please. You look as if it's the early morning after an all night binger." She reappeared with the water and pills. "I felt a punch to my stomach when you started to the ground. And by the way, you have been out cold for over an hour."

"No!" he said, his eyebrows climbing halfway to his hairline.

"I decided to give you another ten minutes, after which time I would have no choice but to call Victory."

"Thanks for holding off. My little episode is all she would need to pull me off this mission."

"Collin, have you stopped to think maybe pulling you off the mission isn't such a bad idea?"

"No, I have to be here. I have to find my sister. Please, Payton. I'll take it easy."

She studied him as she debated what she should do. He watched the thoughts cross her face and patiently waited for her answer.

"All right. But you need to be honest with me. You told me I have to trust you; well you also need to trust me. Deal?" Payton asked.

"Deal," Collin said.

She sat back down on the edge of the sofa. Their bodies brushed together, and he wondered if she felt the tingles of electricity. He put the glass on the table beside them and gently took hold of both of her upper arms and pulled her down toward him. He watched confusion and panic cross her features, yet she didn't attempt to stop him. His lips met hers and he kissed her lightly. In seconds, the gentleness was replaced by a drowning sensation; the physical contact with Payton was his lifeline. Energy crackled and arced between them.

"Thank you," he whispered, his lips softly brushed against hers.

"For what?" she whispered back. Her hazel eyes were the size of silver dollars.

"For being my friend," he said, and smiled up at her.

The front door swung open, and Payton leaped up from the sofa.

"Lucy—we're home," Noah said.

"You're a riot," Collin said. He was already in an upright position.

"Try going on a mission with him," Morgan said.

"Did you find her?" Payton asked.

"No. There are three huge dormitory buildings and a guard on every door. There are at least nine more guards on duty at night," Noah said.

"Why do you think more guards are on duty at night?" Payton asked.

"I'm not sure if they are trying to keep people out or the students in," Noah said.

The computer beeped, and they all went into the kitchen, where Noah connected the call.

"Evening, sir," Noah said to Wyatt. "I thought we were supposed to update you in the morning?"

"We have a development," Wyatt said. "Sarah received a call from Emma."

"What? Is she okay?" Collin asked.

"Emma said she's fine. She also told Sarah some of the students were going on an extended field trip."

"Some of the students? How extended?" Collin asked.

"She wasn't sure; they hadn't gotten all the details. The students all met in an assembly earlier today and were instructed they would be divided up according to how they rank in their class," Wyatt said.

"What in the world does that mean? Only certain students get to go on the field trip?" Payton asked. "The whole idea doesn't sound right to me. Did Emma say when the students would be going?"

"She said they would be informed of the details tomorrow, and at that time they would be assigned to the individual groups. The field trip is scheduled for first thing Friday morning. Payton, we all feel the same way. Something's brewing, and knowing Braxton, it won't be good. Noah, Morgan, what did you guys find out tonight?" Wyatt asked.

Noah gave his captain the full rundown and at the end added, "We didn't really hang around to hear much; we just scouted out the school and guards."

Wyatt looked at his watch. "It's only zero one-hundred. You still have time to head back and try and get into the offices. Put your ears to the ground and see what you can pick up."

"Yes, sir," the two men said.

"Captain—" Collin began.

"Request denied," Wyatt finished. "You look like hell. I know you want to go. We need you to stay behind for now. You can't risk being seen—or worse—blacking out. If things go bad and we have to pull Emma out, we will need you there. For now, go get some sleep, and that's an order."

"Yes, sir," Collin said.

"I will expect to hear back before the night is out. Good luck, men."

With that the computer screen went blank.

"I need to add a couple more toys to our packs. We will be ready to go in five minutes," Noah said.

* * * *

Noah and Morgan split up once they got over the main fence. They had run short on time and decided they could cover twice the ground that way. Morgan headed for the main office, and Noah followed a couple of guards back to their home base. He melted into shadows only a few feet from the entrance to the guard shack.

"Anything going on?" one of the guards inside the building asked.

"Nah, quiet as the proverbial tomb."

"A good thing. Let's keep it that way. I got a call from Dave Anderson today," the first guard said, obviously the one in command. "The timetable has been moved up. Second Wave starts tomorrow. The students selected will be bussed out the next day."

"What's the rush?" the second guard asked. "They've only been here a couple months. Second Wave usually doesn't start for at least six months."

Noah moved closer to the entrance to get a look at the guards.

"I didn't ask. It's above my pay grade, and I want to keep my job," the first man said, giving the other guard an "asshole" look.

"Yes, sir." The first guard took the hint.

"Let's go on a two-man rotation, to play it safe." He turned and looked at a second pair of guards. "You two are on now. Check every door and canvas every building."

That was Noah's cue to pull Morgan out. He slunk back into the bushes. When he'd put enough distance between himself and the guards, he activated his ear bud.

"Morgan, come in," he said, in a low tone.

"Roger," Morgan said.

"You are going to have company shortly. Clear out and meet me at the rendezvous point."

"Roger," Morgan said.

* * * *

"Second Wave is somehow linked to the students," Noah said, as he gave his report to Wyatt and the group. "Morgan sent you some pictures of the files he found. All the students will be placed on busses."

"Did you locate Emma?" Wyatt asked.

"In a way. Emma McBain is on one of the lists, so we can safely assume she is currently at the academy," Morgan said. "It took me some time to get into the building and find the office. The pictures I have are what I found in the paper files on the admin desk."

"I take it you were unable to access any files on the computer?" Wyatt asked.

"I made an attempt. There is one hell of a security block on the system," Morgan said.

"Makes sense. This is an academy full of brilliant students. The staff would have to take great care to keep any wandering eyes out of their system," Wyatt said.

"Sir, there are three different lists here, with a bus number on each list," Jack said, as he reviewed the pictures he'd downloaded.

"Three different busses?" Wyatt asked.

"Do all three have the same destination?" Tristan asked.

"I'm not sure. There is no destination listed on any of them," Jack said.

"If I'd had more time, I might have gotten into the damned system," Morgan said.

"We work with what we have," Wyatt said. "We need to know where all those buses are going. Okay, Collin, your time has finally come. It's your job to locate your sister. Get her out of there as quickly and quietly as you can. I want one of you attached to each of those buses. We need their destinations."

"I'm beginning to think Collin and Morgan's recruitment to Braxton's facility might not be coincidental," Payton said. "Morgan, have you ever noticed whether your sister, Terri, has any special traits or skills?"

"I've been gone for a long time, and she was practically a baby when I joined the army. I haven't spent much time around her, but I can tell you she is extremely smart for her age," Morgan said. "Do you think Braxton will go after her?"

"I think KG International is recruiting gifted children. What if they initially vet the students at the academy and ship them out to some type of training facilities?" Payton asked.

"You might be on to something there, Payton. I wouldn't put anything past Braxton or the Kaleidoscope Group. Let's not take any chances. I'll post a couple guards on Terri around the clock. If we need to, we will put her in a safe house," Wyatt said.

Chapter Twelve

In the darkness of night, the group left the safe house. They rented three vehicles, with each man assigned to follow a bus. After they parked the cars a few blocks away, they all crept up to the academy. The closer they got, the more intense the vibration that flowed through Payton.

Collin picked up on Payton's uneasiness.

"You okay?" he asked.

"I'm not sure. I've never been as inundated by the magnitude and variety of distinctive sources. Your energy is overwhelming because your emotions are extremely intense. What I feel now is totally different. It's still intense, but not with emotions. The energy flows out from such numerous sources, I can't differentiate any of it," Payton said.

"It's a safe bet your instincts are correct, and Braxton is recruiting children with special abilities," Noah said. "Are you going to be able to function, or should Morgan take you back to the house?"

"I'll be okay. I need to breathe and center myself. I want to stay," she said.

Noah gave her a questioning look, but before he said another word she added, "I can do this. I won't put the mission in jeopardy, I promise."

He turned and looked at Collin. "You good to go, Collin?"

"Yes, sir," Collin said.

"Okay, the three of us will find ourselves hidey holes and wait for your signal. With any luck you will be able to snatch Emma and be out of there before anyone notices. Make sure you get a tracker securely mounted onto each bus. If you don't get the opportunity to grab her, you will follow her bus; understand? Good luck," Noah said.

Collin nodded, dashed up to the wrought-iron fence, cleared it with a single jump, and disappeared into the darkness in a heartbeat.

"Damn!" Noah exclaimed. "Collin is beyond fast." He shook his head and gave a little chuckle. "Remind me to get some of those dog genes when we get back."

"That's wolf genes, and they aren't all they are cracked up to be," Morgan said.

"Uh huh, says the other guy who can clear a twelve-foot fence in a single leap," Noah said.

An hour passed and the only action on the grounds was a guard as he made his rounds. He passed within inches of Collin and stopped to light a cigarette. The flash of the match lit up the area around the guard for only an instant, but also illuminated Collin who hid behind the tire of the last bus. The entire team held their collective breath. The guard leaned against the bus and rested a foot on the tire. He took a couple drags on his cigarette, dropped it, stomped on it, and walked away.

"Jesus, that was way too close," Morgan said.

"How are you doing?" Noah asked Payton, who lay prone next to him.

"You mean now that I'm breathing again? The emotional bombardment is about the same intensity, only now I'm finally able to push the energy to the back of my mind, where it feels like an electrical impulse, almost soothing really." Soon she discovered she could actually turn the energy up and dial it back down.

Noah looked at his watch. "Five o'clock. The sun will start to rise in the next hour. We should—" he stopped mid-sentence as the dormitory doors swung open and students started to file out.

A click came through all the ear buds.

"I have eyes on Emma. I'm going in. With the darkness, I think I can slip her out of there," Collin said.

"You better be damn careful," Noah said. "You are only cleared to go if you are sure no one will spot you."

Ninety seconds later, a shadow raced up and over the fence. Collin took cover in the bushes and bent down to let a stunned Emma slide off of his back.

"Emma, these are my friends. You're safe with them. We are here to take you home. Sarah is pretty worried about you," Collin said.

"Pleased to meet you," she said, as she extended a shaky hand out to Payton.

"I've heard much about you. I'm Payton. Don't worry, Emma; you're safe with us."

"Payton, take Emma to the car and wait for us," Noah said.

Emma grabbed Collin's hand and held tight.

"You're okay now, Emma; I promise. Go with Payton, and she'll explain what has happened to you. I'll be right there," Collin said.

"You better," she said, as she hugged him.

"You take them back to the safe house and drop them off. Keep your locator with you and get back here double-time," Noah said to Collin.

The buses were loaded. One at a time they left the academy, each bus followed by a small dark car. All three buses got on the highway and exited a few miles later at the airport in San Francisco.

The men returned to the safe house, and as they reached the door, Payton greeted them. "Shhh," she said. She brought her index finger across her lips. "Emma is asleep upstairs in the spare bedroom."

Noah, Collin, Morgan, and Payton gathered around the computer in the kitchen for one final meeting.

"I'm glad your rescue of Emma came off without a hitch," Wyatt said. "Do you have any idea where the other students were taken?"

"It turned out to be a short trip for us. The children were all unloaded at the airport. One group went to London, one headed for New York, and the other to Hawaii. Unfortunately none of the flights were direct, meaning we really don't know what the final destinations were, or if they would change planes," Noah said.

"At least it's a place to start. I'll get Jack to check out all the flights and see if any of them are close to any properties owned by KG, Kaleidoscope Group, or Biotec. You guys all grab a couple hours of rest. Logan will pick you up early in the evening," Wyatt said.

* * * *

Wyatt, Victory, Tristan, and Sarah, stood at the edge of the helipad and waited for the chopper to power down. The blades on the aircraft spooled to a stop and the door swung open. Emma sprang from the open doorway.

"Sarah. I've missed you." Emma ran into Sarah's embrace and nearly knocked the two of them to the ground.

"Hey there, baby sister, are you okay?" Sarah asked. She rubbed her hands over Emma's body to confirm for herself that Emma indeed had returned in one piece.

"I'm fine. I'm glad Collin came and got me before the buses left. I had a terrible feeling we weren't coming back, and I might never see you or Collin again." Tears trickled down Emma's cheeks as she hugged her sister.

"Hush, little sister. You're safe now. These people are all friends of Collin's," Sarah said.

Collin walked up behind Emma and rubbed the top of her head. Her strawberry blonde hair felt soft beneath his hand, a loving gesture he'd done since the first day he ever met his baby sister.

"You and Sarah go with my friend, Morgan. He will take you back to Sarah's bungalow where you can get cleaned up. I'll see you for dinner in an hour," Collin said.

"Glad the mission was a success," Wyatt said, as they all watched the Jeep pull away.

"Thank you, sir, she's all the family I have left," Collin said.

"Enjoy your time with her. She and Sarah can stay for the next three days. By then all the details of their safe house will be worked out, and we will need to move them. I'm sure Braxton already knows Emma has disappeared. We need to be on high alert. Best case scenario is he will think Sarah hired someone to retrieve her sister. Worse case, we've shown our hand and he will try to locate you," Wyatt said.

"Why can't they stay on the campus? This is secure," Collin said.

"Yes, the campus is secure, but still too many people are aware of it. We will transfer them to a place only a limited number of people will know about," Wyatt said.

"Then you think there is a leak, too?" Collin asked.

"I think it's a distinct possibility, and the reason we need to be so careful with their whereabouts. Outside of our circle, General Roberts is the only other person who knows about Sarah and Emma. As far as the location of the safe house, the actual address will only be known by you, Tristan, General Roberts, the team he sends to guard the two, and me," Wyatt said.

"How do you know for certain General Roberts isn't the leak?" Collin asked.

Tristan looked at his brother. *"He has a good point, Wyatt,"* Tristan said, via their telepathic link.

"I trust Roberts with our lives, don't you?" Wyatt asked.

"Yes, but I don't want to gamble with Emma and Sarah's lives."

"Collin, I trust General Roberts completely. Not to say the leak isn't someone else in his office, but he has promised no written records of our assignment. Sarah and Emma will be safe. General Roberts will send an excellent team," Wyatt said.

"Please don't make me regret trusting you, sir," Collin said.

Chapter Thirteen

Payton lay in her bed, the eerie silence of the house pressing in on her. Willow had yet to return from Europe, and Victory and Tristan were permanently settled into the guesthouse, which now served as their home. Payton found comfort in being surrounded by her own things, in her own bed, with Kes and Asia on one side of her and Parker totally prone along the other, all snoring gently.

Yet she felt restless. The events of the past month raced through her mind, like a movie fast-forwarded, rewound, and played back again: The first time she'd laid eyes on Collin, the sizzle of heat that ran up her arm from the mere touch of his hand, the electrifying kiss they shared in San Francisco, and the week they spent together there. Then she learned from Victory that this grounding ability she never really thought about, a trait she assumed to be a natural ability all humans shared, was not. Not only didn't others share it, her ability might not even be natural. Try as she might, she couldn't clear her mind. She sat up and turned on the table lamp. All three Dobermans stretched, and Parker jumped off the bed, instantly on alert.

"It's okay, Parker; I can't sleep. I thin
have a cup of herbal tea." As she opened th
door, the trio of dogs trotted out in front of

Payton took her cup of tea and went int
room. She placed the cup on the side table
book from the bookshelf, and curled up on th. ˷˷˷. ˷˷˷
read for a bit, and then put the book down to enjoy her
tea. As she reached for the cup, a jab of white hot pain
tore through her stomach. She gasped and tucked into a
fetal position as the agony threatened to consume her.
But as quickly as it hit, it disappeared.

"Collin?" she murmured to herself.

* * * *

Payton spent the morning catching up with work
and she left her office in the early afternoon. She let all
the dogs out to play in the sun, went up to her room and
changed from her designer business suit into shorts and
a tee shirt, slipped on her favorite sandals, and headed
for the attic. The time had finally come to pull all of her
mother's file boxes out of the attic. Until now, she
wasn't ready to deal with throwing any of the files out,
but she knew her sisters; they would have insisted she
get rid of some of the stuff.

One by one she moved all the boxes from the attic
back down to her office. After she dropped the last box
on one of the stacks she made, she felt tired and dirty.
She went back down to the kitchen and made herself a
glass of iced tea and checked on the dogs. She'd picked
Dax up from Victory's on her way home to give the
four dogs a chance to play together. She peered out the
screen door and saw all four of the Dobermans. Basking

. the sun, each slept on their very own padded lounge chair.

"It's a dog's life," she said with a smile. All four of them rolled up into sphinx positions, acknowledging her presence, but refusing to vacate their lounge chairs. She giggled at them, and retreated back into the kitchen, where she filled a large ceramic bowl full of cold, fresh water, picked up her iced tea with her free hand, and headed out to join her four-legged family.

She fell asleep on one of the lounge chairs under a large umbrella. When she woke she felt refreshed and ready to take on her project. Payton spent hours as she fastidiously combed through each file one by one and stacked completed file boxes to one side. She started to think nothing would be found in her mother's files. She stacked the last box she'd finished on the opposite side of the room and sat down on the floor.

She stared at the mountain of boxes she had yet to go through. Anguish filled her as she realized this was the closest she would ever be to her mom again, her mother's files, her life's work stacked in boxes. She held back the tears, for she would not allow herself to go down that dark road. A sensation of warmth wrapped around her, but she startled as her cell phone rang.

"Collin?"

"Payton, are you okay? Do you need my help?" he asked.

"What—how—" she stuttered.

"A wave of grief overcame me. I could tell the feeling came from you, so I needed to make sure you were okay. I guess the work we've been doing also tuned me into your overpowering emotions as well."

"Great, now you can read my thoughts?" she asked.

"No, just your extreme emotions. Are you sure you're okay? If you need me, I'll be right there."

"No, I'm okay, really. And Collin, thank you."

As she disconnected the call, a word on the side of one of the boxes caught her eye. Written in her mother's own handwriting it read, *Trials*. She got up and pulled boxes down and restacked them to one side as she worked to get to the bottom box. At last she reached the box; she pulled it out, dragged it to the center of the floor, and sat back down next to it. She cautiously pulled off the lid, feeling as though all her questions could be found in this brown box. The box overflowed with files. She started at the top and began the process of reading every page.

It was two in the morning when she finished reading the last page. Then she promptly fell asleep.

The light of morning seeped into the room and woke Payton with a start. It was vital that she reach her sisters immediately.

Payton knocked on Victory's door. Tristan answered, already dressed with a cup of coffee in his hand.

"Morning, Payton," he said, as he stepped back to let her enter.

"I'm sorry I'm here so early. I promise not to make it a habit, but what I need to tell Victory is important," she said.

"No worries. Can I get you a cup of coffee?" he asked.

"I would love some coffee."

"Well, this is a nice surprise, albeit early, even for you." Victory smiled as she looked at her sister.

"I know, and I'm sorry. I have some crucial information that I need to discuss with you and Willow. I have already told her, and she's ready to Skype us," Payton said.

"I guess that's my cue to leave," Tristan said, and put the coffeepot on the table.

"No, you need to hear too, if you could stay a while longer," Payton told him. He nodded at her and snuggled in next to his wife.

Payton opened her laptop and connected to Willow. The sisters exchanged pleasantries and waited for Payton to explain.

"To say my 'special abilities' weighed on my mind would be an understatement," Payton started. "I've been obsessed over the idea that Mom used manipulated drugs that might have altered our abilities.

"I've been going through Mom's files. I had nearly thrown in the towel when one box caught my eye, a box labeled 'Trials,' in Mom's handwriting. The papers verified all you told us, Victory, and more. Mom and Dr. Ryker did indeed design the drugs, and Dad didn't know what they were up to at the start."

"How could he not know what they worked on?" Willow asked. "Dad served as the CEO and like you, he made it his priority to be aware of all projects within the company."

"The actual drugs weren't made through our company. Ryker and Braxton were friends, and Biotec produced the drug. I found some information even more astonishing; Mom got pregnant once before she got pregnant with us," Payton said.

"What?" they all asked.

"Mom never told us she was pregnant before us. How could she have kept that a secret?" Willow asked.

"She flew out to England for an important project approximately two months into her pregnancy. She planned to return home no later than seven months pregnant, but she developed problems and was hospitalized in England. Dad flew out to see her, except the company demanded his attention, and he only stayed for a week."

"She went into labor at almost eight months. There were problems, and she needed a C-section; they nearly lost her. Mom remained unconscious for over a week. Ryker called Dad to tell him what happened. Dad was devastated at the loss of their girls and that Mom was unconscious and he wasn't with her. He flew out to England, but by the time he got there his girls were buried. When Mom woke, the twin girls were gone. She was furious with Ryker. Mom spent a few days and sat by the gravesite before she left England, but she never recovered from not being able to say her goodbyes to her daughters."

Payton reached for her coffee, her hand visibly shaking. She took a few sips and allowed time for what she told her sisters to process.

"Makes me wonder if the main reason Mom went back to England as much as she did stemmed from the fact the girls were buried there," Payton said. "She was told she would probably never conceive again. Two months later, she told Dad about the research she had done. With time running out for them, they assumed Mom's research would be their only chance to have a family. Against his better judgment, Dad agreed to fund

155

Mom's research, and she once again solicited Ryker's help. Mom got pregnant with us only four months after the loss of the twins. We were born eight months later."

"You're saying we would have had twin sisters only one year older than us?" Willow asked. "I find it hard to believe Mom and Dad kept this from us. And why does Biotec keep popping into our lives?"

"Exactly what I have wondered," Tristan said. "I wish to hell someone could tell us where Ryker lived, or if he is still alive."

"I can't believe I haven't run across her research," Victory said, she reverted to her scientific self.

"Mom specifically confirmed these files were the only record of her initial research at the time. She talked about incorporating the files into her computer files, but I never found any additional information that verified she did. You know Mom. I'm sure she found new projects to keep her from updating her electronic files," Payton said.

"I'm sure the pain of her loss also played a part in her not electronically recording her initial research. Can you imagine reliving that depth of loss?" Willow asked.

"Is her research all there?" Victory asked.

"I think so, but you know science is not my forte," Payton said.

"Would you mind if I took the box to my lab?"

"I thought you would want it. I spent half the night and made copies of every file. I have locked the originals safely in the vault in my home office," Payton said.

"Good idea, Payton," Tristan said. "To be safe, lock the box in your safe at the lab before you leave at night, Victory. May I tell Wyatt about what you have found?"

"I think you should," Payton said.

"Are you all going to be all right?" he asked the three sisters.

They nodded.

He grabbed Victory up into his embrace and gave her a long kiss. "Well, I need to head out."

"I need to leave too," Willow said. "Please keep me in the loop if either of you find out any additional information. I should be heading home sometime next week. I'm sure we'll talk before then. Love you, 'bye."

"Did you eat any breakfast?" Victory asked Payton.

"No."

"Let's go see what we have."

They got up and went into the kitchen. As they started to make breakfast, Payton asked, "How is Collin doing?"

"He seems slightly more on an even keel. I've run test after test on him and he has passed each one with flying colors," Victory said.

"What about when he is asleep? Have you monitored him when he sleeps?"

"Not yet. Although, I have a sleep study on my schedule for later in the week. Emma leaves tomorrow, and I thought I would give him a day or two get back into his routine. Why do you ask?"

"The past two nights I have been woken up by a stabbing pain to my stomach," Payton said.

"Are you ill?" Victory asked with concern in her voice.

"No. I feel Collin's energy as soon as I wake up. I think he's immersed in some kind of emotional reaction, but I'm pretty sure he has slept through it."

"Damn it," Victory said. "I never considered he might affect you when he is asleep. I'm sorry, Payton. I'll start him on sleep studies tonight."

"Don't beat yourself up, Victory. Like you keep telling the men, this is a whole new world."

"Come on. Let's go to the house and pick up the box. We can ride the cart to the campus together," Payton said.

Chapter Fourteen

"For the love of Pete," Payton moaned as she rolled up into a tight ball. She was ripped out of a deep slumber by an all-too-familiar agonizing pain that attempted to pull her into a sea of torment. Her cell phone on the nightstand rang. She looked at the clock: three-thirty in the morning. She picked up her phone and saw the caller ID. "Victory."

"Hel-lo," she said, nearly unable get the word out.

"Payton? Are you okay?" Victory asked.

"I have been better," she mumbled between panted breaths.

"Wait one minute," Victory said.

Payton held the phone to her ear, unable to move. Within seconds the pain dissipated, and she took in a deep breath and filled her lungs to capacity.

"Payton—Payton, are you okay?"

"I'm fine now. What's going on?"

"I woke Collin. You were right. His emotions run amuck while he is asleep. You should see the result I got off of him." Victory sounded ecstatic.

"Well, I'm glad someone is happy about it," Payton said.

"Sorry. I will need to do further work on the serum I developed," Victory said.

"And how long will that take? I don't know how many more nights I can deal with this."

"I don't think you will have to deal with the pain any longer. I have an idea."

"I'm all ears," Payton said.

"Emma and Sarah are to be moved to their safe house tomorrow. I think we should move Collin into your house. I believe his close proximity might help both of you until I can get this sorted out," Victory said.

"Wonderful," Payton said. She dreaded the thought of Collin living in her home.

* * * *

"I'm really sorry about the entire situation, Payton," Collin said, as Payton met him at her kitchen door. "I'm sure the last thing you wanted was having me move into your home."

"No, actually the last thing I want is to have another fun-filled night, where I wake in a pool of sweat and in unbearable pain," Payton said.

"I'm really sorry about all the pain I've caused you." He dropped his gaze to the floor.

She could see the damnation of himself play across his face.

"Stop all of the apologizing, Collin. You have no control over what happens to me, and it's not like any of what happens is your choice. Let's hope your staying here will help temper the situation. Come on, I'll show you to the guest room."

Collin followed her through the house and up the stairs as he lugged his oversized rucksack behind him.

"Victory told me Emma left today. Did you enjoy your visit with her?" she asked.

"Yes, I wish she could have stayed longer. Emma is a wonderful girl. This is the first time in over two years I have gotten to spend more than twenty-four hours with her. She is brilliant. The topics we discussed blew my mind."

"I'm certain Emma's uniqueness is precisely why Braxton got his hooks into her. He won't be happy to find out she's gone," Payton said.

* * * *

"What do you mean you can't find Sarah? You told me she went to the dog show with a friend of hers," Braxton bellowed into the phone.

"I went to her house and she wasn't there. The place looked as if she packed up some of her stuff and fled. I have men out searching for her as we speak," Dave said.

"You better locate her. If she proves to be an issue, deal with her. Understand?"

"Yes, sir. We have another situation."

"Now what?" Braxton snapped.

"The McBain girl is gone."

"Gone as in she's at the London site?"

"No, sir. She got on the bus to go to the airport and did not arrive in London."

"How the hell could that be? She couldn't have escaped from the bus. Do you think Sarah had something to do with Emma's disappearance?"

"I think it's a good bet Sarah is behind the whole thing. They are probably both on the run. Don't worry; we'll find them," Dave said.

"You damn well better! She is an important part of Second Wave. The board will have my head if you don't retrieve her. Christ Almighty, Dave, how could you let this happen?"

"Try not to worry, Mr. Braxton. I will find both of them."

"I'm counting on it. You'd better if you want to keep your current position in life. And Dave, you have precious little time." Braxton abruptly ended the call.

Now Braxton had to deal with the board and the chairman. Dave had put him in another nasty situation, and this was his final chance to redeem himself. Otherwise, Dave would be done. Braxton despised the thought of replacing Dave, although maybe the time had come. He pressed his thumb to the sensor pad on the front of one of his desk drawers and the drawer clicked open. He reached in and pulled out another phone, a secure line used only to contact the chairman. He punched the button and listened for the familiar voice.

"Yes," responded a deep voice on the other end.

"Good afternoon, Mr. Chairman. I hate to disturb you, but we have a slight setback in our plans," Braxton said.

"That often happens when one deals with science," the chairman said.

"The setback isn't science-related. The McBain girl is missing."

"I see. You are remedying the situation, correct? Even with your limited scientific knowledge, I'm sure you realize she is one of the keys to our success. I have perfected the serum from the blood you took from Collin. With the man dead and buried, you do realize I can't go back to the source to get more blood. She is his only living relative, and she shows advanced abilities. We must secure her."

"Yes, Mr. Chairman. My best people are working on the situation as we speak. We'll get her back," Braxton said.

"See to it. Oh, and Lawrence?"

"Sir?"

"I expect you to clean up your mess. Anyone involved in her disappearance is of subpar standards and not the type of employee Kaleidoscope Group deems worthy," the chairman said, with an icy tinge to his voice.

"I understand, Mr. Chairman."

Lawrence Braxton sat in his office and pondered the current dilemma he found himself in. This did not sit well with him.

"Good help is astonishingly hard to find," he said aloud to himself.

* * * *

Payton's eyes flew open; she lay still and waited for the flood of pain to overtake her. Nothing. *What woke her?* she wondered as she listened to the dogs softly snore.

"No!" Collin's anguished cry rang out.

She sprang out of bed dressed only in a tank top and boy-style boxers and ran for the door, all three dogs in hot pursuit.

"Stay. Go back to bed."

They looked at her, and one by one turned and jumped back on the bed. The last thing she wanted would be for one of the dogs to read the situation as a threat and challenge Collin.

He cried out again as she scurried down the hall to his room.

"Collin?" she called as she tapped on the door. She waited and got no response.

"Collin, it's Payton," she called, and immediately realized it was a dumb thing to say. Who else would be at his door at this time of night? Except part of her feared he might not be aware of where he was or who was around. She cracked the door open and peered into the room.

He'd left the blinds open and moonlight spilled into the room. She could see him in the bed but couldn't determine if he still slept. He moaned pitifully. The sound drew her to him. Without a second thought, she lightly touched his shoulder and gave him a gentle shake.

Before she had a chance to react, he seized her and threw her on the bed, his body towering over hers. Her heart threatened to come up in her throat as it beat a wild, uncontrollable rhythm. His eyes were fixed on her, but instead of looking into the electric-blue eyes she had become accustomed to, golden swirling irises challenged her stare. She completely stilled, as she realized she had come face-to-face with Collin's wolf. By instinct she knew any sudden moves on her part would be seen as confrontational. She fought every defensive instinct and willed herself to remain motionless.

Her mind reeled as she ran through every possible scenario. A gravelly growl emanated from deep within Collin and he leaned into her, inhaling her scent. A tiny plea escaped her lips.

"Collin, please…come back."

Time stood still. Frozen, she waited for his next move.

"Payton? What…how?"

He released her as if she were ablaze and jerked back.

"Damn it all to hell. Did I hurt you?" he asked, while he kept his distance.

The moonlight played along his face, and she watched curiously as his irises changed from golden to a pure sea blue.

"No. You did however scare ten years off my life," she said.

"Son of a bitch, what happened? Why are you here?" he asked.

"You must have been caught up in a terrible nightmare. You woke me, and I came to see if you needed any help."

"I'm sorry. I'm so sorry. I can't stay here. I can't run the risk that I might hurt you."

He rose from the bed and started to pace the room.

"Collin, don't you understand? You didn't hurt me. You heard me call and you came back."

"This time. What about next time? I can't take the chance."

He continued to pace and looked every inch the caged wolf he tried to keep dormant.

"You have to stay here. I called you back. What if you were with Victory or Morgan? Would you have responded to them?" Payton asked.

"I don't know. But I refuse to put you in any further danger," Collin said.

"I truly believe more people would be in danger if you leave here. Come down to the kitchen with me. I'll make us some tea, and we can sit and talk," she said.

He hesitated.

"Tea? Really? I could use something stronger. What about whiskey?" he asked.

She laughed, walked over to him, and took his hand. A soothing sensation swamped his entire body and flushed the tension out of his system. She felt the changes in him as if she shared his skin.

"Much better," she said, and walked with him down the hall.

The living room glowed by the light of a single lamp. Payton sat on the sofa, her long bare legs tucked up under her. Collin sat in a chair across from her and sipped on his whiskey. They sat quietly for a time. Eventually Collin broke the silence.

"I suppose you'll have to tell Victory what happened."

"She needs to know everything in order to help you."

"I know you're right. After tonight she will probably agree with me and not want me to stay here," he said.

"I think you'll be surprised," she said.

* * * *

She yawned and stretched her arms up over her head and as she did her shirt crept up. Collin caught a glint of blue in the area of her belly button.

"Let's go back up to bed. I'll watch over you until you fall asleep," Payton said.

"No one has ever watched over me in my entire life," Collin said, as he returned the glass to the kitchen sink.

"There is a first time for everything," Payton said.

She took his hand once again and led him back up to his bedroom. She sat in the chair across the room from his bed.

"Would you mind sitting here?" he asked, as he patted the bed.

She got up, crossed the room, and sat on the edge of the bed. He took her tiny hand into his.

"Each time I hold your hand I get engulfed with a warm, soothing feeling," Collin said.

"Funny. I have the same reaction."

"Really? I worried my touch would cause you pain."

"No, never has your touch brought me pain. I always feel a surge of heat. It's only when your anger runs rampant and you are overcome with stress and adrenaline that I feel pain."

"It's improved over the last couple weeks though, right? I'm trying to stay in control and I constantly practice the techniques Tristan taught me," he said.

"I would say we have both come a long way."

He studied her. Her auburn hair tousled from sleep fell around her heart-shaped face. Her flawless skin, kissed by the sun, gave her a warm glow. He reached up and cupped her face in his palm. For the first time, he realized her eyes were a starburst of brown that bled into green edges and extremely mesmerizing. He waited for her to protest. When she didn't, he reached up with his other hand and framed her face. Inch by slow inch, he pulled her closer to him and gave her every opportunity to pull away. He leaned in and claimed her mouth. Their tongues danced in each other's warmth, and he moaned softly.

Payton supported herself with a hand placed on each side of Collin's head. As they continued their exploration of each other's mouths, Collin slid his hands down her neck. He stopped at her tank top and played his fingers along the upper edge of the shirt; she shivered. He resumed his thorough exploration, reaching the bottom hem of the shirt where his fingers investigated the hard little nub of the gem at her belly button. Then his hands slid up under her top and travelled up to her breasts. Taking her breasts in his palms, he kneaded and caressed, which filled her body with a fiery demand.

Her arms buckled but Collin's hands supported her. He sat up and pulled her into his lap, his desire for her evident as she felt him press against her thigh. He lifted her top off and leaned his head down to take possession of her breasts; he suckled one while he lightly stroked the bud of the other between his thumb and forefinger. He shifted his weight, abruptly changing position so she was under him on the bed as he kissed his way across her chest until he claimed her other breast. Payton moaned at the feel of him. Using his tongue, he burned a trail down her slim waist and toyed with the blue gem.

He reached her boxers and slowly pulled them down her elegant legs and followed each movement with his warm breath. She lay there completely naked. His gaze burned through her as he memorized every inch of her until his crystal-blue eyes locked onto hers.

"I need to know you trust me, or we stop here," he said, in a quiet, low tone.

"Don't stop now," she panted.

"I haven't been with anyone since I got injected with the wolf DNA, Payton. But I swear on my life I would never hurt you."

In answer, she reached for his tee shirt and pulled it up over his head. She traced his muscles and scars with her fingertips and worked her way to his cotton pajama bottoms. She slid her thumbs inside the waist and ran her hands along the top of his pajamas; she moved closer to pull his pants down. His enormous erection sprang free, and before she even had a chance to cup him in her hands, he pushed her back down on to the bed.

He spread her thighs and trailed kisses up the inside of one leg and around her auburn curls. He pulled her to the edge of the bed, knelt on the floor, placed her legs on each of his massive shoulders, and thrust his tongue deep inside her. Payton cried out. He pulled his mouth away and replaced it with a finger, and he nipped and licked at her. When two fingers entered her, she came off the bed and lifted her hips to meet him. She thrust and bucked, but still Collin's mouth never left her as he heard her whimper his name.

He stood and carefully pushed her back to the center of the bed. He knelt on the bed and once again put one of her legs over each of his shoulders.

"Open your eyes, Payton. You have to go into this with your eyes open," he said.

As she opened her eyes to look up into his face, he thrust himself to the hilt deep within her. She gasped as he remained buried deep inside her.

"You said you trust me," he reminded her.

"I do."

He slowly pulled back completely and buried himself again. He placed his hands around her hips and pushed even deeper into her heat. She quickly started to climax, but he didn't stop. He continued on, his gaze never wavering from hers; he thrust clear to the hilt and totally withdrew from her. He was an expert lover and this deep dance he was performing drove her over the edge…several times. She climaxed once again and brought him with her. He wanted this unbelievable feeling to last forever, but knew it would be but a fleeting moment in time.

Chapter Fifteen

Payton woke to the feel of wet dog kisses as Parker licked her face. She smiled at Collin's arm, which lay possessively across her chest, and his body spooned around hers. She sensed the instant he woke. He reached out with his arm and scratched the top of Parker's head. The two girls sat directly behind Parker, their stubby tails wagging madly as their hips shifted back and forth.

"How did they get in here?" Collin asked.

"There is no door Parker can't open. For future information, if you don't want him inspecting what you're doing, you need to lock your door. Of course if the door is locked, he will pound at it with his paw."

"Good to know. I suppose they need to go out?"

"Yes, the morning ritual must commence," she said, as she yawned and stretched.

"Parker, lay down," Collin said. "They can wait a few minutes longer."

Payton turned to him and gave him a long, lingering kiss. His energy felt altogether different to her today. Her body vibrated at his every touch in a way she'd never in her life experienced.

"You feel…peaceful, a word I would have never associated with you," she said.

"I haven't felt this relaxed…well, ever. Although, since I've spent this time around you, I've been feeling this way more and more. I could get used to this feeling. Have I told you I love the stone in your belly button?" he asked. He reached down and played with the stud. "What type of gem is it?"

"It's a sapphire. I had worn an emerald since I pierced my belly button. I went into town the other day and I peeked in the window at the jewelry store. This stunning light-blue stone caught my attention. I immediately thought of your captivating blue eyes. I asked the jeweler to put the sapphire into a setting. The gem has since become my favorite."

"I like it even more," he said, as he kissed her again.

Payton's phone rang and Collin reached over and grabbed it off the nightstand.

"It's Victory."

She took the phone from him, sat up, and pulled the sheet up under her arms.

"Good morning, Victory."

"Good morning, sis. I thought I would check-in and see how last night went prior to speaking with Collin," Victory said.

Payton looked at Collin, who smiled wickedly; she remembered his keen sense of hearing.

"The night started out a bit rocky, but all is well now," she said, trying to keep her voice nonchalant. She proceeded to relay the events of last night, right up to the point when they returned to Collin's room.

"He went back to sleep and you didn't have any further issues?" Victory asked.

"Ah—yes. Everything is fine, just fine. If you don't need anything else for now, I need to take care of the dogs and get ready for work," Payton said.

"I'll stop by on my way to the campus. I want Collin to walk down with me. We can discuss last night's events. Would you tell him I should be there in about forty minutes?"

"I'll let him know. Bye." Payton ended the conversation and looked over at Collin, who grinned at her. "I assume from the smirk on your face you heard the entire conversation."

"Every word," he said.

"Just how acute is your hearing?" she asked.

"Let's say, I don't miss much."

* * * *

Throughout the day, Payton's thoughts drifted back to her mother's notes. This entire situation had become a little too sticky, with Biotec being the producer of the drug her mother and Ryker invented. It would have been much simpler if her mom had told her father about their research at the start and retained the entire ownership of the drug by producing the formula through their company. Payton couldn't fathom what possessed her mother to proceed in the fashion she chose, and now she would never know. She still retained a couple of contacts in Biotec and weighed the dangers of contacting one. True, Braxton had not been sighted anywhere near Biotec in the past year. At any rate, Dave was still around.

She could call Aimee. They went to high school together and kept in touch, meeting for coffee or lunch over the years. Aimee left Biotec almost three years ago, which added another positive aspect to contacting her, Payton thought, as Aimee's activities shouldn't draw any attention from Biotec.

Three years ago, Aimee had gone to work for another company in Seattle. Payton knew Aimee once told her why she decided to leave Biotec, but she couldn't for the life of her remember what she said—something about not agreeing with their practices. At the time Payton thought nothing of it, but now...

Aimee was a pharmacologist and worked in the department that would have produced the drug her mom developed. Payton wondered why Aimee had never interviewed with the Winters Corporation. Could it possibly be she felt funny about going to work for them? She would invite Aimee over to see the campus. They still had a position open for a pharmacologist, and she would suggest that Aimee submit her resume.

A tickle ran down Payton's back, and a second later a knock sounded on her office door. She usually left her door open, but today she didn't want anyone to see where she hid the copy of her mother's work, and now she didn't want anyone eavesdropping on her conversation with Aimee.

"Come in," Payton said.

Collin pushed the door open and stood in the doorway, his broad shoulders and muscular build nearly filling the entrance. He wore a charcoal gray tee shirt and jeans that fit like they were tailored especially for him. His light-brown hair had finally grown out from the military cut and was streaked by the sun. His five o'clock shadow made him even sexier, and his striking blue eyes ensnared her.

"I thought I would go up to the house and make dinner. What does your sister like?" he asked.

"Oh no, I forgot," she said, as she glanced at the time on her computer screen. "Willow is coming home tonight."

"Yeah, and I figured you would be busy and tired, so I would make everyone dinner," he said. "Are you okay?"

"I'm fine. It's been an unusually hectic day. I'm almost ready to leave. I can take the rest of my work up to the house. Do you want to sit, have a bottle of water, and wait for a couple minutes?"

"My pleasure," he said.

He walked over to the small refrigerator and pulled out a bottle of water, twisted the top off, and drained the bottle in a single gulp. He sauntered over to the sofa, sat at one end, and swung his legs up on to the other end, smothering the entire piece of furniture. He crossed his arms over his chest and closed his eyes.

Payton tore her eyes away and focused on gathering all the files she would need at home.

* * * *

"I could get used to having you for a houseguest if you cook like this every night," Willow teased Collin.

"Good to know I won't crimp your style," he volleyed back.

"I'm glad you're home," Payton said, as she threw her arms around her sister and hugged her for the umpteenth time.

"I'm happy to be home," Willow said. "London is wonderful, but it's not home." She put a hand over her mouth, trying to stifle her yawn.

"I don't think I will ever get used to the jet lag though. If you two don't mind, I'll call it a night."

Willow said her good nights and went up to her room followed by Asia, who never left her side from the time she first walked in the door. Shortly after, Collin and Payton headed to their individual rooms.

A hush filled the house and Payton quietly scolded Parker, demanding he stay put in her room. She rubbed both dogs on their heads and promised to return shortly. She opened her bedroom door only enough to squeeze out and padded down the hall to Collin's room. Thank goodness she put him in the room close to hers and at the far end of the hall from Willow's room. Before she could tap on the door, an arm snaked out and pulled her inside. The room was completely dark, save for a couple of burning candles on the dresser that were reflected back in the mirror.

"I've been waiting patiently," he whispered, as he nibbled her ear.

"I wanted to make sure Willow was asleep," she said.

He kissed her neck and trailed his lips up to meet hers. The sparks flickered between them and ignited. Collin moved his hands down to her shirt and started to unbutton it. Suddenly, his hands stilled and he pulled his lips from hers.

"There's someone outside," he said softly.

"What?" she asked.

"I heard a branch snap. There is someone walking around your house."

He dragged her with him over to the dresser and blew out the candles, plunging the room into complete darkness.

"It's probably one of the security guards," Payton said.

"No, it's not. I know all of their scents, and this one is new. Besides, the security people are told to keep their distance because of your dogs."

He felt her shiver and stiffen in his arms.

"Don't worry, Payton. No one will get by me. I'm going to walk you back to your room. You lock the door and keep it locked until I return, understand?"

She nodded.

"Can you phone Tristan and Morgan for me and tell them what's going on?" he asked.

She nodded her head again.

He opened his door and looked into the hall to make sure the area was indeed clear. He silently led her back to her room. Parker and Kes were glued to the window, menacing growls reverberated from Parker.

"Good dogs, you watch the house," Collin said. He turned back to Payton.

"I won't leave until I hear the door lock. I will lock the backdoor on my way out. No matter what, you stay put." He took her chin in his hand and tilted her head up. He leaned down, claimed her lips, and kissed her with a promise of passion. As he pulled away from her, his eyes were swirling golden pools that instantly flashed back to crystal blue. "Promise me you will stay here."

"I promise. Please be careful," she said.

He slipped out the door and she locked it tight behind him. She grabbed her phone and walked over to the windows, dropped the blinds and threw the room into total blackness. She flipped open the phone and pressed the button.

"Payton, is everything all right?" Tristan answered on the second ring.

"No, there's someone outside the house. Collin has gone out after him and told me to contact you and Morgan."

"Son of a bitch," he said. "You're right. I have just picked up the unfamiliar scent. Are you okay to call Morgan? I'm on my way out to help Collin."

"I'm fine. I'll call him right now."

"Okay, and don't leave the house," he said as he hung up.

"Geez, they certainly all read from the same playbook," she said to her dogs. She punched in Morgan's number, told him the story, and got the same response.

After she finished making her calls she didn't know what to do with herself. She eventually sat on her bed, leaned against the headboard, and absently stroked her dogs' ears. She listened, and strained to hear anything, but could not pick up a single sound. She kept checking the time. Ten minutes passed, then fifteen.

"What on Earth is happening out there?" She could feel energy inundate the area as each man came on scene and realized she was beginning to decode their unique energy markers. Then she discovered there were two or three energies out there that were total unknowns.

* * * *

Collin had circled the house by the time Tristan and Morgan met up with him.

"I heard a branch crack. The broken branch is located by the living room window. There are tracks almost completely around the house," he said, pointing down at the ground.

Morgan looked around, evaluating the scene.

"Look up there." Morgan pointed straight up.

All three looked up at the tree where he pointed. Approximately ten feet up they spotted an object that looked like a small remote camera.

"Bastards," Collin hissed.

Collin took a few steps toward the tree and leaped into the air; he landed on the branch right above the camera. He looked the camera over, switched the power button off, and pulled it out of its perch. After he dropped back down to the ground, he handed the camera to Tristan.

"Nothing special, just your average spy gear," Collin said.

"I wonder how many more there might be," Morgan said.

"We'll worry about the others later. Let's get those assholes," Tristan said. "I picked up two."

"Same with me," Collin said.

"Divide and conquer?" Morgan asked.

"We need them alive, guys. We have to find out who sent them and why," Tristan said.

They split up and started to canvass the grounds. The stars and moon were covered by the clouds, making the night nearly pitch black. It helped them stay hidden, although it made it more difficult to locate the intruders. Despite the darkness, Collin's heightened sight picked up a third set of prints. He tapped his ear bud and whispered, "I picked up a third guy. He must have left the area earlier, or one of us would have picked up on his scent. I bet he's the driver."

"Roger," both Tristan and Morgan said.

As Collin crossed the open yard, he made certain to keep track of his teammates. He reached the tree line ahead of them, stood still straining to hear any noise associated with humans, and inhaled a deep breath to locate a trail. Somewhere in the distance he heard a car door close. He ran in the direction of the sound and hoped to catch a glimpse of the vehicle. Even with his wolf-like speed, he reached the fence only in time to see red taillights fade into the night.

"Shit," he said to himself.

He inspected the fence. When he found no visible breaches, he had to assume they climbed over.

"Find anything?" Tristan asked, as he emerged from the darkness.

"No. I heard a car door close and got there in time to watch them drive off," Collin said.

"Looks as though they were here for one mission: to install some spy cameras," Morgan said. He held up two additional cameras.

"The twenty-foot-tall fence wasn't enough to stop them. They climbed the damn thing," Collin said. "It's time to install some electricity in this sucker."

"What about the dogs? The sisters won't like the idea of an electric fence," Morgan said.

"The dogs will stay clear of it. The electricity will give off a humming sound," Collin said.

Tristan turned his back to the two men and remained silent. A few moments later he turned back to them.

"Wyatt doesn't see the need to wake everyone tonight, and I agree. Tomorrow we will get everyone together and discuss the situation. First thing in the morning, Wyatt will send in a cleanup team. They will scour the entire yard and make sure all the cameras are found. Let's all head back to bed. You two did good work; you might fit in yet," he teased them.

"Gee, thanks, boss. That's the nicest thing you have said to us yet," Collin said.

Collin tapped on Payton's door. She opened it and nearly threw herself into his arms. In order not to wake Willow, he backed her into the room and shut the door behind him as Payton kissed him.

"I was afraid something terrible had happened," she said. "You've been gone for over two hours. What did you find?"

"Makes me glad you missed me," he said. He lifted her off the floor and carried her to the bed. He took off his shoes and slid up beside her, pulled her close, and wrapped his arm around her shoulders. Parker and Kes jumped up and curled into tight balls at the end of the bed.

"We tracked the intruders but didn't even get a look at them. They were here planting surveillance cameras."

"What? How many?" Payton asked.

"We found three. Tomorrow a team will go through the property with a fine-tooth comb."

"Braxton?" she asked.

"I'm thinking more like the Kaleidoscope Group. There's no point in concerning yourself about it now. Wyatt wants us all to meet in the morning, which is going to be here before you know it. We both need to get some sleep. We can't afford to be tired, since that's when our barriers tend to slip, and neither of us needs to deal with those consequences," Collin said.

Collin kissed her on the forehead and started to slide from the bed. Payton grabbed a fistful of his shirt and stopped him.

"Will you stay here and sleep? We can set the alarm, and you can slip back to your room before Willow gets up," she said.

He snuggled in close to her. He reached down, caught her chin, and tilted her head up. He claimed her mouth, while he soaked in the sensation of Payton.

Chapter Sixteen

"I'll give them this; they've got guts. They know Tristan is a resident and don't seem too concerned," Noah said.

"Guess they think there's safety in numbers," Logan said. "At least until Tristan gets a hold of one of them."

"Thanks for bringing in breakfast, Payton," Noah said. He walked up to the serving table in the conference room to fill his plate for a second time. "Captain barely gave us time to shit, shower, and shave. I mean—"

The sisters all broke out in laughter at Noah's comment.

"Noah, are you blushing?" Willow giggled. "Don't give it another thought. We've heard worse—especially since you-all have joined our merry little band."

"Jack, did you get any information from the cameras?" Wyatt asked.

"They were wiped clean. The only prints were our team. Nothing recorded. The guys interrupted them before they had time to finish setting up. The cameras would be turned on and operated from an external site and monitored via a central computer. Don't worry, I've deactivated them. I tracked the registration numbers on them, but nothing there either," Jack said.

"We got a whole lot of nothing is what you're saying." Wyatt summed up. "On the up side, you guys caught them before they got any real information. The team finished up about an hour ago. They located three more cameras. The next step is to discuss how we can beef up security around the house and the campus."

"I say the first thing to be done is to electrify the fence," Collin said.

"No, electrifying the fence might injure the dogs," Payton said.

"It won't; believe me. The electricity will give off a humming sound the dogs will hear. We can easily train them to stay clear of the humming," Collin said.

"I think we should also put in a motion-detector system. We can put a palm sensor pad at both the main house and mine and Victory's. We can turn the motion detectors off when we take the dogs out," Tristan said. "The only trick will be to make sure you ladies turn it back on."

"Very cute," Victory said. "I think we can manage to put our hands on a pad."

"We need to take the generic push buttons out of the carts and install palm scanners there, too, along with changing out the entire keypad system at all the buildings and replacing them with palm scanners," Collin said.

"Those are all good starting points. Let's look at the layout and make a plan. Jack, put the entire grounds on the screen," Wyatt said.

Wyatt glanced at his watch. "That about wraps everything up. Looks like we have come to an acceptable compromise for upgrading the security. And it took less time than I thought it would."

"Great. Then I have to get to work," Victory said.

"I'll walk with you," Willow said.

"Do you mind if we stay here awhile longer?" Wyatt asked, as he looked at Payton.

"You are welcome to stay as long as you need. Feel free to use our campus at any time. If you need to use a specific room or facility, check with Jane, my assistant; she does all the scheduling. I will let her know you are the priority, unless there is a function we simply can't move."

"Thanks, Payton, we appreciate all you have done. It's much easier to have two bases of operation, especially since your campus is fast becoming our focus," Wyatt said.

"We have a new building almost near completion down by the bungalows. We won't be using the building for a few months. If you are interested, it could be set up for your team's use."

"We don't want to impose," Wyatt said.

"You're not imposing," Payton said. "We are happy to have you."

"What do you guys think?" he asked.

"The food's better here," Noah said.

"As are the workout facilities and pool," Logan said.

"Don't get carried away," Tristan said.

"No, really, we already discussed having the team on campus and we are happy to have you," Payton said.

"Okay. For the time being, we'll put a satellite office in your new building. I will need to bring this up to General Roberts for a final approval, but I'm sure he will be on board," Wyatt said.

Payton excused herself and left the conference room. She walked into her office, directly into an ambush. There her two sisters sat on her sofa with grins like children who thought they shared the best secret in the world.

"Aww, what's up?" she asked.

"That's what we want to know," Willow said.

"What do you mean?" she asked.

"What's going on with you and Collin?" Victory asked.

"First you two have issues because we didn't get along, and now you have problems because we do get along? I can't keep up with the two of you."

"You're arguing, Payton. You always do this when you're deflecting," Willow said.

"Stop playing the psychology card on me. I have no idea what you mean," Payton said.

"You're right, Willow. I thought you were off base, but I think you're right. Payton Winters, *what* is going on between you and Collin?"

"Nothing," Payton insisted.

"Liar," Victory and Willow said at once.

"He's a great guy, but you need to be careful. He still has a lot of issues to work out," Victory said.

"Yes, he is a pretty nice guy," Payton said, as her face lit up.

Victory and Willow sprang from the sofa and both pulled Payton up in a bear hug, a type of celebration they'd started when they were young girls.

"We're happy for you, sis," Willow said. "But for your own sake, please, heed Victory's warning and take it slow."

"All right, all right, I admit it. There is something more. We have a connection. I don't know where we are going yet, and that makes me itchy. Enough said on the matter. I don't know how your day looks, but I have a ton of work to do," Payton said.

"Nice deflection," Willow said. "Don't think you're getting out of it that easy. We'll get the all details later."

Payton had a massive amount of emails to return before her six o'clock meeting with Aimee.

Collin stopped by her office. She liked his habit of stopping by at the end of his day.

"Ready to go?" he asked.

"I have a late meeting with an old high school friend and potential new employee," she said.

"I thought Willow did all the interviews?" Collin asked.

"She does all the formal interviews, but all three of us bring someone in from time to time for kind of an informal interview, just to get a feel for them— especially if the person is someone we know."

"I'll head up and throw something together and leave dinner on the stove. I think I will take the dogs for a walk, let them burn off some energy," he said.

"Sounds wonderful and the dogs will enjoy the exercise. Please, I don't want you to wait on me for dinner. I don't know how long I will be."

"No worries. Dinner will be there when you're ready." He winked at Payton before he turned to leave.

* * * *

Payton met Aimee at the guest parking at exactly six on the dot.

"Wow, your campus is truly amazing," Aimee said, as the two hugged. "I've seen pictures, but they didn't do the place justice."

"I'm glad you agreed to come out. Are you ready for a tour?" Payton asked.

"I'd love it."

They chatted like a couple of school girls as Payton showed Aimee some of the labs and offices, along with the amenities.

"You still work over in Seattle?" Payton asked.

"Yes. The company pays well, but I'm beginning to dread the commute," Aimee said.

"You told me once why you left Biotec, but I can't recall any of the specifics."

"We had a difference of opinion. I believe in the code of ethics for my industry," Aimee said.

"And Biotec blurred the lines?" Payton asked.

"Biotec doesn't blur the lines, they totally erase them. If a product will make them money, they will find a way to produce it, ethics and government regulations be damned," Aimee said.

They ended up at the café and were sipping some wine when Payton broached the subject of her mother's drug.

"I recently came across some of my mother's files. She and Dr. Ryker made some changes to a fertility drug. For some reason she kept her research from my father. I suppose she didn't want him getting his hopes up. Anyway, in the files she said the initial drug was tested and produced through Biotec. Have you ever heard anything about Mom's drug?"

Aimee looked at Payton, and Payton could swear she picked up both surprise and uncertainty in her eyes.

"I have. In fact I worked on the drug the first year of my employment with Biotec. At the time, the testing and reformulating of your mother's drug was an ongoing project. They were always searching for new ways to improve on what she'd done. The drug was a top secret project; nevertheless, I assumed you and your sisters were made aware of it eventually, especially given Victory's background."

"No, we knew nothing about these tests or the existence of her drug. There were rumors about Mom using a drug to help her conceive. Of course we were aware of the new fertility drug she developed and we all believed it was her first drug. It wasn't until recently we learned she had invented a drug prior to the one we were all aware of, which made the drug we knew about her second fertility drug. And by some sick twist of fate, the first drug got produced by Biotec."

"I see. That leads me to believe you were unaware of Biotec pirating her work. They renamed the drug and claimed the formula as their own. Eventually, her formula became one of the primary drugs that put Biotec on the map," Aimee said.

Payton sat totally dumbfounded. Why had they never heard about this? And where were the files that would prove her mother's discovery?

"I'm sorry, Payton. I thought you knew. Biotec is notorious for drug piracy. Somehow, someone always covers their butt. I'm positive this someone is powerful and incredibly rich. I never knew whom. Their illegal activities became the reason I left. I couldn't abide by the practice of stealing drugs or rushing them into production without any safeguards," Aimee said.

"Good to know," Payton said, the information finally sinking in. "I assume Biotec mass-produced the drug. How did they manage to use those drugs on people without formal trials and government oversight?"

"Biotec is connected—everywhere. They send out formulas to be produced in secret labs somehow linked with the company. I never discovered what exactly the connection was; I have a feeling the companies involved with Biotec were financially intermingled. The formulas were sent out, produced, packaged, and marketed with the Biotec label. I've often suspected that there was secret human experimentation before they went public," Aimee said. "I am sincerely sorry, Payton. I really thought you knew. I would have told you, had I known."

"I appreciate your honesty, Aimee. I might have only recently become aware of my mother's initial testing and drug, but this is a pursuit I will see to the end," Payton said. "Can I ask you a personal question?"

"Anything."

"Why have you never put your resume in with the Winters Corporation?"

"Part of my condition of employment involved signing a confidentiality agreement."

"I can certainly understand that. The Winters Corporation has them, too."

"Not like Biotec's. Biotec strictly forbids us to take a position with any local company in the same industry for three years. The agreement also states we are forbidden to work for the Winters Corporation *in any* capacity for the same length of time, and we are not to speak of said agreement," Aimee said.

"I see. I guess I have my answer as to why we've had to do so much recruiting from out of state. How did you manage to work for another company in Seattle?" Payton asked.

"Again, they are connected to Biotec in some type of fashion, and I'm not actually making any drugs. I work at a computer all day," Aimee said. She looked down at her wine glass and refused to make eye contact with Payton.

"Your three years is nearly up, in a little over one month, isn't it? I was wondering if you would be interested in coming to work here as the head of pharmacology." Payton said.

Aimee lifted her gaze and gaped at Payton.

"Really? After I kept everything I knew from you, along with having worked for Biotec, you would offer me a position with your company?" Aimee asked.

"Of course I would. You were bound by a contract. You left a company that practiced shady business tactics, and you are a genius at what you do. If you ask me, sounds like a win-win situation."

"I would be honored. I have wanted to work for your company since I graduated. I felt weird asking for an interview; I didn't want to put your family in an awkward position."

"Great. It's settled then. Call Willow's office and schedule an appointment. She's our head of personnel."

"Thank you so much for the opportunity, Payton. You won't regret it."

Payton walked Aimee back to her car, where they said their goodbyes. She knew Aimee would be a great addition to the company. She had certainly given her something to think about. *Why would Biotec single out our company?* she thought. There must have been bad blood for a terribly long time. Tomorrow she would access her mother's computer files and go through them line by line, and do the same with the rest of the paper files up at the house. Hopefully her mother left her a clue.

Chapter Seventeen

Payton walked back to her office, lost in thought as she played back the conversation with Aimee. She nearly jumped out of her skin when she looked up to find Collin sitting on the steps to her building.

"Thinking much?" he asked, as he got to his feet. "I thought you saw me awhile back, when you looked up at the building."

"I guess I wasn't really paying attention." She pointed to the covered dish in his hand. "What did you bring? It smells heavenly." Her stomach grumbled as if in agreement.

"I brought you dinner. Willow and I already ate, and I didn't want you to skip dinner. By the sound of your stomach, I think it is safe to assume you skipped lunch."

She actually couldn't recall when she last ate. The entire ten hours of her workday were a haze.

"Thanks, I really appreciate it. I still have a couple things I need to do."

An hour later Payton shut down her computer and looked over at Collin. He lay on the sofa sound asleep.

She hated to wake him. She grabbed her briefcase and rose.

"Do you mind if we take a detour on the way home?" he asked, his eyelids still closed.

"Sorry I woke you," she said.

"You didn't; my years of training did." He sat up and stretched his arms up overhead.

"A detour? Sure, where to?"

"I need to swing by my bungalow and pick up some clothes."

"You do realize we have a washer at the house and you are welcome to use it."

"I know. I have an assignment tomorrow and I need my work gear," he said.

They left the building and headed to his bungalow.

"That's exciting, your first assignment. Must mean you are getting stronger and Wyatt is convinced you are ready to work."

"It's a test, Payton. They want to find out what type of progress I have made."

"I see. Do you think you are ready?"

"I guess. I won't know for sure until tomorrow. I do feel more in control, thanks to you," he said.

"Great, a good sign," she said. "I met with an old high school friend of mine tonight. She is a past employee of Biotec."

She filled Collin in on the information she found out from Aimee.

"Payton, you need to be really careful," he said. "Braxton is a ruthless bastard. Are you sure you can trust Aimee?"

"I know, Collin. I think I can trust her. I also know there's more to the link between my mom's drug and

Biotec other than the obvious, and I'm going to find out what the link is."

Collin unlocked the door to his bungalow, stepped aside, and allowed her to enter first. She hadn't seen the inside since Collin moved in. The bungalows were small but well laid out. The main room housed the living, dining, and kitchen areas. There were two bedrooms and a bathroom in the back. She noticed he kept his home neat. There were some pictures on the buffet which sat under the bay window, a couple of books stacked on the coffee table, a surf board leaned against the wall in the dining room, and a little stuffed pink bunny sat in the corner of his sofa.

Payton smiled as she looked at the bunny. "I didn't know you were a stuffed bunny kinda guy."

"The bunny is Emma's; she left him here to keep me company," he said.

She smiled at the thought as she walked over to the buffet to get a better look at his pictures. The photos were mostly of Emma, but one displayed an older gentleman; he sat on the porch of a cozy cabin. "Your granddad?"

"That's him. I sure miss the old guy. I took the picture the last time we were together at the cabin," he said.

"It's beautiful. He looks happy."

Collin poured them both a glass of wine. Payton took off her shoes and made herself comfortable on the sofa. He handed her a glass and sat down beside her.

"My sisters know about us," Payton said.

"And I suppose they aren't the least bit happy about it," Collin said.

"On the contrary, they both think you are a great guy. Their only concern is that we don't move too fast; they want us to take our time and give you more time to adapt," she said.

"I certainly can take my time."

He took the glass from her hand, and pulled her close to him for a steamy kiss.

She ran her hands down the front of him and found him already hard for the want of her. She reached for his zipper, pulled it down, and popped the top button of his jeans.

"Hold that thought," Collin said. He pulled away from her and started to drop the blinds around his bungalow. "It's like being in a fish bowl at night."

"I'm glad you thought about the windows," she grimaced at the idea of someone watching them.

Collin stepped out of his jeans and pulled his boxers down behind them.

"And your shirt," Payton said.

He did as she instructed. She stopped him before he could sit back down on the sofa and situated his hips in front of her. She ran her hands gently down the outside of his thighs; his muscles flexed at her touch. She slid her hands back up the inside of his thighs, and when she reached his erection she fondled his full length.

"Your hands feel like heaven," Collin groaned.

She leaned closer and ran her tongue along the tip of his erection, then down the entire length of his shaft. His eyes were fixed on her as she took him into the warm haven of her mouth and started a slow, sensual pace. He reached out and ran his hands through her silky hair. His head started to swim, and he wasn't sure whether to blame the reaction on the wine or the intoxication of Payton.

The fact he stood in front of her totally naked and she still fully dressed spurred him on. He wanted to thrust himself into her mouth, to come apart surrounded by her warm breath. Nevertheless, he couldn't lose total control; he didn't trust what might happen if he did. He fought against the urges of his body, and he pulled back.

"What's the matter?" Payton asked.

"Nothing, I'm in paradise."

He pulled her up to her feet, reached around her, and unzipped the back of her dress. He dropped the garment to the floor. Payton stood there clothed only in her pink lacy bra and matching panties, her fiery auburn hair flowed past her shoulders, and her hazel eyes shimmered with questions. Her beauty stole his breath away; her full breasts, the way her waist tucked in flared out at her hips, and man, those long elegant legs. He loved having her legs wrapped around him.

"Why did you stop me?"

"Payton, you are the only woman I have ever known who has the ability to make me come totally undone."

"Is coming undone such a bad thing?" She smiled up at him shyly.

"Last year you wouldn't have had to ask me the question. I would be all in, no holds barred. Only now—I can't risk losing complete control and possibly hurting you."

"What makes you think you would hurt me? Your triggers are stress—"

"And adrenaline," he finished her sentence. "I have no way of knowing if I will lose control and I refuse to put you in any danger."

"You can't go for the rest of your life holding back, Collin. You need to trust in yourself. You need to trust in me. Does this mean you didn't lose control the first time? We'll have to work on that." Payton pulled her panties down and unsnapped her bra.

Collin pulled her into his embrace and kissed her fiercely. He backed her up until he trapped her between his solid body and the wall. He lifted her off the ground and she wrapped her legs around his waist as he plunged into her, setting a leisurely pace. He could feel the heat inside her starting to build.

He pulled her away from the wall and carried her over to the table. He bent her forward over the table and he entered her again, feeling the heat and tightness of her increase with every move. She matched him thrust for thrust. He felt an inferno building within him, and in an attempt to keep himself in control, he started to pull back once again.

Payton would have none of that. She kept her movements hard and fast, not giving him the opportunity to regain his balance. He felt her climax explode, sucking him in. Colors erupted behind his eyelids and the world fell away. He interlaced his fingers with hers and slid their hands up the table. He extended her arms over her head. He drove himself hard and fast into her again and again, losing complete self-control.

For the briefest of moments, he thought he would black out, as the explosion of his climax overtook him, and for a fleeting instant he noticed the change in his sight and wondered if his irises had actually flashed from blue to gold. Breathing hard, he blanketed his body over hers, both slick with sweat.

"Thank you," he said, when he eventually found his voice again.

"For what?" she asked.

"For trusting me. For knowing you could keep me grounded and still let me come undone. For being you." He kissed the back of her neck and withdrew from her.

"I told you before I trust you, and I meant it. You still need to work on letting go. Don't worry, there's time; we have yet to reach the bedroom, or the shower." Her eyes sparkled with mischief.

* * * *

"I have some work to do," Payton said, as they entered her house.

"It's nearly ten o'clock; can't the work wait until morning?" Collin asked.

"Probably could, but I would toss and turn all night thinking about it. You go on up to bed. Didn't you say you are scheduled to leave first thing in the morning? I'll see you when you get back."

He wrapped his arms around her, leaned down, and kissed her. "Try not to be too late; you need to get your rest."

Parker and Kes followed Payton into her office. When they realized she meant to stay awhile, they both jumped up on the sofa and went to sleep.

Payton stared at the remaining stack of boxes. Victory had made a couple trips up and taken the boxes Payton already reviewed, and she knew her sister was like a kid in a candy store, not able to decide which of their mother's scientific studies she wanted to start on first.

This left twenty or more boxes yet to go through. She started to read the labels on the side of each box, and hoped something would jump out at her. She found a box that piqued her interest. The label was written in her mother's hand and said *Journals*. She knew her mother; journals could mean about anything—her mom was known for journaling everything, both personally and professionally—but it was as good a place as any to start.

She unburied the box from the stack and carried it over to her desk. Collin had made a valid point that she should get some sleep; she made a promise to herself this would be the only box she would go through tonight. Before she made herself comfortable, she walked over to the buffet and poured a cup of tea from the electric teapot and took the cup back to her desk. She removed the lid from the box and set it on the floor and stared into a box full of composition notebooks.

"Oh my God, there have to be over fifty notebooks in here," she said.

She'd hit the mother lode, unless it was another box full of scientific research. Even so, this box would still be a find, albeit one for Victory. She pulled the first notebook out of the box. The notebook was labeled with a date and research number. Great, Victory would be happy, but what she had discovered didn't help her in the least. She repeated the process five more times, and got the same result each time.

"Victory will be like a kid at Christmas when I show her these notebooks tomorrow," she thought.

She smiled. Maybe there would be a formula or study in one of them that could offer a clue to help Collin and Morgan.

She pulled the next notebook out and read the label *Personal*. She gasped, which caused the two dogs to raise their heads and stare at her. She sat back in her chair, opened the notebook, and read about her mom's hopes, dreams, and concerns. Payton realized she'd stumbled upon one of her mother's diaries, which was dated four years after the girls' birth.

As she sat and read into the wee hours of the morning, she felt wrapped in her mother's embrace and engrossed in her hopes and dreams. Love and pain were etched on the pages in her hands. They made her smile and weep as she read each entry of her mom's most inner thoughts.

Payton dropped her feet off the desk and sat up straight in her chair as she read and re-read the next entry: *I am beginning research on the girls' DNA. I now fully believe Edward tampered with the drug in ways other than we agreed on.*

Payton placed the notebook next to her keyboard, booted up her computer, and pulled up the past employee files. She skimmed through the names, until she located the name she was looking for—Dr. Edward Ryker.

"Bingo."

In the remainder of their mother's notebook, she cited situations where she witnessed the girls demonstrate traits that created questions or apprehension in her mind.

* * * *

Payton arrived at the office two hours late. After she discovered the notebooks, it had taken her hours to fall asleep. Now she was on a mission to locate Victory and Willow and fill them in on what she'd discovered. She found Victory in her lab, engrossed in her latest experiment. Payton asked her to stay put while she rounded up Willow. She dropped the file box next to one of the overstuffed chairs and knew full well Victory would not even notice it.

"What's going on, Payton?" Willow asked, as they walked across campus.

"I want to wait until we are all together to get into it," Payton said.

"Are you okay? You appear rather agitated today."

"I'm tired is all; I'm running on four hours' sleep."

"You have to stop doing that to yourself, Payton. Go see Dr. Russell and have her give you something to help you sleep for a couple of nights."

"Maybe I will."

Payton gathered her sisters together to reveal what she had discovered.

"I found a rather interesting box of Mom's last night. It was packed full of composition notebooks," she said, as she lifted the lid to the file box. Victory and Willow peered inside.

"Tell me more of Mom's work is in there," Victory said, as her eyes lit up.

"Yes, there is. Victory, you will be in heaven. I also discovered other information. There are three notebooks labeled *Personal*. I read through the first one last night."

"What did it say?" Willow asked.

"I found the most comforting yet disturbing information. I could feel Mom's pain and joy in every word, especially with regard to us. The first time she mentions anything unusual about us is when we were a little over four years old."

"What do you mean, unusual?" Willow asked.

"Willow, Victory is on the right path. Mom began to feel something was unique about us right after we turned four. Remember the blood draws she would take from us?"

"Yes, every six months. She said she did the draws to keep up on our health screens," Willow said.

"The primary reason she did those blood draws was to study any changes that might have taken place in our systems and to have our serum available for her research. She felt extremely guilty each time she drew blood from us. The whole situation ate her alive because all along she was lying to us," Payton said.

"You must have misinterpreted something. Mom would have never lied to us." Willow scrubbed her cheeks to remove her frustrated tears.

"She needed to keep us safe, Willow. You don't have to believe me, honey. I'll give you her notebook and you can read Mom's words for yourself," Payton said.

"How could she? How could she have kept such an important secret and lied to us our entire lives?" Willow asked.

"She desperately wanted to find answers for us. She needed to figure out what Ryker did to our DNA," Payton said.

"And our special abilities?" Victory asked.

"She writes about our abilities and how certain she became with each consecutive year that they grew more intense, due to the enhancement of the drug."

"Enhancement?" Victory asked.

"Yes, for some reason I have yet to come across, she thought each of us possessed an initial ability or 'nature' as she often referred to it, and our abilities became greatly magnified by the drug. Maybe you can discover more in her other notebooks," Payton said.

"Based on this information, I wonder if our abilities could continue to develop and change as we mature," Victory said.

"I'm not sure. Like I said, I only read the first book. There are two more notebooks in the box, and there could be more in the other boxes."

"Maybe now we can find some answers for ourselves and a possible lead to help the men," Victory said, as she looked at Willow.

"How could this information help the men?" Willow asked.

"The studies focus on the possibility of manipulating DNA, based on the introduction of foreign DNA. I have a sneaky suspicion that Mom thought that way too. I'm hoping she will provide me with a starting point. Can I keep this box for a few days?"

"Of course. Make sure you lock it in your safe when you're gone. These are our only copies. I will have everything put on flash drives over the next few days and make another paper file. We will need to lock all the originals away for safekeeping," Payton said.

* * * *

Payton rubbed the kinks from her neck—another long day at work, topped by another late night poring over the computer files. Usually when she planned to stay late at the office, she walked back up to the house and brought Kes and Parker back down with her. She glanced at the clock on her computer. It was a few minutes before ten o'clock; where had the time gone?

She wasn't concerned about going back up to the house alone. She'd walked home late and alone hundreds of times. Besides, the guys completed all the upgrades in their security, and now the campus was even more secure than when first built. She would grab one of the carts and be home in less than five minutes. As she finished shutting things down and readied her desk for the next day, she realized she was the only person left in the building.

"Don't be silly," she chided herself. "Security has been beefed up and there is absolutely not one thing to worry about."

Still an uneasy feeling grabbed hold and wouldn't let go. She looked out her window to make sure a cart was available. The night was clear, stars filled the sky, and the moon was a meager sliver. Everything took on a sinister appearance. There were no carts sitting under the streetlight, where they were supposed to be. She decided to contact the front gate and make sure there would be cart and a security guard out front when she wanted to leave.

She pressed the intercom button to the gate and let it ring for a bit. She waited and pressed the button again.

"Strange."

She pulled the file out of her desk drawer to see who was on duty. Frank, the shift boss, was on. He was one of the first people they hired when they started to staff the campus and one of their most conscientious employees. Payton sat back in her chair.

I'm being silly. I'm sure it's been a busy night, and Frank has probably stepped away to get a cup of coffee.

She grabbed her purse out of her desk drawer, double-checked to verify her cell phone was in her jacket pocket, and left for the main gate to get a cart. The gate sat directly across the parking lot, and the entire area was well lit with streetlights. An ominous dread slithered down the back of Payton's neck. Was there someone else in the vicinity? She scanned the entire area. No one.

"These blasted psychic abilities," she mumbled.

She thought she had more control over them. She needed to heed Victory's advice and work on honing her skill on a daily basis.

As she approached the gate, she noticed there appeared to be no one in the security shack. Not unusual, this often happened at night. When it was quiet and the gate was locked, instead of sitting in the tiny shack, the guards would stay in the security office across the street from the shack. There were lights on in the office, making it a safe bet Frank was there. She pictured a cup of coffee in his hand as he watched his favorite talk show.

Payton veered toward the office building; she gave one last backward glance at the shack. She stopped in mid-stride. Something seemed off. Then she noticed the door was ajar. The door was equipped with an automatic close-and-lock feature. The only way for the door to be left open was if someone stood in the doorway or something prohibited the door from closing.

She walked up to the shack and reached out to take the doorknob. Her eyes tracked down the length of the door until she saw what kept the door from closing. There was a black shoe wedged in the doorway. She stared at the shoe, her mind unable to decipher what she was seeing. Her eyes traveled from the shoe, to the dark blue pant leg, to the matching shirt…Payton gasped.

There lay Frank, crumpled across the floor, a dark wet spot on the left side of his chest. She reached into her jacket pocket and fumbled for her phone. She finally pulled the phone out and pressed the power button as she felt the strangest prick at the side of her neck. She turned to her left, where she noticed movement. Her head started to spin and her eyes blurred. She caught a blurry image of a man right before she hit the ground.

Chapter Eighteen

A few minutes after midnight Collin made his way back to Payton's house. His day turned out to be long and draining, but the team appeared pleased with his progress. He felt a weight lifted off him at the knowledge his teammates and commanding officers were finally beginning to trust him. Wyatt told him at his current rate of improvement, he could be completely back on active duty in the next month.

He silently entered through the kitchen door, not wanting to wake the dogs, who in turn would wake the sisters. He turned the light off in the kitchen and headed into the living room to switch the lamp off. As he entered the room he stopped short. Kes and Parker sat on the bottom stair.

"Hey guys, why are you up?" They ran to greet him. "You two should be in bed. Did you open Payton's door, Parker?"

Parker wagged his short black tail. "Come on, I'll tuck you in."

The two dogs bounded up the stairs ahead of him.

Light spilled into the hall from Payton's room. He thought she would be sound asleep by now. He stepped into the doorway and instead of finding her sitting in bed reading, he found her bed still made. A bone-deep feeling of foreboding choked him. He jogged back down the hall and tapped on Willow's door.

"Willow, it's Collin." He heard Asia jump from the bed and head to the door. "Willow, wake up."

"Collin?" came her drowsy voice. "It's late, Collin," she said. She still did not sound fully awake.

"Where's Payton?"

In a heartbeat, the door flew open. Willow stood there, tying her robe.

"She isn't in bed?"

"No."

"She probably lost track of time and is still working at the office. She was engrossed in Mom's files when I left the campus.

"Let me phone her office," Willow said. She walked back into her room, picked up her cell phone, and dialed Payton's office. "It's ringing—her voice mail just picked up." She pushed the disconnect button and hit the speed dial. "I'll try her cell. Darn it, voice mail again. Do you think she could have fallen asleep?" she asked.

"It's possible. I'm going down to her office. You wait here and keep your cell phone with you."

Collin shot out the door and ran full speed for the campus, racing at three times the top speed of the carts. As he approached Payton's building, he could see all the lights were off except for an insignificant glow in Payton's office window. He bounded up the front steps and stopped dead at the entry. He closed his eyes, concentrated on the interior of the building, and listened. He heard only the high-pitched humming of the security system. He forced that sound from his mind and refocused. He listened for breathing, snoring, or any other sound associated with a human.

Not a single sound.

He placed his hand over the scanner next to the door. The color turned from red to green and the lock release clicked. He crept soundlessly down the hall and didn't bother to turn on lights, as his eyes immediately adapted. He could feel the wolf inside him; it fought to surface. Payton's office door was closed, and the blinds were up on the windows that framed the door. He scanned the room, lit only by the nightlight she always left on, which sat on her credenza. He placed his palm on the security sensor and her door clicked open. He walked into the room, and quickly and thoroughly surveyed his surroundings. Nothing looked out of place. Collin pulled his cell phone out of his pocket and punched in a speed-dial number.

"Farraday here; this damn well better be life or death," Tristan growled.

"Payton's missing."

"What the hell? Where are you?" Tristan asked.

"I'm at her office. She isn't here. Nothing looks out of place, but she isn't here."

Collin used every bit of self-control to keep himself focused. He could feel the adrenaline begin to pump through his body. He knew if he lost himself now and blacked out, he would be of no use to Payton. She trusted him and he needed to live up to her trust and find her.

"And before you even ask, no, she's not at the house," Collin said.

"Christ Almighty," Tristan said.

Collin could feel a buzz through the phone and knew the instant Tristan started to communicate telepathically with his brother, Wyatt.

"What'd he say?" Collin asked, unable to wait.

"What the—" Tristan began.

"I can pick up the energy," he explained. "What did he say?"

"He wants us to start the search of the campus. He'll contact the rest of the team. They should be here within the hour. I'll call Morgan and we'll meet up with you. Don't move, Collin. We'll be there shortly."

Collin inhaled a deep breath and filled his lungs with the familiar scent of Payton. The scent was subtle, yet still permeated the office. He stepped out into the hall, closed his eyes, and inhaled once again. He caught the scent cone, it was weak, but he picked up Payton's scent. She left by the side door. He ran to the door, threw it open, and assessed the area. His eyes scanned the security building and guard shack across the far side of the parking lot. It looked out of place to his wolf-enhanced eyes. He headed for the security office.

Where the hell were all the guards? Surely, Tristan had contacted them by now, he thought.

He'd jogged halfway across the parking lot, when something caught his eye. He couldn't make out what was on the ground, yet deep inside dread iced his bones. He picked up his speed and reached the shack in seconds. On the road a couple of feet from the guard shack lay Payton's purse and cell phone. Collin's world spiraled around him, his vision blurred, and he dropped to his knees.

Payton. He yelled her name; only his mind heard the plea.

Tristan and Morgan arrived on the scene to find Collin crumpled on the road. Morgan ran up to him stopping within arm's length.

"Collin, Collin," Morgan said.

"Has he been shot?" Tristan asked.

"I can't tell," Morgan said. "I need to roll him over. Stand back a couple of feet in case he comes up swinging."

"Collin, it's Morgan. I need to see if you've been injured." Morgan reached down and placed a hand on Collin's shoulder.

Collin spun into a crouched position, his eyes emitting a golden glow. A menacing growl reverberated through his body.

"Holy hell, Collin, get a grip. You will be no use to Payton if you check out now," Morgan said.

"Does he do that often?" Tristan asked, and pointed to Collin's eyes.

The sound of Payton's name pulled at Collin...beckoned to him. He should know that name. But the thick haze in his brain stopped him from connecting the dots. Slowly, Morgan squatted down by him and reached out to pick up the purse. He never broke eye contact with Collin as Morgan lifted the purse to Collin's nose. On instinct Collin inhaled.

"Payton needs you, Collin. You told me only today that she believes in you. You need to find your way back," Morgan said.

Collin's eyes flashed from bright gold to dark blue and back to gold. Eventually they settled on his natural light blue, with streaks of gold. He looked into his partner's eyes and slowly registered the situation. Collin looked over Morgan's shoulder at the guard shack.

"There is a dead man over there," he growled in an aggressive tone. "I'm going to kill Braxton."

The other two men followed Collin's stare to the partially open door of the guard shack. Tristan made the first move; he walked around the two men and over to the shack door.

"God damn it all to hell," he hissed. "They shot Frank. I know exactly how you feel right now Collin, and what I need to know is, are you going to be able to hold it together and help find Payton, or do I have to demand you return to the house?"

Collin reached out and picked up Payton's cell phone, and then he and Morgan rose to their feet. "I've got a handle on this, sir," he said.

"Good. You and Morgan go take a look inside the security office. I couldn't get anyone to pick up the phone. Wyatt will be here in five minutes; he and the rest of the team are at the house."

* * * *

Morgan reached the door first and entered the security office.

"Shit," he said, as the two men took in the devastation.

The main office looked like a wrecking ball had ripped through. Three men were sprawled out, each one with a single gunshot to the head.

"How the hell did this happen? Why didn't they radio anyone?" Morgan asked.

"How many others are on duty?" Collin asked.

"I'm not sure, maybe four or five on a walking rotation."

"Have they all been accounted for?"

"Let's go ask Tristan."

"It's a mess in there," Collin said, as they reached Tristan. "Three guards each shot in the head."

"Damn it all to hell," Tristan snarled. "Guess that explains why no one answered when I phoned them."

"Why were there three men in the office?" Morgan asked.

"They must have gotten caught in-between shift changes. The outgoing team leader always gives a verbal report to the incoming team leader," Tristan said.

"There are five men on patrol. I made contact with each of them and told them to be alert for intruders. They are to maintain their route and report anything suspicious immediately."

"Fill us in," Wyatt said, as he, Logan, Noah, and Jack arrived on the scene.

Tristan gave a complete account of what had happened, leaving out the part about Collin.

"Who was the last person to see Payton?" Wyatt asked.

"Willow, I think," Collin said.

"No, Victory. She said she stopped by Payton's office around nine o'clock and tried to get Payton to ride up to the house with her. Payton promised Victory she would head home shortly," Tristan said.

Wyatt looked down at his wristwatch. "It is one forty-five now. Collin, what time did you reach Payton's office?"

"I'm not certain. I do know I wasn't at the house too long before I left for her office," Collin said.

"He contacted me at twelve thirty-five," Tristan said.

"We have a three-and-a-half hour window when no one saw Payton," Wyatt said.

"She could be anywhere by now," Collin said. "We need to start the search."

"Everyone spread out and look for any clues. Morgan and Collin, you stay inside the campus. Logan and Noah, search the outer perimeter and see if you can find anything. Jack, you head over to our office. Look through the security feed and see what you can find. I want everyone back at the office in one hour," Wyatt said.

The team dispersed, leaving Tristan and Wyatt behind. Wyatt looked at Tristan.

"Let's take a look around the security office," Wyatt said. "Do you think Collin will be able to handle Payton being kidnapped? Seems he and Payton have grown rather close."

The two brothers started toward the building, heads down; they scoured the ground for footprints, debris—any kind of a clue.

"You don't know the half of it," Tristan said. "They're involved."

"What? I thought the two of them couldn't stand the sight of one another."

"Things changed."

"Obviously…I'm feeling a little out of the loop," Wyatt said.

"Don't take it personally. Remember, I'm married to Victory. I know about all the goings-on by default, whether I want to or not."

"I can't even imagine what you deal with on a daily basis, given a new wife and two sisters." Wyatt chuckled and shook his head.

They got to the door and looked for any evidence of forced entry.

"No forced entry means one of our intruders wasn't a threat and was welcomed in," Wyatt said.

"Someone they knew did this," Tristan groaned.

"What a damn mess," Wyatt said, as they entered the office. "Clean shots, straight through the head. The place is an absolute disaster. Wonder what the hell they were looking for?"

Tristan felt for a pulse on each of the three men, even though he knew full well the task was futile.

"Bodies are cold, must have happened a couple hours ago. Victory left the campus by herself around nine. They could have taken her, Wyatt."

"She's fine, Tristan. I moved her and Dax over to the main house with Willow. I brought four additional men with me. The women will be fine. Right now we have to focus on finding their sister, or we will both be up shit creek," Wyatt said.

"This can't happen again. We need to insist they have escorts if they stay late on campus."

"We will, but for now we need to get back to the office and figure out who the hell took Payton and why."

"You know damn well Payton's kidnapping has Braxton written all over it or someone associated with Kaleidoscope Group," Tristan said.

* * * *

216

"Tell us what you found, Jack." Wyatt said. He grabbed his cup of coffee, went to the table and sat down with the rest of the team.

"You were right, sir. Whoever killed those men was no stranger and knew enough to erase the security feed. On the other hand, they were not technically advanced enough to know to wipe the backup."

"Did we actually catch a break?" Collin asked.

"Sorta." Jack tapped a couple keys on his computer, and the screen on the wall in front of the team lit up.

The interior of the security office appeared on the screen. The three guards sat and watched the television. A beep sounded and notified the guard someone was at the door. One guard got up and walked behind the desk to look out the door.

"Hey, what are you doing here?" he asked, as he pushed the button to let the unseen person in.

The next thing they heard was a thump, thump sound.

"Silencer," Jack said. "And I assume that's why the other two guards didn't react instantly. They were turned away from the door and didn't hear the shots over the television."

"Well, the layout of the office will change. Who the hell moved the camera? We situated that particular camera to record everyone who walked into the building," Wyatt said.

"And the person who entered knew that," Jack said.

Next they saw a single person dressed in black with a black ski mask on the monitor.

"Hey. What the—" The second guard rolled off his chair dead before he could finish his sentence. The last guard jumped to his feet and attempted to pull his gun. Another thump sounded, and a small crimson spot appeared between the man's eyes before he collapsed to the ground in a heap.

They watched as the assailant tore through the office, reading files and checking the computer. He stopped and read the screen, and then he flicked the computer off and left the office.

"Jack, can you see the last thing the intruder looked at before he shut down the computer?" Wyatt asked.

"Already did." Jack tapped another key, the computer came into view and filled the entire screen. The last open file showed the list of buildings and what employees were still inside each building. The middle of the screen, where the gloved finger of the assailant stopped, read: Payton Winters, clocked out of her office at ten fifteen.

"The new security was supposed to keep them safe, not broadcast their comings and goings, God damn it." Collin growled.

"We also thought the whole security team had been vetted. Seems obvious we have a leak," Wyatt said. "Jack, has the entire team checked in?"

"Every one of them. The leak must be someone on one of the other shifts. I've left messages for all of them to check-in," Jack said.

"Have you heard from everyone?" Wyatt asked.

"Still waiting on three to get back to me," Jack said.

"Odds are it is one of those three guards. The guard who buzzed the intruder in showed no sign of real surprise. The only person he wouldn't be surprised to see at that time of night would've been one of the guards who just came off duty. He probably thought the intruder forgot something or wanted to fill them in on an event that took place during his shift," Wyatt said.

"Start with the three you can't reach. Do a background search, check their computer traffic, do a cell phone dump, credit checks…the whole nine yards. I want an entire workup on each of those people. In the meantime, Morgan, Logan, and Noah, each of you take an address of one of the three guards and see what you can find," Wyatt said.

"Yes, sir," the men responded.

Wyatt turned and looked at his brother and Collin. "And now, we have to go and inform Victory and Willow that Payton has been kidnapped."

* * * *

"Why would they take Payton? I could see if they tried for me again, but not Payton. She doesn't have a scientific bone in her body," Victory said. She absently wiped at the tears that continued to cascade down her cheeks.

"I don't think they want her for the same reason. I believe they took her for leverage," Wyatt said.

"Not again," Willow mumbled. "Why can't they leave us alone?"

Victory got up from her chair, sat down beside her sister, and hugged her close.

"You guys will get her back, won't you?" She stared at her husband for confirmation.

"We'll get her back," Collin said. "I promise."

Wyatt's cell phone vibrated. He pulled the phone from his pocket and hit the button.

"What do you have for me, Logan?"

"I think I found our leak," Logan said. "But he isn't going to be of any help to us. Same MO, single gunshot to the head, no break-in, and no struggle."

"This just keeps getting better and better," Wyatt said.

Chapter Nineteen

Payton floated in a twilight sleep, entangled between actual sleep and wakefulness. Her head throbbed, and she found herself caught up in a terrifying nightmare. She willed herself awake, the pounding in her skull intensifying the closer she moved toward consciousness. She reached down her side and expected to feel Parker and Kes lying beside her. She felt only the cool sheet draped over her body. She opened her eyes. The shades were drawn on the windows and shafts of sunlight bled through them.

This is not my room, was her first fully conscious thought. *Where am I?*

She looked up at the ceiling fan and tried to piece together the last thing she could remember. She'd left her office, headed for the security shack, and—

Oh my God, Frank is dead. The terrible scene replayed in her mind.

The door to the room clicked, and Payton closed her eyes and pretended to be asleep. She heard someone walk in and set something on the table across the room from her.

"I know you're awake, Payton. We have a camera in the room," Dave Anderson said. He pointed up at the tiny black circle in the upper corner of the far wall. "I brought you a bottle of water and some aspirin for your headache. The drug you were given leaves a nasty aftereffect. There's also coffee and some food if you're hungry."

She opened her eyes and turned her head to get a look at the man who spoke to her.

"Where am I and who are you?" she asked. She slowly slid up to a sitting position and used the headboard to support herself.

"My name is Dave Anderson. Perhaps you have heard of me?" he asked with an unwarranted smile.

Payton felt panic begin to well up inside of her, but she refused to give Dave Anderson the satisfaction of seeing it. She scowled back at him, not such a hard thing to do, given that her head and chest were attempting to throb out of her body. Dave had coal-black hair with piercing eyes that matched his hair. Neatly dressed in a gray suit, he looked as if he might be on his way to attend a business meeting. Payton felt no energy radiate off of him; he seemed dead inside and out. But the scent of his cologne nearly overwhelmed her. The scent was familiar—Polo.

"Where am I?" she demanded.

"All in good time," Dave said. "There are clean clothes and the items you need in the bathroom. Get yourself cleaned up. I'll be back to get you in half an hour. And don't get any crazy ideas about leaving. There are guards outside both your door and windows."

He shut the door behind him, and she heard the lock click back into place. How could she have been kidnapped right off their campus? They'd upgraded all the security systems and increased the number of guards. None of this made any sense to her. Maybe one of her employees kept Braxton and his motley crew updated. The thought made her cringe: Someone she and her sisters spent every day with betrayed them; she could see no other logical explanation. Her sisters must be panicked by now, and unfortunately, she knew firsthand what they were going through. *Poor Willow, having to deal with yet another sister kidnapped. Damn you to hell, Braxton.*

Dave led her out the door of the building; two men followed them. She assessed her environment. It looked as if they were in a massive compound, possibly somewhere tropical. There were buildings scattered along the many paths that led in all directions. Each building and trail was clearly marked with beautiful hand-carved signs, and foliage was expertly placed throughout the entire compound, giving it a tropical flair. Payton inhaled and took in the fragrances of plumeria, orchids, and tuberoses.

She followed Dave in silence as they passed the skeleton of a building all but completely burned to the ground. A sick feeling started in her stomach. Could she conceivably be on the exact same Hawaiian island Victory was taken to? *Impossible, Braxton could not have gotten on the Hawaiian Islands undetected.* She knew his presence would alert the authorities the instant he came back into the States.

Dave turned and walked up a short path to a building. He opened the door and gestured to Payton.

"This way," he said.

The building contained one large room with a couple of doors to one side, the room sparsely, yet elegantly decorated. The slate floor was covered by an oversized Oriental rug and a few antiques were scattered throughout. Payton's attention was drawn to a massive antique mahogany desk that nearly swallowed an entire wall.

A man sat in the chair behind the desk; his elbows rested on the chair arms and his fingers steepled together as he stared down at a computer screen. He looked like any other middle-aged businessman, his salt-and-pepper hair neatly cut, bangs brushed to one side. He was dressed in an expensive three-piece suit, which looked custom-tailored. She couldn't tell what color his eyes were, as he appeared to make it a point not to acknowledge her presence as she entered the room.

Typical power play.

"Payton Winters, I didn't think we would get the opportunity to meet. Allow me to introduce myself—"

When he finally raised his eyes to meet hers, Payton could fully understand Victory's anger of him, for his true nature showed in his cold dead eyes.

"I know who you are, Lawrence Braxton." She cut him off.

"Well, I see my reputation precedes me."

"Please, don't flatter yourself," Payton said. *What was she doing, poking the bear?*

"I certainly see your resemblance to Victory. I'm looking forward to meeting Willow." Braxton smiled.

"Don't hold your breath! You are never going meet Willow." She could barely keep her temper in check. The horror stories Victory had related bubbled up to the surface. Braxton was making her relive the weeks of anguish she and Willow went through, not knowing if they would ever see their sister again.

"You know the old saying, 'never say never.' Please sit down."

She remained planted on her spot. Dave yanked her by the upper arm, dragged her to the closest chair, and physically forced her to sit.

"I'm usually a bit more patient with my guests, however, I haven't the time to play your little games," Braxton said.

"You're right; you don't have the time. I'm certain it won't take long before I am found on the same island you brought Victory to."

"Believe me; no one will even think to look here. As far as they know, the complex is abandoned. All the pictures and reports about my facility show the area as uninhabited."

"Not possible," she said.

"Oh, but you're wrong. I can attest that it pays to have friends in high places, and Carl is a good friend of mine."

Carl? Payton thought.

She had no idea who Carl was, but she filed his name in her mind. Maybe Braxton slipped up and told her more than he planned, or maybe he wasn't concerned because she would never leave the island.

"You do realize I have no scientific background and no ability to pick up where my sister left off?"

"I'm especially well-versed in your abilities. In truth, I have extensive knowledge of all the Winters sisters' education, experience, and accomplishments. I did not abduct you for lab work. You are here merely for information, or at the very least—leverage. You and your friends took someone from me and I want her back," Braxton said.

"I assure you, I have no idea what you are talking about," Payton said.

"On the contrary, I believe you do. I want Emma McBain, and you are going to tell me where she is."

"Who?" She prayed the nerves she felt weren't reflected on her face.

"You know damn well who," Braxton snapped. "Emma. At first I thought Sarah took her from the school. However, after further evaluation, I realized Sarah could not have pulled off such a plan alone. She met Victory at the offices. I'm sure she has seen her recently in the paper with regard to your gala. If I know Sarah, she would go to her, hoping Victory's influence could be of use."

"I have never even heard of this Sarah, and I have no idea what you are talking about."

Braxton rose abruptly from his chair. The desk chair skittered over the floor and smashed back against the wall. He slammed his open palms on his desk.

"I have no time for these childish games. You will tell me where she is, or I will force the information from you," he snarled at her. All semblance of calm and sophistication was gone. "Take her to the lab."

Dave opened the door and the two men who'd escorted Payton and Dave rushed in, each grabbing one of Payton's arms and dragging her from the room. She gritted her teeth to keep from crying out in pain. She wouldn't give Braxton, or his thugs, the satisfaction of seeing her pain or her fear. They threw her into a cart and climbed in after her, caging her between them.

Dave jumped into the driver's seat and sped away from the building.

When the cart came to a halt, the two men yanked Payton out and hauled her into a different building. Payton could feel Victory's energy still infused inside the lab; it confirmed her fear that this laboratory was indeed where Victory had worked. Payton was in the lab where Victory initially met Collin and Morgan, and where her sister feverishly worked to try to save the lives of the two men.

"Put her over there," Dave said. He pointed to a desk chair.

They sat her in the chair and stepped back from her. She recognized another trace of energy; it encompassed the chair she sat in and almost brought a smile to her lips. Tristan had spent a great deal of time in this chair. Even immersed in her dire situation, Payton's thoughts turned to her sister as she hoped she would get the opportunity to tell Victory about the strides she appeared to have made in sensing energy signatures.

Time slowed almost to a standstill as Payton sat and waited to see what Braxton's next move would be. She prayed he still saw her as an asset. The door to the lab opened and Braxton entered, followed by a woman and another man. The man was dressed in a white doctor's coat, the woman in black jeans and a skintight black shirt that accentuated her well-toned body. Her hair was blonde and cut in a short bob. She was quite stunning, except for her icy stare. The woman brandished an air of darkness and danger. Payton was immediately unnerved by the terrifying emotions she picked up from the woman's aura.

"Take her into the other room," the doctor said.

Payton looked around.

What other room?

One of the men pulled her off the chair and ushered her to the wall covered almost entirely by a mirror, and for the first time, she noticed the door at the far side. The man opened the door and tossed her into what looked like an exam chair, and he and his buddy strapped her arms and legs down.

As soon as her skin made contact with the chair, she was swamped by Collin and Morgan's emotions. The pain, helplessness, and sheer anger they felt invaded her entire body and mind. She struggled to breathe through the emotions while, at the same time, she felt an energizing sensation vibrate throughout her body. Evidently she was learning how to transfer intense emotional energy to her benefit. Victory had explained that as she honed her skill, she would eventually learn how to use it for her specific needs. Payton didn't believe her at the time. She prayed what she now felt were Victory's words coming to fruition, for she knew she would need every mental weapon she could conjure to make it through this nightmare.

Braxton strolled into the exam room, followed by the other two.

"Now Miss Winters, let's try this again. Where is Emma McBain?" Braxton asked.

"I told you; I have no idea what you are talking about," Payton said, as she stared at Braxton.

"Fine, you leave me no choice. Granted, your lack of co-operation has provided me with the perfect opportunity to test one of my newest weapons."

Weapons? What the hell was he talking about? He truly is insane, she thought.

"Let me introduce you to Tessa," he said. He gestured to the woman who stood to one side of him. "Tessa can retrieve anything I ask her to from your mind."

"A mind reader?" Payton asked. "There is no such thing."

"Oh, but I assure you there is. Tessa, locate Emma."

Tessa stepped close enough to touch Payton, and locked on to her eyes. Tessa's eyes whirled from gray to black, and Payton could feel herself being sucked into their vortex. Without a conscious thought, she threw up her mental barriers and centered herself. Her entire focus was to keep this woman out of her mind. Tessa's eyes flashed a surprised look for a split second as she refocused on her task.

Payton didn't back down or give in, and the two women fought a mental battle. Seconds slipped into minutes; their faces became covered in a sheen of sweat. Payton prayed she could withstand and outlast this parasite. For a single heartbeat, her barrier slipped.

"Collin."

At last Tessa pulled away, both mentally and physically, and her once healthy complexion now appeared noticeably pasty.

"She is a strong-willed one," Tessa said.

"Are you telling me you can't retrieve the information I require?" Braxton asked, both curious and upset.

"I did not get what you wanted. After I rest, I can try again. I did however discover some information that might interest you."

"Spit it out, girl," he snapped.

"Collin is alive," Tessa said.

Stunned, he looked down at Payton.

"Really? Well, now that is of interest to me."

* * * *

The team had moved back to the naval base, and the next morning Collin started to brief them in the Situation Room.

"Collin."

He swore he heard Payton's terrified voice scream through his mind. He stopped mid-sentence and grabbed the table. The only thing that kept him from falling to the ground was that he was already sitting down.

"Collin, do you need a break?" Wyatt asked. "We don't want to push you too hard or too quickly."

Collin didn't answer.

"Collin," Wyatt said, the volume of his voice increased a few notches.

Collin's vision cleared and he looked around the room. All eyes were trained on him.

"I asked you if you need a break, Collin," Wyatt said.

"No, sir. I could swear I heard Payton," Collin said.

Wyatt looked from him to Tristan. Collin felt a mild buzz in his head and knew the two brothers conversed telepathically.

"You have developed telepathic skills?" Wyatt asked.

"No, sir. Still, I am positive I heard Payton. She's alive but in immense pain. Her pain felt—mental. We need to locate her, now. I don't think she will be able to withstand many more assaults."

Chapter Twenty

"Collin has been hidden on your campus along with Morgan," Braxton said.

"Who?" Payton asked.

"Really Payton, playing dumb infuriates me. You should consider yourself lucky I still need you because people who irritate me the way you have don't usually live long."

Braxton turned to the doctor.

"How long will it take Tessa to recover?" Braxton asked.

"I'm not certain. This is the first time she has extended herself in a real-life situation," the doctor said.

"I need an estimate, doctor; otherwise you are of no use to me."

"My best guess is she will need until tomorrow morning, maybe as late as the afternoon."

"Fine. Dave, take our guest back and put her in a room with no windows. I don't want any screw-ups. We will all meet back here tomorrow at nine in the morning."

"B-but," the doctor stammered.

Braxton spun around and pinned the doctor with a formidable stare. "Did you or did you not assure me Tessa would be ready tomorrow?"

The doctor appeared extremely nervous as he slowly nodded his head.

"Good. We have precious little time to solve our problem. If Tessa can't retrieve the information I need tomorrow, I will have to find other alternatives."

Braxton stormed out of the lab.

* * * *

Payton sat on the bed and nibbled food from the tray of dinner left for her. She wasn't the least bit hungry, yet she knew her body needed all the fuel she could absorb. After dinner she took a warm bath, went back into the bedroom, spread a blanket on the floor, and started her yoga practice. She worked on her breathing, focus, and centering her thoughts for over an hour. Both physically and mentally exhausted, she climbed into bed and fell asleep within minutes.

She was already strapped in the same exam chair by the time Braxton arrived the next morning.

"Where are Tessa and the doctor?" he asked.

"I sent one of my men with a cart to hurry them along. They should be here any minute," Dave said.

The door to the lab opened and the doctor and Tessa walked in. As soon as they walked into the lab, Payton became hyper-aware of Tessa. Her energy didn't feel as hostile as the day before but she didn't look as if she was fully recovered. Payton hoped all those factors would help her cause.

"Is she ready, doctor?" Braxton asked.

"She hasn't had time for a total recovery, although I think she will do fine," the doctor said.

"Fine. I need more than fine. Did you give her any steroid?" Braxton asked.

"No, sir, I didn't think you would want me to tamper with her by giving her an artificial stimulant." the doctor said.

"Give her the damn steroid, now. Can you not understand the importance of Tessa's ability being at its most powerful? Make a note in your research so everything is correctly recorded."

The doctor scurried over to one of the medicine cabinets, unlocked the metal door with his key, and prepared a syringe. He injected Tessa with the drug.

Payton could swear she saw Tessa's eyes light up and her breathing quicken. Payton began her deep breathing. She focused herself on her mental image, and shut out everything and everyone around her. Tessa approached her, only this time Payton did not give her the opportunity to make the first move. Her entire concentration centered on her mental image, and she hardly registered when Tessa's gaze locked onto hers.

Payton felt the mental push, the intensity grow as Tessa tried to force her mind open. Payton ignored the invasion and remained centered. Minutes slipped by; again she and Tessa were bathed in sweat, yet the mental battle raged on. More time passed and blood began to drip out of Tessa's nose.

"She must stop," the doctor said.

"I need the information," Braxton said.

"Are you willing to trade the possible retrieval of this information at the cost of an entire year's work? We have no one with her advanced skills. What if you need her again, sir?" the doctor asked.

"Fine. She's getting nowhere. End this," he said, with the wave of his hand.

The doctor walked up to Tessa and put a hand on each shoulder.

"Tessa, you are done. You need to rest. Leave her."

Payton was conscious of the instant Tessa withdrew, exhausted and grateful the agonizing battle at long last came to an end. Tessa collapsed on the floor, blood running from both nostrils and a tiny trickle starting from one eye. She glared up at Payton, hate radiating in her eyes.

Payton felt sorry for the girl. How did she come to be here? Was she recruited from the Wright Academy as a young child or did she willingly volunteer to take part in these horrible ventures? What kind of life did she have?

"Help them back," Braxton said, to one of the men. "Well, Payton, you have greatly surprised me, and if I weren't limited on time, I would study you more extensively. It is regrettable that at this point in time I need to retrieve my property."

"She's not your property. She's a little girl," Payton said. She immediately realized the error she had made in her admission. *Damn it, Payton. There are times you need to keep your mouth closed.*

"You do know Emma. No matter. I will have her back soon. Clean her up and bring her to my office in an hour," Braxton said to his men.

Payton sat in Braxton's office and waited for him to arrive. Braxton appeared to be agitated, and that did not bode well for her survival. He entered the office without an acknowledgment and he walked over to his desk. He picked up a phone, dialed a number, and waited.

"Lawrence Braxton speaking. I need to speak with Victory."

Payton sat up straighter in the chair and intently watched Braxton's every move.

"Good afternoon, Victory. I'm sure by now you have surmised I have Payton. Contact Wyatt and his team. Tell them that I have a proposal for them." He looked at his watch and continued. "You have five minutes to patch me through, and I want to speak to the whole team, including Collin. That's right; I know he's alive, and I know he is there. Do it now, or Payton suffers."

Now what was he up to? Payton wondered.

Payton never in her life experienced such a sinister individual. She realized Braxton would stop at nothing to reach his goals.

Payton was desperate. She began to wonder if she focused on the phone, maybe Victory or Collin would pick up her energy and feel her presence. She thought about a mental message, and an idea sprang into her mind. They were both endowed with supersonic hearing. Could she send them a message? She might run the risk of being seen or heard by Braxton or Dave. She would have to be extremely subtle. Her message needed to be simple—one word, a snippet of a clue to help point them in the right direction.

"Do you have everyone patched in?" Braxton asked. "Good, put me on speaker phone."

While Braxton was engrossed in his call, she glanced over to see Dave. He stared down at his phone, probably checking his messages. She pretended to sneeze into her hands, and whispered a single word— "laboratory."

"Collin, I'm delighted you survived your fall. How have you progressed?" Braxton listened and chuckled.

"I see you still have that same spirit. Good to know; your spirit will come in handy. Okay, enough of the pleasantries. I want Emma, and in return you may have Payton back. I will send a helicopter to the helipad at the Biotec offices on the San Juan Island. You have until tomorrow morning at ten o'clock to get her there. As a bonus, I also want you, Collin. Payton will not be on the helicopter. She will be returned to you after I get Emma and Collin."

He stopped for a moment and listened. "You have my word she will be returned to you. Keep yours, or Payton's life will be forfeited."

* * * *

"Payton was there in the room with Braxton," Collin said.

"You're right, I heard her sneeze," Victory said. "I thought I might have imagined her."

"Is the sneeze all you heard?" Collin asked.

"I can't be certain, but I think she said—"

"Laboratory," Victory spoke the word at the same time he did.

The team stared at Collin.

"Laboratory. Did either of you hear anything else?" Wyatt asked.

Collin and Victory shook their heads.

"But you are certain Payton was there and you heard her say 'laboratory'?"

"The word has to be laboratory. We both heard the same word, which means Payton is physically with Braxton, and she is okay," Collin said.

"What do you think she is trying to tell you?" Wyatt asked.

Collin mulled the word over in his head, as he knew Victory did too, and then Victory spoke.

"The first thought that came to mind is the lab on the island," Victory said. "I know Payton, and she used the best word she could think of that would relate to the both of us to trigger an image in our mind. She would want to tell us where she was, hence 'laboratory.'"

"It must be another lab. It can't be the lab on the island. I have downloaded pictures from the satellite. The place is deserted, abandoned right after you guys left. We've monitored it ever since. Besides, that would mean Braxton is in the United States and hasn't been flagged," Jack said.

"Are you saying it's impossible to tamper with a satellite or to fabricate photos?" Collin asked.

"Not impossible, but pretty damn tricky. There are probably only a handful of people with the capability or authority to work with the satellites. You're talking someone very, very, high up in the government food chain," Jack said.

"We now possess one more piece of evidence to prove the Kaleidoscope Group has an extensively deep reach," Wyatt said. "Okay, we go with what we have.

We need a plan." He looked at his wristwatch. "Let's synchronize our time. Victory, what time do you have?"

She glanced at the antique clock on her desk, "Quarter past seven," she said.

"We have ninety minutes. The C-27J Spartan will be fueled and ready to go in an hour and a half, and you gentlemen will be on that plane. By the time we get you over the island, it will be dark," Wyatt said.

"Who's going, captain?" Collin asked.

"The whole team, if you are sure you can handle this, Collin," Wyatt said.

"I can, sir, thank you."

"Okay, gentlemen, wheels up in ninety minutes."

* * * *

"It's been awhile since either of us have done a HALO jump," Morgan spoke though his intercom to the rest of the team.

"It's like riding a bike," Noah said.

"Okay, guys, we're going in totally dark. Our mark is approximately half a mile from the compound. The distance should keep us clear in case they have managed to keep the lights on," Tristan said.

"Didn't Jack say the security system went down?" Morgan asked.

"Yes, he did," Logan said. "It's not as though I don't trust Jack…I do, but he also thought the place was abandoned."

"You're right, Logan. Until we have eyes on the ground and can verify what we are walking into, we assume the worse," Tristan said.

"Target in ten minutes," the pilot's voice broke in.

"ETA five minutes," said the pilot.

"Time to dance," Logan said.

"Okay, guys, let's make one final check of our gear," Tristan said.

The team pulled on their oxygen masks, checked their gauges, and put on their helmets. A HALO jump, High-Altitude-Low-Opening, meant they would jump out of the plane at over twenty thousand feet so as not to be heard or seen from the ground. They would not open their parachutes until the last possible minute. That would limit the amount of time they could be spotted in the air. They walked to the tail of the plane where Logan pushed a button and watched the floor of the plane open up to the inky night sky.

"Go," they heard the command from the pilot.

Noah looked at Tristan, Morgan, Collin, and Logan. All five gave the thumbs-up sign, and one by one they did a free fall from the plane.

Tristan counted four tiny flashing lights spread out below him. Each man's helmet displayed a light, they would stop blinking the moment they disconnected their oxygen masks, which kept the lights from being seen on the ground. He checked his altimeter. At ten thousand feet, he removed his oxygen mask and checked in with his team.

The men hit the ground and wasted no time gathering up their parachutes and locating a place to hide the gear they wouldn't need.

"What do you got, Noah?" Tristan asked, as they all watched him pull a device from his bag and attempt to find their bearings.

"We hit the mark, right on. We head west for a half mile to locate the compound."

"Let's go," Tristan said.

They travelled in absolute silence. When they were within sight of the compound, they stopped.

"Sure looks different from the last time we were here," Logan said. "I don't see any guards at the main gate, and there are only a few lights scattered throughout the compound."

"Collin, do you hear any buzzing from the fence?" Tristan asked.

Collin focused on the fence and listened for the hum of electricity.

"No, the fence is dead."

"Okay, we go over the fence and spread out and search the compound. You are not to make any contact," Tristan said, as he locked eyes on Collin. "In thirty minutes, we'll head to the guard shack right inside the high security area, where Morgan and Collin were held. The outer perimeter looks totally deserted, and the gate is wide open. Everyone test their mikes."

They did as they were instructed and scaled the fence, except for Collin and Morgan, who preferred to clear the fence in a single leap.

"Damn show-offs," Noah grumbled.

Like ghosts, all five men melted into the night.

Collin's assigned area was the laboratory and the buildings that surrounded it. There wasn't a single light burning as he approached the facilities. The buildings were black figures in the night, but, compliments of his wolf DNA, he had excellent night vision. The darkness presented him with no trouble as he searched the area. He crept up to the back door of the lab, and an involuntary shudder ran up his body.

When he escaped from this prison over a year ago, he promised himself to never lay eyes on the place again. His wolf DNA protested, and he started to feel slightly off-balance as his vision began to blur. He would not allow the wolf inside him to rule his judgment, decisions, or his consciousness.

Right here, right now, he must resolve the struggle within himself and use the wolf as a weapon, not a distraction. He was the leader of his pack, not the wolf. As if the wolf understood the determination deep within him, Collin's vision cleared. His sense of smell became more acute and his sight sharper.

Working the lock with his tools, he opened the door and slunk inside. As he entered the exam room, he was instantly bombarded with the scent of Payton. She'd spent time in this hideous room. The thought brought him despair. He vowed to make Braxton pay for everyone he hurt and every insane action he'd done.

"Report," Tristan said. The men gathered inside the guard shack.

"I only saw a handful of men, ten tops," Morgan said.

"I counted four in the area I was assigned," Noah said.

"No one in my area," Logan said. "The dorms were all empty."

"Collin?" Tristan asked.

"No lights, no people. Nevertheless, Payton definitely occupied the area recently."

Chapter Twenty-One

A soft knock sounded on the door. Braxton looked at the clock on the nightstand: three twelve in the morning.

This better be good, he thought.

"Who is it?" Braxton asked. He switched on the lamp.

"Sir, it's me, Tessa," she said, in a quiet, muffled voice.

"Come in," he said as he sat up.

She opened the door only enough to squeeze in and silently closed the door behind her.

"What in the world has brought you here at this hour?"

"Sir, someone has entered the compound," Tessa said.

That got his full attention.

"How do you know?"

"I feel their consciousness."

"Can you read their minds, determine who they are?"

"No, sir, I can only feel their presence."

"How long ago and how many?" He sprang from the bed, grabbed his clothes, and headed for the bathroom.

"Four, maybe five individuals, and they all feel male. I first noticed them about thirty minutes ago, only at the time I wasn't certain they were strangers. Now I am certain," Tessa said.

"You've done well, Tessa. Go update Dave. Have him secure Payton and tell him to meet me at the helipad. On your way, wake the pilot and tell him to be quiet and careful. I want you to get the doctor, and the two of you are to leave by boat. Do you understand?"

"Yes, sir. Would you like me to alert the guards?" she asked.

"No. You only alert the people we spoke of. If you alert the guards we run the risk of tipping off the intruders. The guards will know soon enough. Now go."

Tessa nodded in understanding and slipped out of the room.

The guards deserved whatever happened next. They had failed in their jobs, and now Braxton must vacate this blasted island before Tristan's team caught up with him.

"They're all a bunch of morons," Braxton said. "If they think they are going to rescue Payton, they have another thing coming."

* * * *

"Okay. The majority of guards are gathered close to the canteen. There are four buildings in the area. I saw six guards. There is one small dorm. If I were a betting man, I would put my money on Payton being held in that dorm. I didn't see Dave, but I assume he is also here, probably guarding Payton," Tristan said.

"Noah, I want you to keep watch, make sure no one gets in the way of our extraction. Logan you head up to the helipad, no sense in us calling in a retrieval if there is a perfectly good chopper hanging around," Tristan said.

"I'll update you as soon as I reach the hangar. If there isn't a usable bird, I'll call for a pick up," Logan said. He pulled down his night-vision goggles and took off into the night.

"Collin and Morgan, it's your job to locate Payton. Keep an eye out for Dave. I suspect he is here. I'm going to check all the other buildings and find Braxton. Good luck," Tristan said.

* * * *

Braxton had only just reached the lab when he saw movement a few steps ahead of him. Could it be some of Tristan's men? He flattened himself against the building and watched. He could make out two people. He watched for a moment longer until he was positive the two were Dave and Payton.

"Dave," he whispered into the night.

The figures stopped. One, the taller of the two, turned.

"Mr. Braxton?" Dave asked.

Braxton let out a breath he didn't even realize he'd been holding.

"Yes," Braxton said, as he emerged from the shadow of the building. "Have you seen anyone?" As

Braxton reached the two, he noticed Payton was gagged, and her hands were tied together.

"One of the men ran past the building an instant before we came out, but I haven't seen anyone since." He nodded his head in Payton's direction. "I didn't want to take the chance that she would call out."

"Good thinking. I don't know how the hell they found us. This facility is shown on all of their reports as abandoned," Braxton said.

"We can worry about the details later. Right now we have to move and move quickly if we want any chance of getting off this rock," Dave said. He tugged at Payton's arm and started to move up the hill to the helipad.

In the distance they could hear the rotor blades start to gyrate.

"Sounds to me like the pilot is almost ready to take off. Let's get up there," Braxton said.

* * * *

Morgan and Collin split up; each approached from opposite ends of the small dorm and covered both exits. Collin was the first to enter. The hall was partially lit by a few small, yellow-domed night-lights scattered along the bottom of the wall.

"All clear," he whispered into his ear bud to Morgan.

Collin started down the hall, stopping at each door to listen and inhale a deep breath in an effort to pick up Payton's scent. About halfway down the hall he got a hit. He saw Morgan approach and gestured to him that he'd found her room. Morgan acknowledged Collin's signal and positioned himself to cover Collin's six. Soundlessly, Collin picked the lock and opened the door. As the door opened, light spilled out of the room, and in one fluid motion, Collin stepped through the threshold, gun held at the ready. He swept the room with his gaze and gun—empty, except for Payton's scent, which permeated the entire area.

"For Chrissakes," Collin said. "How did they know we were here?"

"You don't know for sure they are aware we are here," Morgan said, as he came up behind him. "Could be they moved her for another reason."

"Yeah, right."

"We got a problem." Logan's voice whispered through their ear buds.

"What's happening, Logan?" Tristan asked.

"There is a pilot here, and he's started the helicopter. How do you want me to handle him?"

"Is he alone?"

"Yes—wait."

The connection went dead for a heartbeat; it felt like eternity to Collin.

"There's movement down the hill—Braxton, Dave, and Payton are heading this way," Logan said.

"I can be there in two minutes," Collin said.

"Morgan?" Tristan asked.

"I can keep up with him," Morgan said.

"All right, Logan maintain your position; don't engage until Collin and Morgan arrive. Don't do anything stupid, Collin. We'll be right behind you."

"Yes, sir," Collin said.

Collin ran full tilt for the helipad, Morgan hot on his heels, the last vestiges of darkness not slowing their progress a single pace.

"Braxton," Collin yelled, as he got within distance.

The trio turned toward his voice. Dave pulled his gun and positioned the barrel up against Payton's temple.

The sight of Payton bound and gagged caused the wolf inside Collin to fight to break free, but he demanded control. Even in his intense fury and fear, he would not fail Payton.

"Well, Mr. McBain, you look good for a dead man," Braxton said.

"We'll let you leave the island, but only if you leave Payton," Collin said.

"Oh, we're leaving, and we are taking Payton and you."

"He's not going anywhere," Logan said, as he emerged from the hangar.

"So, where's the rest of your merry gang?" Braxton asked. "Surely they can't be far. As I said, we're leaving…and if any one of you so much as twitch, Dave will put an unsightly hole in Payton's head."

The team stopped, frozen like statues.

"Don't any one of you move a single muscle," Tristan said, through their ear buds. "We will be there in five minutes. We ran into a slight snag with a couple guards. Stay put."

"Collin, you are coming with us," Braxton repeated. "If you aren't on that helicopter in the next minute, Payton's death will be on your head."

Braxton, Dave, and Payton continued to back step to the aircraft, and one by one stepped up into the helicopter.

Collin dropped his gun and headed for the aircraft.

"Collin, stop," Morgan said.

Collin looked back at Morgan and over to Logan. "I'm counting on you two to explain to Tristan and to get us out of this mess."

Collin jumped up into the chopper and sat down next to Payton, his deadly stare transfixed on the two men.

"I'm going to remove her gag," Collin said.

"If you must," Braxton said, with a slight nod. "Nice to have you back, Collin. Give Dave your arm."

Dave produced a hypodermic needle and started toward him.

"What the hell is that?" Collin growled.

"Merely something to keep you quiet until we reach our destination. Now, be a good boy," Braxton said.

Collin eyed Dave, the promise of revenge reflected in his glare. He relented and leaned forward. The last image Collin saw as his vision faded and blurred was Payton's beautiful smile.

Collin slumped into Payton's lap.

"What have you done?" She scowled at the two men.

"Don't fret. It's a little something to keep him out for the trip. He's easier to deal with when he is out cold," Braxton said.

"So why did you want Collin? I thought you wanted his sister?" Payton asked.

"Oh, I do. Have no fear; I intend to retrieve Emma. For the moment, Collin is my prize."

"Why do you want only Collin? What about Morgan? You injected him too."

"You are correct. But much to my dismay, he has not shown the advancement in abilities that Collin has."

* * * *

Tristan watched helplessly as the helicopter lifted into the sky. Dawn broke, and the early morning sky filled with purples, pinks, and streaks of sunlight. He and Noah started up the hill to the helipad and the remaining two team members.

"Shit," Tristan said.

"Sorry, sir," Morgan said. "There was no stopping him. If it's any consolation, I really do believe Braxton was prepared to shoot Payton. He gave the impression of being much more on edge, as though he reached his breaking point."

"Collin did the right thing. I'm pissed Braxton got the jump on us. How the hell did that happen? Did anyone see him prior to Logan?" They all shook their heads. "Any chance you tagged his bird?" he asked Logan.

"Sorry, I had planned on us taking the bird," Logan said.

"I figured, though it couldn't help to hope. Tell me you contacted our ride?"

"The first instant I saw Braxton. They should be here in another ten minutes."

"Good. Contact Jack and have him track that bird," Tristan said.

Chapter Twenty-Two

Lack of sleep and the constant tension of the last few days wore on Payton. Try as she might to stay awake throughout the flight, she drifted off to sleep. Collin's presence gave her a sense of safety, even though their situation showed no signs of improvement. She woke up as she felt the aircraft start to descend. The geography below them sparked an awareness of familiarity.

"Are we in Northern California?" she asked. She half-expected them to ignore the question.

"And what if we are?" Braxton asked.

"What makes you think Tristan's team won't locate you here in a matter of hours?"

"They have no idea where we are. Our helicopter is untraceable, and the ranch is off the grid—just another ranch owned by a local rancher, nothing out of the ordinary."

'The ranch,' as Braxton referred to it, sat on the edge of a forest. It was a massive one-story house made of cream-colored stucco with a red clay tile roof, materials typical in that area. There was a helipad with an adjacent hangar and two additional outbuildings, along with what looked like a barn. The entire ranch was contained inside a security fence, with only one well-guarded gate to the outside.

As the blades on the helicopter spooled to a stop, two men approached.

"Where shall I tell the men to put Collin?" Dave asked.

"On level three in one of the rooms. Put Payton in another room on the same level," Braxton said.

Braxton exited first and headed directly to the main building. The two men lifted Collin out of the helicopter and each grabbed one of his arms. As they carried him, his feet and lower torso dragged the ground.

"Can't they even put him on a stretcher?" Payton asked.

"Why? He's out cold," Dave said.

"He's going to be sore when he wakes up." She glowered at him.

"I sure hope so." Dave sneered at her.

As they entered the main house, Payton was totally caught off-guard. This was no typical ranch. The floor was white marble, with veins of black running through it. The foyer was massive and held a sitting area with a large Oriental rug, oversized leather chairs, and side tables. On the left sat a desk with a receptionist who typed away on her computer. She looked up as Dave entered.

"Good afternoon, Mr. Anderson. I notified everyone when I got your call. Your room is ready, as are the two for our guests."

"Guests?" Payton snorted. "I think the proper term is 'prisoners.'"

The receptionist ignored Payton.

"Everything is on schedule. Dinner will be served at six, as Mr. Braxton likes it."

"Good. Our two guests will be dining in their rooms," Dave said. "Follow me," he said. He motioned for Payton to follow him.

They left the foyer. One of the living room walls was floor-to-ceiling glass. A couple of the sections were open and allowed for the fresh air to drift in. An outdoor kitchen, complete with chefs and seven tables sat on one side of the enormous patio; on the other side there were fountains, benches and fireplaces. The open-air patio was entirely enclosed on the three sides.

Payton wondered how many people actually worked in this facility and what they could possibly do. They approached a bank of elevators on the back wall. Dave pressed the only button.

"Where are we going?" she asked.

"The only way to go—down," Dave said.

She looked at the panel and read: main, sub one, sub two, and sub three.

"I guess I won't have an ocean view," she said.

"You could say that. Not a window anywhere, but if you are a good girl, I'm sure Mr. Braxton will let you come up to the patio to eat."

Smart-ass, she thought to herself.

The elevator doors opened and halls on sub three took off in three directions like a typical hotel.

"Follow me." He led her down the hall straight in front of them and stopped at a door; he pulled his ID card out of his breast pocket and swiped the card over the electronic lock. The door clicked, and as he opened it, the door next to Payton's opened. The two men who had dragged Collin off the helicopter walked out, one locking the door behind them.

"He's all tucked in," one of them said.

"Good. See he gets a dinner tray. I'm sure he will be waking up in the next hour," Dave said.

He followed Payton into her room. She was surprised at how posh the room looked. There was a spacious bath off to one side, complete with a large soaking tub. A small sitting area contained a love seat and a couple of chairs, a bookshelf full of books, and a small refrigerator. The king-sized bed encompassed the far wall.

"Dinner will be brought to you in a few hours. For now, make yourself comfortable. If you require anything, use the phone. It connects to the main desk."

"What, no cameras?" she asked.

"No need. There is only one exit. This door is the only way in or out, and rest assured there will be a guard posted twenty-four hours a day."

Dave stepped back into the hall and locked the door behind him.

"Peachy," Payton said to herself. Collin would find a way out of this mess. She was taken aback that she actually missed Collin. He had become a good friend to her...or maybe more. *Don't be silly. We've developed a friendship, with some great fringe benefits. This is only natural, considering all the time we have spent together over the past weeks*, she thought.

* * * *

Collin fought to pull himself out of the drug-induced sleep. He opened his eyes and took stock of his surroundings. He put his hands on his temples. *What the hell did they give me?* he thought. *It feels like my damned head is about to split wide open.* He replayed the last few minutes he could remember.

"Payton? What happened to Payton?" He swung his legs off the bed and sat up.

"Shit, that was a mistake." His head continued to throb and made it all but impossible to focus on anything except the pain.

He heard the door click open. The overhead light snapped on, which intensified the drumbeat inside his skull, and nearly blinded him.

"What the hell," he said. "Next time warn me before you blind me."

A man entered, holding a tray, followed by a second man, gun at the ready.

"You're awake," the man with the tray said.

"Lucky me. I need something for my blasted headache."

The man set the tray down on the table.

"There is a medicine cabinet in the bathroom. You will find some aspirin in there."

"Where are we?" Collin asked.

"Northern California."

"Shut the hell up you idiot," the man with the gun said.

"What? It's not like he's going anywhere."

"Leave the tray and let's go."

After the men left, Collin stood and the room started to spin. "Not now," he said, as he sat back on the bed. Finally he understood how Payton had felt when she'd first been around him. "If Braxton or Dave puts even one bruise on her, I'll kill them twice; once for Emma and again for Payton." He promised himself.

He forced himself to stand and shuffled to the bathroom, feeling like a ninety year-old man. He found the bottle of aspirin, dumped out four, and tossed them back. He needed to eat something to keep the pills from burning a hole in his stomach. He would get something to eat, lay back down for a few minutes to let the pills take hold and hopefully turn the throbbing in his head to a dull ache. Only then would he be able to work out a plan.

Collin woke and took stock of his body. The pounding in his head had all but disappeared, but his shoulders, arms, and neck were stiff. No telling what Braxton did to him while he remained out cold. He sat up, switched on the lamp that sat on the nightstand, and looked at the clock. *Six the following morning?* In that case, he'd slept for over twelve hours or maybe he'd even slept for a more than a day.

You jackass, Collin! He chastised himself. *You were supposed to be watching out for Payton.* In an attempt to calm his rising anger, he forced himself to slow his breathing. He took in deep cleansing breaths and cleared the growing storm from his mind. There, he could feel Payton's essence. She was here and close by. He stood up and walked the length of the room. When he reached the wall, he turned his head, and placed his ear and hands on the cool surface. He listened and reached out for her energy.

He heard her breathing right in the next room. By the pace and rhythm of her breath, he surmised she was still asleep. The tension and terror melted away from his body. She was safe. In that precise instant he realized

Payton had become more than a mission. She kept him grounded in both his mind and heart. At what point in time had she become so essential to his well-being? Could these feelings be what love felt like?

Get a grip McBain. She had spent a couple of nights with him; it didn't mean he was in love with her or she with him. He backed away from the wall. First, he would grab a shower and food. Then he would get the lay of the land and start to work on a plan to get them both out of there.

As Collin emerged from the bathroom, he heard voices in the hall. He walked up to the door and concentrated on those voices. Dave stood outside his door, giving the guards instructions.

"Take Payton and Collin up to the patio for all their meals today. Keep a constant eye on them," Dave said.

"Will they stay here for long?" one of the guards asked.

"No. This place is nowhere near secure enough to keep Collin. We are only using the ranch as our stopgap. This was the only available place for us to transport them under the circumstances. We are playing the odds that Payton is his mission and his focus will be to keep her safe. With any luck he won't try one of his half-assed tricks. There is not another soul for miles around, just forest, state land, and mountains. We have to keep up the facade that this is a high-security facility for a few days while we wait for the final touches to be done on security at the new facility. After we get the go ahead, they will be transferred."

"How do we keep up the hoax?" one of the guards asked.

"We let them out to eat their meals together. They will be locked down for the remainder of the day. Collin is reminded at each meal Payton is here and she is his mission. Stay on your toes every minute; your only concern is to keep Collin in line," Dave said.

"Yes, sir," the two men said.

Collin heard Dave's footfalls fade down the corridor. The door to his room clicked as the electronic lock disengaged. He sprang for the love seat and snatched a nearby magazine.

"You ready to eat?" the guard asked, as he stuck his head in the room.

"I'm starved. What did you bring me?" Collin asked.

"You get a treat. We're taking you up to the main floor to the central patio."

"Great. Is Payton eating too?" Collin asked.

"She's already on her way up."

The patio was full of people. Collin scoured the area for Payton. She sat at the far side, her back to him; she appeared to be admiring one of the fountains. He made his way through tables and people to reach her. He reached down and gently laid his hand on her shoulder.

"Payton, are you okay?"

She turned to him, and a smile spread over her face. She rose and started for him, but he stepped back. He frowned and she dropped her outstretched arms.

"They already know your safety is my priority. We don't need them to know there is anything more between us," he said.

"Is there?" she asked. "Other than the few nights we spent together, is there anything more between us?"

"You know there is. I worry about you every minute we are apart. You mean the world to me."

Her frown turned back to a smile, but she said nothing.

"Let's go get something to eat, and hopefully we can find a quiet place to sit and talk. Make sure you keep all the guards in sight. I count four; it shouldn't be difficult to stay far enough away from them to make overhearing our conversation impossible, but we must be discreet. Act nonchalant, as if we are talking about the weather."

She nodded that she understood and started to the dining area. They found a small empty table in the middle of the area.

"Are you sure you are all right? You sounded as if you were mentally drained when I heard you on the speakerphone the other day," Collin said. He stared at his plate, not making eye contact.

"All in all, I'm fine now. I have recovered after being burned out the other day. I fought the toughest mental battle against Tessa. She is a master at reading minds, and for a time I thought she would break me down. But I held fast. She broke before I did, both times," Payton said.

"I'm proud of you, Payton. Sounds like you have definitely mastered your ability. That is a huge accomplishment."

"Thank you." She smiled shyly over at him.

"Who is Tessa?" he asked.

"Didn't you see her when you were on the island? She is one of Braxton's experiments. If I were to make a guess, I would predict she came out of his academy."

"No, none of us saw her. We only saw Braxton's men. We didn't even see Braxton until he appeared at the helipad. How the hell did he know we were there?"

"Tessa. She went to Dave's room. They stood in the hall and talked. I heard them. She told Dave she sensed intruders on the island. We were to meet Braxton at the helicopter."

"Explains how he got the jump on us," Collin said. "What I can't figure out is why he brought us here. I listened to Dave and the guards, and from what I have seen thus far, this place has limited security. And why stay in the States? The team will be here before they know it."

"No, they won't," she said. "Braxton told me, thanks to his special friend, there would be no way to track the helicopter, and the ranch is in a local rancher's name."

"Must be one hell of a special friend to offer a stealth helicopter and an off-the-grid ranch. I would hazard to say his friend would have to be someone way, way up in the government or very rich with important friends."

"I have no idea who he is, but back on the island he told me he has a good friend named Carl. I don't know if Carl owns this place or not."

Collin practically spilled his coffee.

"Are you sure Carl is the name he told you? Did he give you a last name?" he asked.

"No. I think he said Carl without giving any thought to me hearing the name. After he said it, he kept talking, like he wanted to try and erase his name from my memory. Why, do you know a Carl?"

260

"I know a few. The one that jumped to mind is Carl Sterling."

"Why him in particular? Does he have access to those types of things?"

"Those and much, much more. Carl Sterling is the CIA director," he said.

"Impossible. Do you have any idea what you are saying? The Kaleidoscope Group has infiltrated the uppermost echelons of our government. How could the Kaleidoscope Group command such power?" she asked.

"Stay calm, Payton, we don't want to draw attention. Let's forget about Carl for the time being. For now, we have to concentrate on getting out of here. They plan to move us to a top-secret facility in a few days. I'm guessing said facility will probably be out of the country. We need to get out of here before they have the chance to move us. Stay alert, and tell me everything you see or hear. I will work on a plan to get us out. For now, we play their game. We act as if we are in a high-security facility and we behave, understand?"

The two guards who brought Collin up to the patio approached them.

"Okay, you are through eating. Let's go," one of the guards said.

Chapter Twenty-Three

"Have you learned anything new?" Collin asked Payton as they stood in line and waited for dinner.

"Not as far as security is concerned, but on our way up here, a guard got on the elevator. He told my guard that Braxton has left the facility for the next few days," Payton said.

"Then it's decided. We go tonight. With Braxton away from the facility, the guards will be more lax."

"I hope you have a plan."

"I do—at least as far as getting us out of our rooms. Earlier in the afternoon when I got escorted back from lunch, I jammed a tiny piece of a Band-Aid in the lock. The door clicked closed and obviously read 'locked' on the outside. When I heard my guard go down the hall, I tried the door, and it opened," Collin said.

"The Band-Aid gets us out of our room, but what about out of the building?" Payton asked.

"Don't worry. I'll get us out. Be ready late tonight. The guard usually heads out for coffee around two in the morning. I'll be at your door as soon as he is gone. If everything goes according to plan, we will have a six-hour head start."

Payton tossed and turned in her bed. She knew she should try to sleep, but the anticipation of their escape tonight made her antsy. She heard a click and looked at her clock—one thirty in the morning. The guard must have left early. She lay still in her bed. She didn't want to give herself away in case the person who entered happened to be a guard—or worse yet, Dave.

"Payton, are you ready to go?" Collin whispered from the doorway.

She threw the covers off and hopped out of bed.

"Thank goodness it's you. I started to worry for a second."

"Come on. We only have a few minutes before he's back."

She closed the door to her room and started for the elevators.

"No, this way," Collin said, in a hushed tone. "We'll take the stairs, and you need to stay right behind me the whole way. Not a single peep, got it?"

She nodded in response.

Collin opened the door to the stairwell and listened, and then motioned for her to enter. He closed the door behind them and signaled for her to stay put. They stood there soundlessly as Collin closed his eyes and focused. He searched for anyone who might be on the stairs above them. When he heard nothing, he waved Payton forward and started up the first flight. They repeated the process for each floor until they reached the main floor.

He pulled her into him, his hot breath on her earlobe and whispered, "You wait here. I'm going to check out the main floor and find the best way out. I'll be back as soon as I can."

She nodded and stepped away from the door.

Collin cracked the door open only enough to squeeze through. He scrutinized his vicinity. No one occupied the front desk or the immediate area. The most difficult feat would be to get past the patio unseen, which came up immediately to his right. He stayed in the shadows and crept closer to see how many people were out on the patio. A small group of men was gathered at a table in the far corner playing cards. One of them faced the entrance and there were two other men talking near the kitchen area.

"Looks like seven men on the patio," he whispered in Payton's ear. She nearly jumped out of her skin. "Sorry, I thought you heard me. We are going to have to move to the far side of the main floor to keep to the shadows. Let's go."

They snuck out of the stairwell and stopped next to the patio. Not a single man looked their way. Collin grabbed Payton's hand and pulled her swiftly down the hall to the main door. He did a quick check for security sensors and guards. He saw neither, opened the door, and motioned for her.

Unconscious when he entered the building, Collin did not know the layout of the facility. He knew the odds that he could get away unseen with Payton would be against them. If only for the fact the sky was clear and filled with stars, along with the damn moon being full and shining like a spotlight. He got them to the first bunch of bushes and pulled her to the ground with him.

"Do you remember if you saw any vehicles when you arrived?" he whispered.

She looked around.

"There were a couple of SUVs back by one of the outbuildings. I think I remember seeing some kind of vehicle up by the gate. Maybe a Jeep?"

"It's too dangerous to try for one of the outbuildings. We would likely run into a guard or two on patrol. How far is the gate?"

"A mile or so, and there aren't any other buildings between here and the gate. However, there is a guard shack at the gate," she said.

"Okay, we move fast and we stay in the shadows. You hear anything, drop to the ground," he told her.

They followed the road down to the gate. Collin could hear Payton breathing as they ran, and he kept checking back on her to make sure he wasn't running too fast. The guard shack came into view, and he picked up the voices of two men. Instantly he veered off to his left and jumped down into the gully that ran along the road.

"What's wrong?" she asked, as she dropped down beside him.

"We're near the gate and there are two guards inside the shack; it sounds like they are watching television or listening to a radio."

She poked her head up and looked toward the shack.

"I can't hear them. I see a light down the way, but nothing more. Boy, your hearing is phenomenal," she said.

"They're there. You stay here; I'm going to take a closer look."

Collin stayed in the gully and headed for the shack. He got close enough to get a good look around and listen to the men inside. One sat watching a small television and the other read a magazine. The Jeep was parked on the far side of the shack. He would have to take down both men in order to get to the Jeep.

The phone in the guard shack rang, and Collin crouched lower to the ground.

"What's up?" one of the guards asked as he answered the phone. "Why? Now, really? Fine, we're not going anywhere." He hung up the phone in a huff.

"What's the problem?" the other man asked.

"Maintenance decided to work on the problem with the Jeep now."

"What the hell? At this hour?"

"Yeah, Braxton will be on his way back in the morning. They don't want the damn Jeep to act up while he is here."

Collin heard a slight humming sound and a light shone on the road up toward the facility. He hoped to hell Payton had plastered herself to the ground. He would have to trust in her because now it would be far too risky for him to make a single move.

An electric golf cart came into view, bumping down the road. Collin hugged the ground as the headlights on the vehicle passed near his position. The cart came to a halt next to the shack and two men dressed in coveralls got out.

"We'll probably have the Jeep for most of the morning," one of them said.

"So we get stuck with the kiddie cart?" one of the guards groused.

"Either the kiddie cart or you walk back to the ranch."

"Fine," the guard said, and tossed the keys to the mechanic. "You couldn't wait two more hours?"

"We could, but apparently the boss couldn't."

The mechanics got in the Jeep and tried to start the engine. The vehicle coughed and sputtered in protest, but finally the engine turned over. The driver put the Jeep into gear, backed away from the shack, and at the same time he popped on the headlights. The bright lights flooded the ground above Collin. He sucked in his breath as the vehicle rolled a few feet closer, illuminating even more of the area around him. One more inch and his cover would be blown. The Jeep made a sharp turn to the left and started up the hill.

One of the guards went back into the shack. The other lit a cigarette and sat on the front fender of the cart. Collin slithered out from his hiding spot and headed for the man on the cart. In a flash, he stood next to the vehicle, within an arm's length from the guard, a ghost in the night.

"Didn't your momma ever tell you cigarettes could kill you?" he whispered in the guard's ear.

"What the—"

Before the guard could react in any way, Collin snapped his neck. The man's body went limp in his arms, and he dragged him away from the cart. He crept up to the shack. The other guard, engaged in the television, made the major mistake of sitting with his back to the door. Collin came in low, so as not to throw a reflection on the windows behind the television.

When Collin was directly behind the man, he stood up and his reflection appeared in the window. The man's eyes widened the second he saw him, but it was a second too late. Collin wrapped his arms around the man's neck; he strangled him and left his body in the chair. He searched the guard and found a cell phone, the keys to the cart, and a sidearm. He walked out of the shack, and took off at a full run back to Payton.

"Payton, let's go."

She popped out of her hiding spot and ran to him. Collin caught her as she leapt up into his arms, and she hugged him fiercely.

"I thought for certain they found you," she said. She pulled back. "Do you know that your pupils change from blue to gold when your wolf emerges? It used to frighten me, but now I find it rather comforting." She smiled at him as she leaned forward and kissed him.

Collin let himself give in to the sensation and warmth of Payton. Begrudgingly, he pulled away from her as he set her feet back on the ground.

"Nah, it would take better men than that to find me," he said. "But make no mistake you can welcome me back this way every time. Right now, we need to go."

"The guards?" she asked.

"They won't be a problem. We need to hurry. The sun will begin to rise in another couple of hours, and Braxton is on his way back this morning. There's a good chance the guards will visit our rooms earlier."

They took off for the guard shack.

"Get in," Collin said, as they reached the cart.

He heard a slight gasp as Payton saw the guard's body. He waited for her condemnation, but none came.

"Take the driver's side," he said, and motioned to her. "I'm going to push the cart through the gate and down the road a stretch. The farther we are from the facility when we start the engine, the better off we will be. Put it in neutral."

He pushed the cart through the gate and down the road. The cart started to pick up speed as it rolled down the hill. Payton placed her foot on the brake.

"No brake, let it roll," he said.

"What about you?"

"Don't worry about me; I can keep up."

He pushed the cart for a while longer as their speed began to increase.

"Slide over," Collin said, as he ran up to the driver's side.

He vaulted into the seat, started the engine, and popped the cart into gear. At top speed with no lights, they flew down the hill. Payton said nothing, as she gripped the side bar next to her.

Chapter Twenty-Four

"Mr. Braxton, I have Sarah and Emma," Dave said.

"Good. Give me the details," Braxton said.

"Sarah called me yesterday morning when I was still at the facility in California. While she and Emma were out for a walk, she used the excuse of needing a restroom and managed to steal a phone from some woman's purse. She used the stolen phone so no one could trace her call to me. She said she went to Collin to get Emma back, and her only goal is for them to stay together. She doesn't want to spend her life in hiding. She still wants to work for us, but she is now making some demands. The only way she is willing to come back is if she is transferred to the New York office so Emma can live with her while she attends our academy in the city. She is also asking for a raise and a promotion," Dave said.

"What did you tell her?" Braxton asked.

"I said yes. You said to do whatever was necessary to get Emma back. There is one slight problem."

"Only one?" Braxton asked, with anger edging his voice.

"Sarah said Wyatt's team asked her to list all the business and personal contacts of yours she could recall."

"I don't see a problem. We kept her out of the loop with regards to Kaleidoscope Group," Braxton said.

"Yes, sir, we did. Nevertheless, they did question her about the group and made her suspicious," Dave said. "She has figured out who one of the members is, and she thinks she can use the information as leverage with us."

"Wonderful. Did she tell Wyatt's group who she thinks the member is?"

"She says she didn't. She gave them a tidbit of information with regard to a couple of times she recalled scheduled meetings with KG, but she gave them no other details."

"Smart girl," Braxton said. "How did you retrieve them? No doubt they got assigned a guard."

"Yes, they did. Last night after dinner, Sarah made a list and set one of the guards off to restock her supplies. She then said good night to the other guard. The guard sat stationed in his vehicle at the front door. Sarah and Emma snuck out one of the bedroom windows, and I picked them up a half block away."

"Good work, Dave. Where are they now?"

"In the helicopter. We are about ready to take off."

"Take them to the California facility; I think it's time for a McBain reunion," Braxton said.

* * * *

The guard knocked on Payton's door and waited. Not hearing a response, he knocked again and unlocked her door. He noticed the door to the bathroom was closed, and he assumed she got a late start.

"It's time to go up to breakfast, Payton," the guard said.

Again he didn't hear a sound, so he crossed the room and tapped on the bathroom door.

"Payton, are you almost ready?"

A terrible dread overtook him as he opened the door and found the bathroom empty. He ran from the room into the hall.

"Payton is missing," he said, to the guard assigned to bring Collin up to breakfast.

"Did someone else already take her to breakfast?" Collin's guard asked.

"No, I'm assigned to her today," he said, as he unlocked Collin's door.

They found his room completely empty and the door to the bathroom wide open.

"Aw hell, we are in a shitload of trouble," Payton's guard said.

The alarm started screaming throughout the facility. "I don't think we are the only ones," Collin's guard said.

* * * *

Collin stopped the cart and got out to stretch his legs. The sun had come up a couple of hours earlier and even with all the evergreens, the day's heat had already begun to rise from the ground.

"My guess is we are somewhere in the Shasta Cascades. We could go for miles before we see another person," he said.

He pulled the cell phone from his pocket and checked for reception. "Damn. No reception and just about as much electricity left in the cart."

"Are you saying we are stranded?" Payton asked.

"No, we still have our legs. We are going to have to dump the cart in the next few miles. We need to make sure it can't be seen from the air. We don't want Braxton to locate the cart, which of course means Wyatt and the team won't see the cart either. Let's keep heading west; I think it is our best option for finding civilization."

Collin took the back plate off of the phone and pulled out the battery and GPS chip. He stuck the phone back in one pocket and the battery and chip in another.

"What are you doing?"

"Attempting to slow Braxton down. As soon as he discovers that we took one of the guard's phones, he will be able to track us using the phone's GPS. I pulled the battery out to help save the charge."

"Then why not destroy the GPS?" she asked.

"We have no real idea where we are. This GPS is the only way for the team to locate us. Judging by the lack of reception, it would be highly unlikely they could triangulate our location."

Twenty minutes later the cart started to sputter. Collin pointed the nose of the vehicle deeper into the trees and stopped.

"We have gone as far as we can with the cart," he said. "Time to get out."

Payton got out and Collin drove it farther into the forest. He returned on foot and brushed pine needles from his arms.

"Now we walk. We need to keep an eye out for a stream or spring. We don't want to get dehydrated," he said.

They continued to walk until late in the afternoon.

"Collin, I need to take a rest," Payton said. "We've been walking for hours now."

She sat down in the shade of one of the giant evergreen trees. She looked pale and worn. Collin knew the lack of food and water would quickly make her situation worse. He pulled out the cell phone, put the battery back in, and checked for reception yet again. He frowned, pulled the phone apart and stuck it back in his pocket.

"I think you should go on without me," Payton said.

"What? No, I will not leave you out here alone," Collin said.

"Think about it, Collin. You can engage your wolf traits, and with them you will cover a massive distance on your own. At the very least, you can get to a place with reception where you can contact home."

Payton, nothing if not practical, he thought. They could be out there for days before anyone found them, or, for that matter, got phone reception.

"All right I'll go, but not until tomorrow. It's too late in the day for me to make any real progress and return before dark. I refuse to leave you out here alone at night. You stay here and rest. I'm going to find us some water, something to eat, and a safe place to spend the night."

* * * *

Her surroundings were peaceful and quiet, Payton felt exhausted, so she drifted off to sleep. Startled by a flash of intense emotion, she opened her eyes but didn't as much as flex a muscle. The tension in her body released as she recognized Collin's energy. She heard a rustling in the trees a distance away, and she sat up as Collin emerged.

"I found a vacant cave near a stream about a mile away." He reached down to help her up. He kept his hand locked with hers as they headed for the cave.

On arrival they both had their fill of water, and then he showed Payton where they would spend the night.

"I realize we are not talking the Ritz, although the way the cave is situated we can have a small campfire close to the opening. The fire will help to keep the chill at bay."

"What about the fire being seen during the night?" Payton asked.

"Don't worry. I'll hear the approach of any aircraft long before they see our fire. You look around for firewood; I'll get us some fish for dinner and maybe a few berries."

"Thanks for dinner," Payton said, as she popped the last couple of berries in her mouth. "I would say I'm enjoying myself, if we weren't in our current predicament."

"Don't worry, Payton; I'll get us out of here. There's no reason not to savor the special moments."

They chatted effortlessly through the early evening. Collin checked the campfire from time to time and made sure they had gathered enough wood to get them through the chilly night. He took Payton by the hand and led her to the opening of the cave. He sat down and leaned against the wall of the cave, far enough inside to keep the brisk breeze off, but close enough for the heat of the fire to reach them. Collin gently pulled her down to sit next to him. He tucked her shoulders under his arm and pulled her into the heat of his body. She snuggled close and relished the feel of him.

Out in the darkness, the owls hooted and a pack of coyotes barked and yipped. Far off in the distance they heard the growl of a cougar. Payton shivered at the eerie sound. Collin placed his hand on her chin and tilted her face up to meet his. He leaned in and claimed her lips, kissing her with pure gentleness. He pulled back and looked into her enchanting eyes.

"You are safe with me, Payton. I would lay my life down to protect you and your sisters. I was terrified I might not ever hold you again," he said. "The night at the campus, when I found your purse and phone on the ground next to Frank's body, I thought I'd lost you forever. A terror filled my body and soul the likes of which I have never experienced before. Only my desperate need to get you back kept me from losing myself to my wolf."

He kissed her again, and Payton could swear she felt his passion and need rage within him.

She woke early in the morning to find her head in Collin's lap and her arms wrapped around his waist. His head lolled back against the cave wall. A minute later Collin yawned and stretched his arms over his head. He brushed a few strands of her hair out of her face.

"How did you sleep?" he asked.

"Better than I thought I would. How about you?"

"Same here. I hate to do this, but I need to get going. I want to get back to you long before dark," he said.

* * * *

"It's about time," he said to himself as he punched in to the cell phone the only number he retained in his memory.

"Morgan."

"Damn, it's good to hear your voice, partner," Collin said.

"Collin, is that you? The connection isn't very clear," Morgan said.

"Yes, and at least I have a connection. I was really beginning to wonder if I would have to run clear back to Washington State."

"Is Payton with you? Where are you? I'm putting you on speaker."

"Yes, Payton is with me. I'm not exactly sure where we are. If I were to hazard a guess, I'd say somewhere in the Shasta Cascades. We were taken to a facility owned by some rancher, located about fifty miles south of my current position."

"And Braxton?" Wyatt asked.

"Super pissed, I bet," Collin said.

"Whose phone are you on?" Tristan asked.

"A guard's. He won't need it any more. I stuck the GPS chip back in," Collin said.

"I can track your position," Jack said.

"I figured as much. You better be quick about it, though. Braxton could be doing the same thing. There's another problem. I left Payton probably forty miles back. I need to get back to her. When I leave the vicinity, I will lose reception. I'm going to pull the GPS back out and smash it. Hopefully that will slow Braxton and his goons down."

"Give us the details regarding which direction you are travelling and we'll plot a course. You get back to Payton and retrace your steps back to your current position," Wyatt said. "The helicopter is fueled and ready. The team will head out immediately."

"Roger. Does Jack have a lock?"

"Yes," Tristan said. "Jack has your coordinates plugged in and is working on your current location. Needless to say, Braxton and his men are much closer than we are. We need every second we can get to reach you first."

"Collin," Wyatt said.

"We lost him, sir, but I'm still picking up his signal for the moment. Wait, the signal is gone," Jack said.

"You didn't tell him his sister is missing," Logan said.

"I know. He can't do a thing to change it right now. He needs to stay focused. We'll tell him after we get the two of them safely on board the aircraft," Wyatt said.

Chapter Twenty-Five

"Have you located the guard's phone yet?" Braxton asked, for the hundredth time in the past two hours.

"No, sir. I believe you were correct with your assumption that Collin took it with him. I have the men searching for the GPS signal. As soon as we have the signal, we will know where Collin and Payton are," Dave said.

"This is unsatisfactory, Dave. You'd better locate them soon, or more than those two idiot guards will be fired. Why don't you send out a search party?"

"There's too much ground to cover, and we don't have the manpower," Dave said. "Don't worry; they are as good as found, as long as they carry that phone."

A brisk knock came from the door.

"What now," Braxton said.

Dave went over to the door and opened it. One of his men stood in the doorway.

"Sir, you told me to let you know the second the phone was tracked," the man said.

"Spit it out, man," Braxton said as he pulled the door out of Dave's grip.

"We found the signal, and it's moving," Dave's man said.

"How far away are they?" Dave asked.

"As of a few minutes ago, they were approximately fifty-three miles away," the man said.

"How do you want to handle the retrieval?" Dave asked Braxton.

"Send all but four of the men out in the all-terrain vehicles, this instant. Have the two helicopters ready to take off in thirty minutes. Put Sarah, Emma, and two guards in one helicopter and you and I will be in the other with two guards."

* * * *

The day had turned out to be simply gorgeous, full of gentle breezes and birdsong. Payton moved away from the cave and sat under a nearby tree. Abruptly, the birds stopped their song and the breeze stilled.

Payton's eyes snapped open and she canvassed her surroundings. At the edge of the stream she zeroed in on what caused the change in the forest's mood. An exceptionally large cougar sat there and stared directly at her. Payton's blood ran cold. She knew she couldn't possibly outrun or out climb the cat, and her only weapon was the walking stick she'd picked up that morning. She was being stalked, and nothing she could do would deter the cat.

* * * *

Collin suddenly became overwhelmed with a feeling of fear and panic. *Payton*, she was in trouble. He reached deep within himself and focused. He willed himself to run faster than he had ever run before. Even though it felt like it took hours to reach her, he arrived at the unfolding scene in minutes. As he approached the area he saw that Payton had moved under a tree and a cougar stalked her. She'd managed to gain her footing and she held a stick directly out in front of her.

Payton.

She must have felt the push of his energy and turned her head in his direction. Her features were pale.

"Hold the stick out. I'm going to grab it from you as I go by," he said.

The stick was torn away from Payton's hands, and the next instant he placed himself directly between Payton and the cougar. The cougar seemed startled by his inhuman speed. The cat gathered itself and traded menacing glares with Collin.

* * * *

A deep gravelly growl sounded. Payton couldn't tell if the sound emanated from Collin or the cougar. She focused on Collin and caught fragments of self-assuredness, total commitment, and a need to force the cat away from her by any means necessary. She willed her psychic energy to him and hoped she could somehow aid in his mission. Her terror left her, replaced with attainment, conquest, and control. For a brief time, she felt she and Collin shared the identical psychic wave, as if she amplified his psychic powers.

The cat began to stalk Collin. Each time the cat moved, Collin jumped in the same direction and covered five to ten feet in an effortless leap. His actions confused the cougar, and it growled and hissed at Collin. The cat snapped its tail back and forth in agitation. Collin growled back and lunged toward the animal; he jabbed the stick in the cat's direction. The cougar hissed again and pounced toward Collin. Collin didn't back down. Each time the cat leapt at him, he returned the gesture.

Finally the cat growled one last time, flicked its tail back and forth, and turned to saunter into the cave. Collin held his ground, making sure the animal did not return.

Payton didn't wait until Collin reached her. She covered half the distance and jumped up into his waiting arms. She kissed him madly, and when she pulled back she saw his pupils were the golden wolf-color she had grown accustomed to, which indicated he had completely engaged his wolf.

"Are you okay?" he asked.

"Yes, thank you for saving me...again," Payton said.

"I can see you are going to keep me on my toes," he said, as he kissed her once again. He carried her for a bit and then set her back down on her feet. "We need to keep walking and get away from the cougar's den."

They walked in silence for a couple miles. Collin reached out and took Payton's hand. He sat down in the shade. He pulled her into his lap, and she felt his bulge press against her upper thigh.

"I got the strangest sensation when I confronted the cat. I felt your energy aid me, not only grounding my emotions but actually focusing my abilities. Have I finally lost my mind?" he asked.

"I felt the same thing. Over the past couple of weeks, my abilities have evolved. Not only in grounding you but also in aiding you, a totally new twist to my skills. I have never experienced such an awareness," she said.

"Have you noticed the same skill when you are around others with abilities?"

"No, I can still feel others' energy, and I seem to be able to ground them, but I can't increase or expand their natural energy. With Tessa, I felt her flow of energy and managed to use it against her. I concentrated on weakening her impact on me."

"Wow, that ability could come in handy."

"Did you reach anyone?" she asked.

"Yes, I got a hold of Morgan. Thank God I remembered his number. The team is on their way. They should be here in a few hours. In the meantime, we need to head back to the area where I contacted them. The team will start looking for us there."

Payton and Collin walked hand in hand. She smiled and looked up at Collin.

"What?" he asked.

"You seem…peaceful. Even with everything that has happened over the past few days. What were you thinking about?"

"I was thinking that if someone would have told me two months ago that you, Payton Winters, would become such a crucial part of my life, I would have told them they were nuts."

She stopped walking and waited for him to turn in her direction. She rose on her tippy toes and kissed him with the sweetest of kisses.

"Thank you. That was strangely the sweetest compliment I have ever received."

* * * *

The distant sound of engines jerked Collin away from their conversation.

"Shit, we are about to have company," he said.

"What? Where?" Payton asked, as she looked around.

"Sounds like a group of vehicles coming from behind us and heading our way. We are heading straight into another open meadow. This is the last place we want to get caught. Great, someone else has joined the party. I hear a helicopter, and it's closing in rapidly."

Payton caught the sound and looked up. She pointed up in the sky. "Collin, they're here," she said. She started to run out into the meadow.

"Payton, no." Collin grabbed her around the waist and yanked her back into the tree line. "That's not the team; it's too soon." He knew as he pulled her back into the cover of the tree line the effort had been futile. Chances were more than likely they were seen from the air.

Collin looked around them as he tried to find a place to hide. The only spot he saw was some dead trees. As they wedged themselves under a couple of dead trees, two helicopters landed in the meadow. The blades on both aircraft slowed to a stop. The side door of the first helicopter slid open, and Braxton stepped out. The four all-terrain vehicles stopped a short distance behind the two.

"Son of a bitch," he mumbled to himself.

"Maybe we can stall them," she whispered into his ear.

"The team is at least an hour out. I don't think we can stall Braxton that long."

"Collin," Braxton bellowed from the meadow. "I know you can hear me. You have nowhere to go. You might as well make this easy on yourself and come out where I can see you."

Collin placed his finger to his lips and indicated to Payton to be quiet.

"I haven't the time or patience for your antics, Collin." Braxton spoke into a walkie-talkie, and the door to the second helicopter opened. A man jumped out, turned back to the aircraft, and pulled out a child.

"Sadistic bastard," Collin hissed. He didn't care that he could be overheard. "He has Emma."

"How is that possible?" Payton asked. "They were at their safe house. No one knew about them but our small group."

"Sarah, that's how," Collin said.

"Collin, I have your sister Emma here. If you don't show yourself right now, the day might not end well for her," Braxton said.

"Dickless bastard," Collin said. "I'm going out; you stay here." He pulled out the gun he'd taken from the guard and tossed it away.

"I'm not staying. He knows I'm here. I have nowhere to go. I'm coming with you."

He knew she was right, so he nodded and the two crawled out from their hiding spot.

"We're right here, Braxton." Collin said. He spread his arms out wide in front of him, palms up, as he started into the meadow.

"Well, I'm glad you've seen things my way," Braxton said.

"You've got what you wanted. I'm here. Now send Emma back."

"You're right, Collin. I have got what I want, and you are only part of the equation. Emma is the other part," Braxton said.

Chapter Twenty-Six

"Sarah, please take a seat," Braxton said. "I have a few questions for you. Oh, how rude of me. Allow me to introduce you to Tessa."

Tessa stood in the far corner of the room in black jeans and a skintight gray shirt. Sarah thought she was quite stunning except for her bone-chilling stare.

"Nice to meet you, Tessa," Sarah said. She was still concerned about how Braxton would react to her taking Emma and leaving, but it looked to her as if everything might work out for them.

"You might want to wait on your sentiment," Braxton said. "Tessa isn't really someone people are pleased to meet." He nodded and Tessa moved closer to Sarah.

"What's going on?" Sarah asked, as she bordered on panic.

"I want to know what you told Wyatt and his team. Tessa here is going to get the information for me."

Tessa moved closer still, and Sarah tried to get out of the chair, but found herself restrained by a guard as his large powerful hands pushed down on her shoulders.

"I already told Dave everything."

Terror overtook her as Tessa bent closer and her eyes bored into Sarah. She mentally fought to pull her gaze from Tessa but found herself locked in place. Tessa invaded Sarah's mind; she could feel her there. Sarah's thoughts and memories were now an open book to the woman.

In her mind, Sarah pleaded and begged to be free from this insane woman. Tessa probed and pushed and forced the information she wanted to come to the surface. Pain started somewhere deep within Sarah's brain and intensified with each passing second. The more Tessa invaded Sarah's mind, the more extreme the torment.

The torture continued, and Sarah could feel her mind unhinge, reality recede, and her brain begin to misfire. Tessa never slowed her persistent mental push. Farther and farther she ripped into every memory and left a wake of destruction in her path. Sarah clenched her jaw. She continued to grip the arms of the chair with such force that the bones in her fingers broke and her nails tore away. A single bloody tear trickled down Sarah's cheek. Agony engulfed her and she started to convulse; her heart beat erratically, and then...no more pain.

* * * *

Tessa pulled away from Sarah. She gasped and looked at Braxton as she stammered, "S-Sir, I believe she is dead."

Braxton pressed a button on his desk and the doctor rushed in.

"See to her," Braxton said.

The doctor listened for Sarah's heartbeat, checked her eyes, and looked up at Braxton.

"The indications are that she suffered a brain bleed," he said.

"I see. I believe you and Tessa still have some fine-tuning to do. Her new skill is useful, but I don't necessarily want her to kill every person I ask her to read," Braxton said. "What did you find out?" he asked Tessa.

"She gave the team a list of contacts." Tessa repeated the names to Braxton. "She also thought she knew who one of the members of Kaleidoscope Group might be."

"Well, who did she say?"

"Carl Sterling. But she never told the team his name," Tessa said.

"Clever girl," Braxton said. "Just as well events turned out the way they did. She wouldn't have left the facility with the information that she knew."

* * * *

"Any sign of them?" Tristan asked Morgan as he met up with the group.

"None. I ran a good thirty miles, but they are not in the area," Morgan said. "I did see evidence of them though. A couple miles back I found a stream and a large area covered in prints. It looks as though Collin got in a little dance with some kind of cat."

"Any blood?" Logan asked.

"Nope. I think he only wanted to scare the animal off."

"I found tire tracks to the east a ways back. The tracks look like they belong to some type of all-terrain vehicle, and they are fresh," Noah said.

"Shit," Tristan said. "I lay odds that bastard, Braxton, beat us here. Noah, call Jack and see if he located the ranch Collin mentioned."

Noah left the group to retrieve his pack and dig the SAT phone out. Minutes later, he returned.

"Jack says there is only one ranch within a fifty-mile range. That ranch is to the south of us," Noah said.

"Looks like we caught our first break," Tristan said. "How close can you get the helicopter to the ranch without being heard?" Tristan asked Logan.

"Depends on the topography and where we can put our bird down," Logan said.

"Jack said the terrain is similar to where we are now. He could only locate two possible landing spots. The first is five miles from the ranch; the second is thirteen miles out," Noah said.

"To stay on the safe side, I say we land the chopper at the second spot. I realize Collin didn't see a great deal of security, but we would risk being heard or seen by someone if we get any closer," Logan said.

"We are running out of daylight. Is there any chance someone would spot our lights?" Tristan asked.

"I couldn't say for sure, but if we leave now I still have plenty of daylight to get us safely to the landing spot without aid," Logan said.

"This is the spot," Logan said, as he put the helicopter on the ground.

"Let's check our gear and stow everything possible into our packs. We need to be ready for anything," Tristan said. The team took off on foot for the ranch.

* * * *

Hands tied behind his back, Collin was escorted to Braxton's office. The door opened and he found Payton. She was sitting in one of the chairs with a guard towering over her.

"Collin, I've been worried sick something happened to you." She stood as she greeted him, only to be roughly grabbed by the guard and shoved back into the chair. She caught a glimpse of Collin's eyes as they flashed gold, and shook her head. Cautiously, she mouthed the word, "Emma."

Collin willed himself to remain calm and allowed himself to be forcefully pushed into the other chair.

Braxton entered the room. "You certainly have been a thorn in my side, Collin. No matter; your days of pranks are long over."

The two waited for Braxton to show his hand.

"Tomorrow we leave for my new facility," Braxton said.

"Sure, as long as you release Emma, Payton, and Sarah, I'll gladly go," Collin said.

"You are in no position to make demands. Emma is an important factor in our plan, and all three of you will join me on this adventure."

"Three of us?" Collin asked.

"In a manner of speaking, Sarah has already left. She engaged in a conversation with Tessa earlier this evening. Things didn't turn out well for her."

"You despicable prick," Collin growled. He jumped up from the chair and started toward Braxton.

"Tsk, tsk, there will be none of that," Braxton said. He pointed in Payton's direction.

Collin's gaze followed Braxton's hand and horror filled his heart. The guard tightened a rope around Payton's neck. She desperately tried to tear the rope away from herself as the guard pulled the rope taut and caused her to gasp for air.

"All right, stop hurting her now," Collin pleaded.

Payton's lips started turning blue.

Braxton nodded to the guard, who loosened the rope. Payton sucked in a huge breath of air and tried to rip the rope from her neck.

"Good, now we understand each other," Braxton said.

"You have me and Emma; you know I wouldn't do anything to put Emma in danger. You can at least let Payton go; she is of no use to you," Collin said.

"Oh, but she is. This couldn't have worked out any better if I had planned it. I certainly do not want to do anything to hurt Emma, so we will need Payton to control you. Emma and dozens of others are being groomed for our Second Wave. Don't look so surprised." Braxton paused. "I have no reason to not to tell you. The facility you are all being taken to is escape-proof, and you will never be left alone with your sister. You should feel honored, Collin. You and Emma play a major role in our future."

Collin glowered at Braxton, frustration seething from every pore. If he could get even one chance, Braxton would die.

* * * *

Tristan, Morgan, and Logan crouched in the gully a few yards from the main gate to the ranch and evaluated the layout. Noah had dropped back a few feet behind them and was on the phone with Jack. He disconnected the SAT phone, after which he slunk up beside the three men.

"What'd you get, Noah?" Tristan asked.

"Well, you know Jack, not enough time to complete a thorough investigation, blah, blah, blah. He says the place is pretty low security, which makes it a strange place to keep Collin, if you ask me."

"They were pressed for time when they left the island. I guess the ranch happened to be the only available place to stash them," Logan said.

"Besides, he's not alone. Payton is in the mix. He won't try his extreme escapes with her to consider," Morgan said.

"Jack did manage to dig up some blueprints on the ranch. He told me there are three floors underground," Noah said.

"Safe bet that is where Collin and Payton are being kept. The security may not include all the bells and whistles, but when you are underground, there are only so many ways out," Tristan said.

"The entire ranch is enclosed by an electric fence and there are keypads on all the doors," Noah said.

"And by the looks of things, it's pretty heavily guarded. I count seven men," Tristan said, as he pulled the night vision binoculars away from his face.

"I saw three men guarding the outbuildings," Logan said.

"Plus the two guys here at the gate," Morgan said.

"Do we know what kind of firepower they have inside the guard shack?" Tristan asked.

Noah shook his head. "No. Funny thing though, the shack doesn't show up on any of the blueprints."

"So, we're going in blind. We need to be fast and clean," Tristan said. "Morgan and Logan, you take the two men at the shack; Noah and I will watch your six."

Morgan and Logan soundlessly drifted up to the shack without generating a single ripple in the atmosphere. Both men were plastered against the side of the shack, one on each side of the window. Logan peered inside. He pulled back and signaled Morgan with hand signals. Morgan nodded he understood, and the two crept up to the door.

As Logan reached up to turn the handle, the door banged open, and the two men melted into the shadows.

"I know, I know," said the guard, as he walked out of the shack. "I'll be back in a minute; I can't think if I don't get a couple of drags."

The guard fished cigarettes from his pocket and headed right toward Logan. He stopped just short of him and flicked his lighter. The guard froze in shock, hardly registering what was happening as Logan grabbed him, yanked him to the ground, and sliced his throat. Simultaneously Morgan entered the shack, low to the floor. The other guard had his back to him, watching the television. Morgan was on the guard in a flash; he stabbed his in the heart, and the body slid to the floor like a rag doll.

Logan signaled to Tristan, and the other two men joined them.

"Not much here," Morgan said. "Cameras on the main gate and the front doors of all the buildings. I don't see any signs of motion sensors. I'd say we are pretty clear."

"Let's get this done," Tristan said.

The team made their way up to the main building and then scattered to scout out the layout.

"There are two men walking the perimeter around this building," Morgan said. "I found a way to enter. On the other side of the building there is an enclosed patio. You would have to scale the stucco wall, but I got up in a single jump. I could get up and throw you three a line."

"Very funny," Noah said. "I think we are all capable of climbing a wall."

"We better be, or it's time to retire," Tristan said. "What did you find, Logan?"

"The three men I spotted on the way here are inside one of the buildings playing cards. There are two additional men walking the perimeter of the outer building and the helipad," Logan said.

"Then we have a way out of here and we won't have to huff it back to our chopper," Morgan said.

"I would say so, as long as Logan can fly that bird," Noah said.

Logan glared at his partner. "You know damn well I can fly anything."

"Okay guys, let's get down to business. You know the plan, two-man teams; Morgan you'll be with me. We gain entry into the building, split up, and locate Payton and Collin. They're our only priority. After we secure them we get the hell out of Dodge," Tristan said.

"What if Braxton is still around?" Logan asked.

"We'll leave him for now; our mission is Payton and Collin. Let's do our sound check."

They all pulled on their headsets and made sure they were in proper working order, and slid down their night vision goggles. The team waited for a guard to disappear around the far side of the building before they started for the patio. Morgan jumped up the wall and made sure the area was still clear. The four men jumped into the patio and spread out against the walls.

Tristan edged his way up to the glass doors and glanced out into the main foyer. A few dimly lit lamps were scattered throughout the area. A guard sat at the main door. Tristan turned back to the men and signaled his findings, telling them to hold their positions until he returned. He slipped out of the patio and slunk up behind the guard. He pulled his knife and crept closer, stopped and listened. The guard snored softly. Tristan turned back and returned to his team.

"The guard is fast asleep," he whispered. "I left him be. No sense in killing him if we don't have to. Besides, if someone else shows up before we get out, finding a dead guard would raise an alarm."

The team kept to the shadows as they made their way to the stairway and started down. Logan and Noah started their search on the first level. Tristan and Morgan proceeded to the third level, with the idea of meeting up on the second level.

Chapter Twenty-Seven

Payton tossed and turned. With all the activity she'd experienced that day, she thought she would drift to sleep as soon as her head hit the pillow, but sleep eluded her. Tessa's mental ability to cause Sarah's death haunted her in the darkness.

She imagined Sarah's dreadful struggle, and it gave her chills and made her stomach threaten to rebel. She personally knew the pain of Tessa's mental intrusion, and if it weren't for her psychic barriers, she too would have suffered the same fate. She couldn't suppress the horror. Energy pulsed through her. *Collin must be awake or having a bad dream,* she thought.

"Wait a minute," she whispered in the darkness. "That's not Collin."

* * * *

Collin picked up the scent of Tristan and Morgan the instant they arrived in the stairwell on the third floor. He leapt up from the bed and dressed in seconds. He waited patiently until they were outside his door and whispered, "Morgan."

"Collin?" Morgan asked.

"I'm here."

The electronic lock clicked, and the door swung open.

"I'm glad to see you two. Braxton plans on shipping us out first thing in the morning; nothing like cutting it close."

"Where's Payton?" Tristan asked.

"She's nearby; I feel her energy," Collin said.

* * * *

Payton felt certain the rest of the team was there. She placed her ear to the door and listened. She thought she heard mumbling.

"Collin, are you there?" she whispered.

Collin turned to his left and walked past a couple of doors. He stopped in front of one.

"Payton," he said.

"Yes, I'm here."

* * * *

Tessa opened her eyes and stared out the window into the star-speckled night. Something woke her from her slumber, but she couldn't put her finger on it. She closed her eyes and reached out with her mind. There. She was familiar with the new energy that drifted in the atmosphere. It was the identical signature she first came in contact with on the island. She hurriedly dressed, padded down the hall, and tapped on the door.

"Mr. Braxton."

"What is it, Tessa?" Braxton asked as he pulled the door open.

"Those men who invaded the island are here in the building."

"Damn them. How long have they been here?"

"I noticed their presence about ten minutes ago."

"Go retrieve Emma and Dave, and meet me at the helipad."

"What about Collin and Payton?"

"Chances are they have already been discovered by their team. Tell Dave to lock the door to the stairway and lock down the elevators on your way through. Hopefully you can slow them down. Go now; our priority is Emma," Braxton said.

Braxton grabbed his phone and dialed the helipad.

"Yes, sir," said the pilot's voice.

"We have intruders. You need to prep the aircraft and notify the guards. I want two guards to leave with us; the rest should detain the intruders."

* * * *

"Package is secure," Tristan spoke into his mouthpiece. "We are exiting the building."

"Roger," Logan and Noah said.

"Wait," Collin said. "We can't leave yet; we have to locate Emma."

"Did he say Emma?" Logan asked.

"Emma is here?" Tristan asked.

"Why else do you think I would willingly come back to this hellhole of a place," Collin said.

"Okay, spread out and locate Emma and Sarah," Tristan said.

"No, not Sarah—only Emma. Tessa killed Sarah while trying to retrieve information from her mind."

"The bitch," Tristan said. "Okay guys, we need to locate Emma and get the hell out of here," he said into his headset. He looked at Collin and Payton, "Let's go get her."

Both Tristan and Collin filled their lungs and tried to pick up a trace of Emma's scent. Payton closed her eyes and freed her mental barriers. She searched for Emma's psychic signature. The sudden onslaught of energy took her totally by surprise. Finally she comprehended what Victory tried so desperately to drum into her. Her mental barriers were now subconsciously part of her, and her mind had erected them without a single cognizant thought. She thought Victory was crazy when she told her the barriers would at some point react without being prompted. Victory had compared her barriers to breathing and said she would hold them in place without any conscious effort.

Now, she opened the floodgates and sensed a number of energy signatures, which included each of the team members. She stumbled backward, overwrought from the blast of emotional energy. Astonishment stopped her cold. Could the team's abilities be the common thread and the reason General Roberts had brought these particular military men together? Was he even aware of each man's abilities?

"Payton, are you okay?" Collin asked. He caught her in his arms and pulled her back to the present.

"I'm fine. Just got slightly overwhelmed, is all. Surprisingly, my mental barriers have become a part of me, without me even realizing," she said.

Payton pulled away from him and stood erect.

"Are you sure you are going to be okay?" Tristan asked. "If not, I will get one of the guys to get you out of here. We can't take any risks or have any distractions. Never mind the tiny matter that your sister will kill me if anything happens to you."

"No need. I'm fine, really. Give me a minute to adjust," she said.

Her discovery of the team's psychic abilities would have to be put on hold. Once again she cleared her mind and refocused on locating Emma. She first noticed Emma's powers when they met out at the academy. Her powers were still weak, unfocused, and confused, as if Emma's own mind fought against them. Payton surmised Emma was not even really aware of her abilities yet.

"I have her," she said to the two men.

Tristan and Collin looked at Payton.

"Don't look so astounded, guys. I've been honing my skills for months now."

"Where is she?" Collin asked.

"Second floor."

"Emma is on the second floor," Tristan said, into his headset. "We are on our way to her. You two meet us on the landing of the second floor."

They ran down the hall silently and up the flight of stairs to the next floor, where they met Noah and Logan.

"Payton, stay here with Noah and Logan. Collin and I will get Emma and meet you back here," Tristan said.

The two men started down the hall.

"Are you picking up what I am?" Collin asked.

"Unfortunately. I hope I'm wrong," Tristan said.

"No, Emma traveled through here recently."

"Let's check her room to make certain."

They got to her room and noticed the door was ajar. Tristan pulled out his Ruger .38 and twisted a silencer on the end. He nodded to Collin, and the two men rushed into the room. They found drawers opened, clothes scattered about, and an unmade bed, but no Emma.

"For Chirssakes. How does Braxton stay one step ahead of us?" Tristan said.

"That would be Tessa," Collin said.

"I thought you said she reads minds?" Tristan asked, as they ran back to the stairwell.

"She does, and apparently she can sense energy signatures just like Payton. She is extremely dangerous, and I shudder to think what Braxton might have planned for her."

"Braxton knows we're here. He has Emma and I'm sure he is heading for the chopper. Let's get the asshole," Tristan said into his headset.

They bounded up the stairs. As the two men came into view, Logan pushed on the door leading to the main floor.

"Son of a bitch, someone locked the damn door. It's going to take me a minute, if you want me to get this opened quietly," Logan said.

Seconds later they stood in the hall of the main floor. Nothing looked disturbed, except the guard was awake and stood near the door. The group quickly melted into the shadows. Tristan tapped Collin on the shoulder and signaled for him to take care of the guard. Collin acknowledged the command and shot off. The guard stood and looked out the door, but a moment later he disappeared and Collin returned to the group.

"Shit man, give me some of those special dog genes," Noah said.

The team fanned out as they reached the outskirts of the helipad. Dave and Braxton came into view pulling Emma along between them. The trio was only steps away from the helipad. Tessa slid the large door open on the helicopter and then moved into the passenger's seat next to the pilot.

"Braxton," Tristan called loudly, trying to be heard over the sound of the chopper's rotating blades. "We have four guns trained on you. Take one more step and we'll shoot."

Braxton turned slowly back toward the group and kept hold of Emma, using her as a shield. Dave pulled a gun from his holster and stood behind Emma and Braxton.

"Drop the gun, Dave," Tristan said.

Dave aimed the gun at Emma and waited for instructions from Braxton.

"Well gentlemen. Seems we have a standoff. If you want Emma to stay alive, I suggest you let us leave," Braxton said.

"We can't let you take Emma," Tristan said.

Payton felt Collin's anger and fear accelerate to a feverish pitch. She sensed his terror that Braxton would once again escape with Emma. He felt powerless to stop him.

"Dave, put the damn gun down, now," Tristan said.

Payton shut out the events that unfolded around her and focused exclusively on Dave. She'd spent enough time around the man to know he had weak mental resolve. *Maybe I can force him to drop the gun*, she thought. She focused and pushed Dave mentally, trying to will him to loosen his grip and drop the gun. Immediately she felt a shift in her power, an increase of command. *Collin*. She felt his essence wrapped in her mind.

Dave's face blanked; all emotion left his features. He started to move his arm to his right and line up the gunsight with Braxton's head.

They watched in utter shock as Dave's gun slowly moved from aiming at Emma to aiming at Braxton.

"We are leaving this instant. The first person who moves will cause Emma's death," Braxton said.

Collin reached down and took Payton's hand. "There is no other way," he whispered. "You know if Braxton leaves with Emma, we may never find her. He will turn her into another Tessa."

"You can't do this," she whispered back to him. "We only need him to drop his gun."

Still, somewhere deep inside her, she knew Collin was right. This madman needed to be stopped once and for all.

They could see Dave's face as the realization of the situation dawned on him. He attempted to lower his gun, pushing on his arm with his free hand. His arm wouldn't budge. Braxton turned around and stared directly down the barrel of Dave's gun.

"What the hell are you doing? Get that damn thing out of my face," Braxton demanded.

"I-I-I -ca-ca-can't," Dave stammered.

Payton felt the surge tear through her as somewhere in the distance she registered the sound of a single shot, followed by Braxton crumpling to the ground.

Shock filled Dave's face as he dropped the gun. The helicopter took off behind him as he stood transfixed by Braxton's body.

Collin released Payton's hand and ran to rescue Emma. The team encompassed Dave and confiscated his gun. Tristan bent down to check for a pulse, making sure Braxton was indeed dead. The macabre scene moved in slow motion, and everything blended into a blur as Payton fainted and fell to the ground.

Chapter Twenty-Eight

"Payton?" Willow sat on the edge of Payton's bed. She gently brushed her hair from her face. "Hey, sweetie, welcome back."

Payton's eyelids fluttered open.

"Willow, how'd I get home?" Payton asked, still feeling a bit queasy.

"What's the last thing you remember?" Willow asked with concern.

"Hmm, I remember we chased Braxton to the helipad, and Tristan tried to convince him to give up Emma. Emma, how is she?"

"She's safe and sound, thanks to you and Collin. Is there anything else you can remember?"

"I-I'm still really tired. I think I need to sleep a little longer." Payton drifted back off to sleep.

Willow sat for a while longer, trying to assure herself that her sister would indeed return to them. She stood up and walked out of the room and headed downstairs. Victory and Dr. Russell sat in the living room having a cup of tea.

"She woke up," Willow said.

"Wonderful," Victory said. She put her cup on the table and started to rise.

"She went back to sleep again."

The two sisters looked at Dr. Russell.

"Don't worry, ladies, she will come around. She has to come to grips with what happened in her own way and time. She's dealt with a great amount of trauma and her mind is trying to protect her. When she gets stronger, she will wake up."

"I questioned her to find out what she remembered last, like you told us to do. She recalled that she tried to save Emma, and then she drifted back to sleep," Willow said.

"Good. She's not blocking the entire incident from her mind. She's still in shock, but she will come around. Give her more time," Dr. Russell said.

"It's been two days," Victory said.

A knock sounded on the back door. Willow got up and walked into the kitchen. She returned with Collin.

"Willow told me Payton woke up," he said.

Each in turn reiterated the events to Collin.

"It's my fault. I'm sorry. My complete focus stayed on Emma. I was deathly afraid Braxton would take her again. I would never, ever have done anything intentional to hurt Payton."

"We know you would never hurt Payton, Collin," Willow said. "You have already apologized over and over. We don't blame you. You didn't need to move out of the house."

"Yes, I did. I don't want to put any more pressure on Payton. Can I go up and sit with her?"

Victory smiled at him. "Of course, and you don't need to ask our permission."

The three women watched him climb the stairs. It looked as if his whole world lay in ashes around him.

"How is he doing?" Dr. Russell asked.

"He's been by Payton's side almost constantly. If he's not working, or in Victory's lab with her, he's here with Payton," Willow said.

"True love," Dr. Russell said.

"The big question is how Payton will feel," Victory replied sadly.

* * * *

Payton woke in complete darkness and tried to orient herself. She felt the familiar weight of Kes and Parker, her body wedged between them. She reached down and rubbed their heads. It felt wonderful to be in her bed with her dogs beside her, she thought as she drifted back to sleep.

She woke the next morning to find both Victory and Willow in her room. They smiled when they saw her eyelids flutter open.

"Good morning, sis," Willow said.

"What a surprise. Good morning to both of you. Why are you in my room?" she asked.

"We've been worried," Victory said.

"About what?" Payton asked, as she sat up in her bed. The severe ache in her head forced her to place a hand on each temple.

Willow went over to the dresser and picked up a pitcher, poured a glass of water, and grabbed a bottle of aspirin.

"Here, take these," she said, as she shook a few pills from the bottle and handed her sister the water.

"How are you feeling, other than the headache?" Victory asked.

"A little sluggish, and a tad foggy, but not too bad. Why?" she asked again eyeing her sisters.

"You've been asleep for three days," Willow blurted out.

"What? No, that can't be," Payton said.

"It is. What's the last thing you remember?" Victory asked.

"I remember all of us chased Braxton to the helipad. He had Emma. How *is* Emma?"

"She's fine, Payton. She is in a new school where she's totally secure and happy. Collin got her settled in and told her he will visit her anytime she would like," Victory said.

"What about her mom? Didn't she even wonder about Emma when she couldn't reach her daughter?"

"Emma's mother is on vacation with her newest beau. She's been out of touch for the past few months. Wyatt spoke with her the other day, and he filled her in on all that happened," Victory said.

"Including Sarah's death? Did she come home?" Payton asked.

"No. Guess she's not really the motherly type, more the self-centered type. She seemed upset by Sarah's death and happy Emma is safe, but didn't want to disrupt her schedule. She said she needed more time away to grieve," Victory said.

"I'm happy Emma has Collin; otherwise, she would be all alone in the world," Payton said.

"Emma is being taken care of, Payton, don't worry. Tell us what happened when you reached the helipad," Victory said.

"Dave and Braxton were trying to get on the helicopter with Emma. Tristan tried to talk them down, but Braxton wasn't having any of it. Dave held a gun aimed at Emma's head." She stopped and took another sip of water. She lowered the glass back in her lap and stared into it. She raised her head and looked at her sisters, tears filled her eyes. "I don't want to talk about what happened. I need to get up and get ready for work. I've been away for far too long."

"Payton—" Victory said.

"Let her be for now," Willow said, as she placed her hand on Victory's shoulder. "She will tell us what happened in her own time. Let's go feed the dogs and make ourselves some breakfast. Come down when you're ready, Payton."

They took Kes and Parker and closed the door behind them. Payton sat quietly for a bit longer, and then she broke down and wept. Revenge had gotten the best of her and she had killed a man. Now she would be forced to live her entire life with this terrible nightmare.

Eventually she pulled herself together. She got up from her bed and headed for the shower. She would have a quick breakfast with her sisters so they didn't worry and then head to the office.

Willow and Victory tried to get her to ride with them down to the campus. She refused the offer, telling them she wanted to stretch her legs and get some fresh air—partly the truth, but mostly she didn't want to be questioned. So much had happened over the last month, and she needed time to process all the events in her own mind. How could she have slept for three days?

She smiled and greeted each person who crossed her path on the way to the campus and as she walked the hall to her office. When she reached Jane's desk, Payton informed her she had a great deal of work to catch up on and didn't want to be disturbed.

An hour later she heard Jane on the phone. "I'm sorry, Mr. McBain; Payton is in meetings all day today. Yes, I'll be sure to tell her."

Payton's thoughts drifted to Collin. She'd used him as a tool to kill Braxton and felt horrified and ashamed of herself for what she had done to both Braxton and Collin. She would not be surprised if Collin never forgave her for using him in such a grisly manner. He probably called her to give her a piece of his mind. *He moved out of the house, for goodness sake. Didn't his actions speak louder than his words?* At the very least, Collin would never look at her in the same way; of this, she was sure. She had single-handedly destroyed his trust in her. She needed to stop these thoughts and focus on her work. She certainly had more than enough to keep her busy.

There was a soft knock on her door and Jane stuck her head in. "Payton, is there anything else you need?"

Payton looked at the time on her computer. She was surprised to see it was after six.

"No, Jane, I'm good. You should go home; it's been a long day."

"I wanted to make sure you didn't need anything," Jane said. "I also wanted to tell you Mr. McBain called earlier today. He wanted to let you know he will be away for a few days."

"Thank you, Jane. Have a nice evening."

Payton started to clean up for the day. She had promised her sisters she wouldn't stay late and she would join them for dinner. She wished she hadn't made the promise. Another knock sounded on the door.

"What did you forget?" Payton asked, expecting to see Jane.

"Pardon?" Dr. Russell asked as she opened the door.

"Oh, sorry. I thought you were my assistant."

"I wanted to see how you were doing," Dr. Russell said, as she walked in and took a seat. "How did you do on your first day back? I hope you didn't push yourself."

"I'm fine, and no, I didn't overdo." She wanted Dr. Russell gone as soon as possible. The last thing she needed right now was to rehash her ordeal.

"Do you want to tell me what happened, Payton?" Dr. Russell asked.

"You know what happened." Now she started getting antsy.

"I know what everyone else has told me, but not from your point of view."

"What does it matter whose point of view you heard the story from? What happened, happened." Tears started leaking and trickled down her cheeks; she wiped furiously at them.

Dr. Russell went over to her, took her by the hands, and led her over to the sofa. She sat Payton down, went to the credenza, pulled out the brandy snifter, and poured two small glasses. She walked back to the sofa and placed one glass in Payton's hands and sat down next to her.

"Your point of view matters a great deal. Talking about mishaps is painful, but it will also help you to heal." Dr. Russell sat back and waited.

312

"I killed a man; that's what happened! How could I have possibly killed him? How will my sisters ever forgive me? How will Collin ever trust me again?" Tears cascaded unchecked down her face and she shook all over.

Dr. Russell leaned forward and took the glass from her shaking hands and brought it up to Payton's lips.

"Take a sip," she said.

She gave Payton a few minutes to cry it out and started again.

"Payton, start from the beginning and tell me what happened."

Needing to expose her demons to someone, Payton told her story. She got to the part where they were all at the helipad and hesitated.

"Go on," Dr. Russell prompted her.

"Dave held a gun to Emma's head. Tristan tried to talk Braxton out of getting on the helicopter with her. I remember that I thought, 'oh God, Braxton is going to get away with it again. He's destroying the life of someone I love.'

"First, he was involved with the making of my mother's and Dr. Ryker's drug. Then, he stole the formula and produced the drug under the guise of his own company, reaping all the benefits. Next, he kidnapped Victory and forced her to participate in his immoral research. He injected Morgan and Collin with foreign DNA, which will endanger their lives forever. He has recruited children, for goodness' sake—children with special abilities—and tried to create his own hit squad and who knows what else he planned to do with them?

"Braxton kidnapped me and Collin, and threatened to kill me. He did kill Sarah. He stood in front of me and held Collin's baby sister at gunpoint. I couldn't let him take her; it would have destroyed Collin. At first I thought if I could get Dave to lower the gun, the guys would have a chance at him. I remember I thought if I focused all my energy on Dave, I might get him to drop the gun. Suddenly, the strangest sensation came over me, a burst of energy, as if Collin and I were sharing the same psychic force. In that instant I knew in my heart that getting Dave to drop the gun wasn't enough. Braxton needed to be stopped once and for all, and the only way to make certain he would never hurt anyone else again would be if he was dead."

"So, because of what you did you no longer think you are worthy of love, or of your sisters' respect?" Dr. Russell asked. "You were protecting your family. Anyone in your position would have done the same."

"No, they wouldn't. No one else would have the ability to do what I did," Payton said.

"Collin does, and he aided you."

"No, he didn't. I drew from his energy, but *I* turned the gun and made Dave fire all on my own."

"You need to discuss what happened with Collin, Payton. You need his story to complete all the pieces to the picture and to get through this process."

"Well, I won't be getting Collin's story anytime soon, now will I? He has left and I have no idea where he is or when he will be back."

"Isn't his leaving the nature of his job?"

"He moved out of the house. He doesn't want to see me. I can't really say I blame him. If I was given the chance, I wouldn't want to see me either."

314

Payton's phone vibrated in her pocket. She reached in and looked at the display screen.

"It's Willow. I promised her and Victory I would join them for dinner."

* * * *

Payton was greeted at the kitchen door by all four dogs, each pushing the other to reach her hand first.

"Wait one minute," Payton said, to the brood as she emptied the contents of her arms on to the table. She turned back to them and warmly greeted each and every dog.

"What on earth did you bring home?" Willow asked. She stood at the kitchen island where she was putting a salad together, and she stopped to pour Payton a glass of wine.

"Thanks," Payton said taking the wine. "I need to catch up on a few things, is all."

"Payton, you have put in more than eight hours already today. You need to take it easy for a couple of days," Willow said.

"I am. You know me; work relaxes me."

"Yeah, right."

"Where's Victory?" Payton asked abruptly, as she tried to change the subject.

"She went over to her house to take a quick shower. Tristan is home and will be joining us for dinner."

All the dogs jumped up and ran to the front of the house. The door opened and Victory's laugh floated in. Payton went out to greet them.

"I thought you were on a mission?" Payton asked Tristan. She knew if Collin were really on a mission, Tristan would be gone too, since he was the team leader.

"Who told you I was on a mission?" Tristan asked.

"Jane said Collin will be away for a few days," Payton said.

"Yes he is, but not on a mission. General Roberts wanted to debrief him in person. He and Wyatt flew off to D.C. a couple hours ago. They should be home in a few days."

Willow stuck her head out of the kitchen door. "Let's get dinner on the table."

"How are you feeling, Payton?" Tristan asked as the four of them sat down at the table.

"Still slightly out of it, although better than earlier today," Payton said.

"Give yourself time, Payton. You've been though a horrendous ordeal," Victory said.

"Are you willing to tell me what happened?" Tristan asked.

Payton sat back in her chair as she thought about his question. She nodded.

"Good. When Collin debriefed the team, he said you mentioned a name of one of Braxton's good friends," Tristan said.

"Yes, Braxton told me it paid to have friends in high places, and Carl was a good friend of his. He also said you wouldn't look for me on the island where Victory and you were taken to because the photos were doctored. He said they gave the impression that the facility remained totally abandoned."

"Did he ever give you Carl's last name?" Tristan asked.

"No, just Carl; that's it. Collin believes he's the CIA director. I think the director of the CIA might be a leap," Payton said. "There must be a number of men named Carl working for the government, but the CIA director? I can't believe he would or could double-cross the government."

"I can see how that may seem farfetched; nevertheless, stranger things have happened. This person has to be someone with a great deal of political pull who has access to top security areas. The director of the CIA would certainly qualify. I think Collin might be on the right track. I know one thing for sure; if this friend is Carl Sterling, General Roberts will be one pissed-off guy. As of now we have precious little to go on except a first name Braxton threw out," Tristan said.

"Can't you question Dave? He was Braxton's right-hand man. I'll bet he heard the name a time or two, maybe even met the guy," Payton said.

"You didn't tell her?" Tristan asked Victory and Willow.

"She didn't want to talk about what happened, and today we didn't have any time to get together," Victory said.

"Tell me what?" Payton asked.

"The helicopter Braxton and his team planned to escape in managed to take off before we had a chance to stop it."

"Meaning Tessa got away. She is an extremely dangerous woman," Payton said.

"I realize she is dangerous, and we are trying to locate her. But as of now, no luck. It's almost as though she fell off the face of the Earth. Anyway, Logan and Noah went back and got our chopper and picked us up, including Dave. We radioed in and were told to drop off Dave with one of our contacts. We needed to stay under the radar as much as possible. We were told our contact would take him to a holding facility, and he would be transferred the next day to a more permanent place."

"And what were they holding him for?" Payton asked.

"The murder of his boss, Lawrence Braxton," Tristan said.

"I'm sure he's done his share of horrendous deeds. This one wasn't his fault. I forced him to do it." Guilt started to seep into Payton's every pore.

"It wasn't your fault either, Payton. A number of factors entered into the situation, and you can rest assured Dave has killed in the past."

"You and I both know he will say Braxton's murder wasn't his fault," Payton said.

"And do you really think anyone will believe him? Besides, we are debating a moot point now. Before Dave was transferred, someone murdered him. Dave got placed in a local prison, where he was inadvertently let out into the general population at breakfast the following morning. A fight broke out in the dining hall. Apparently he was stabbed and bled out before any of the guards saw what happened to him," Tristan said.

"Seems too coincidental," Payton said.

"My thoughts exactly. Somehow, someone got him placed in there and didn't want him to get out and now we have lost our most promising lead. Dave's murder confirms there is a definite leak in the system. Everyone who might have known the person named Carl is now dead—Sarah, Braxton, and Dave," Tristan said.

"What about me? I heard the name. Are you saying I'm the only one left?" Payton asked.

"It would seem so; although no one except the team, your sisters, and General Roberts are aware that you heard the name. You are safe Payton, and we will make sure you stay that way."

"You know I trust you, Tristan; even so the whole situation makes me extremely nervous."

"I understand how you feel. Rest assured you have my word nothing will happen to you. Now please explain to us what happened as you approached the helipad," Tristan said.

Payton explained the scene exactly as she had earlier to Dr. Russell.

"Collin didn't explain the events in the same way, Payton," Willow said.

"Collin said he felt your energy focus on Dave. He knew you were trying to get him to drop his gun. He said he overpowered your direction and forced Dave to shoot Braxton," Tristan said.

"No. It didn't happen the way he told you," Payton said.

"I think you and Collin need to talk," Willow said.

"That's precisely what Dr. Russell said; but facts are facts, and they can't be changed. I think I will skip dessert tonight. I'm feeling rather drained." Payton said her good nights to her family and went up to her room.

"Poor Payton," Willow said. "She is distraught with guilt and blame. The sooner she and Collin can talk, the better it will be for her."

"I hope their problems will be worked out as easily as you think," Victory said.

Chapter Twenty-Nine

The week crept by, and Payton heard no word from Collin. She woke early Saturday morning and decided to stop her moping and refocus on moving forward. She would have to deal with the reality that Collin was no longer part of her life. She tried to keep herself occupied the entire weekend with household chores and bathing the dogs.

She sat out on the back patio and soaked in the warm rays of the late afternoon sun as she sipped on her iced tea. She read all her mother's notes that she had accumulated on her laptop, and let the information flow freely through her mind. There had to be something more. Her mother was known for copious notes, and there were too many holes in the information she had collected.

Her mind filled with thoughts of the drug her mother created and its repercussions. She had gathered a number of the pieces together regarding her mom's research and her feelings. "Pieces" was the operative word. If only she could find her mom's actual formula. Victory could study the formula and get some answers, which would secure a future for all of them, including her, her sisters, Collin and Morgan. She really thought she would find the formula in her mom's computer files, but no such luck.

"The will," she said to herself. She didn't know why the thought came to her out of nowhere, but now she couldn't shake it free.

After the loss of their parents, the sisters' grief was all encompassing. Not one of them had looked over the will since the initial reading. Could her mom have given them a clue in the will that had stared them all in the face since her death? Payton closed up her computer, carried it into the house, dropped it on the nearest counter, and headed back out the door, Parker and Kes right behind her.

"All right, you two can come with me since it is late Sunday afternoon and the place is deserted, except for security people. Nevertheless you both have to be on your best behavior, understand me?"

Payton grabbed their harnesses and leashes and opened the door. They shot out the door, barking and leaping at each other. Kes ran to the outer perimeter of the yard; she covered the massive distance in seconds and repeated her pattern. Parker fought to keep up, but his sheer size slowed him. Payton laughed at the two as she headed for the campus. She allowed them to run free and burn off their pent-up energy until they all reached the wrought-iron gate. There she called them to her, snapped their harnesses on, and hooked their leashes. Tails wagging and tongues hanging, they trotted by her side down to the campus.

Her building was empty, so she unhooked the dogs and allowed them to roam the halls. Of course, being Dobermans, they made a few passes to check out the building and then settled in her office, the better to protect her.

Payton pulled open a drawer in her credenza and located the file containing her parents' will. She walked back to her desk, sat down, and stared at the gray file folder. She summoned all her conviction and reverently opened the file. Anguish overcame her, but she fought to drive her pain into the background as she began reading her parents' last words to them. Her parents had left the sisters all equal shares in the company, the family home, and all other assets. Although, there were a few items her mom and dad specifically wanted each sister to have.

She leaned back in her chair, disappointed nothing popped out at her. She picked up the file and once again read through the individual items. Each was a family heirloom or picture, except for the clock. Why would her mother have specified the clock when she owned many more important items?

The little antique clock had sat on her mother's desk for as long as Payton could remember, except the clock was neither expensive nor a family heirloom. The clock was made of sterling silver in the shape of an old Victorian picture frame. Her mom bought it on her eighteenth birthday during her first trip to England. Sure, it held sentimental value, but if their mom wanted a particular sister to own the clock, the recipient should be Willow. Willow was the one that spent so much time in England. Why would she specifically want Victory to have it, and want it enough to list the clock in the will?

"Let's take a walk," she said to Parker and Kes. Payton grabbed the leashes off the chair and headed out the back door to Victory's labs. She placed her palm on the scanner and was surprised to discover there was no one in Victory's building either. There was always someone here, running some kind of test—usually Victory. She repeated the same process and allowed the two dogs free rein. She headed for Victory's office, placed her hand over the scanner and opened the door.

The clock sat on one corner of Victory's desk. Payton picked it up and turned it in her hands, and studied it intently, as if this were the first time she had ever laid eyes on thing. There were two panels on the clock, one on the bottom housing the batteries, and the second on the back. It looked to her as though both panels could be opened with a screwdriver.

Payton crossed the hall to Victory's main lab and found a couple of screwdrivers that could open the panels. She carried them back to the office. She sat down in Victory's desk chair and went about opening the bottom panel. She didn't really expect to find anything out of the ordinary in that compartment. She was positive Victory had replaced the batteries a number of times since she took possession of the clock. Nonetheless she wanted to confirm there was nothing there with her own eyes. Satisfied the compartment held only batteries; she closed the panel up and reattached the cover plate.

She turned the clock over and started to loosen the screws on the back plate. Gingerly she pulled the plate free from the clock and examined the inner workings. She didn't actually know what the inside of a clock looked like, but nothing seemed out of place. She opened Victory's top desk drawer, removed a small flashlight, and used it to get a better look at the interior—nothing.

Payton slumped back in the chair, disappointed that the clock was yet another dead-end. She picked up the back plate and started to put it back over the opening when one of her fingertips ran across something. She put the screwdriver back down and turned the plate over in her hands. In one of the upper corners she found a small USB drive, taped to the back of the panel. Her hands started to sweat, which made it almost impossible for her to get a hold of the tape. Finally after several attempts, she pulled the tape along with the USB drive from the back of the clock. Hurriedly she screwed the plate back on the clock, dropped the drive into her jeans pocket, and she and the dogs headed back to her office.

Her computer took forever to boot up as she wondered what new clue she'd found. Her mom had gone to great lengths to hide much of her findings, and for the first time, Payton wondered whom she had tried to hide all her research from. The only possibilities that came to mind were the obvious—Biotec and Braxton.

The computer came to life and she plugged the drive in. File after file popped up. Familiar with her mother's shorthand from going through all the file boxes, she knew she had found additional research studies. One file in particular caught her eye, and when she opened it, she found herself staring at a huge formula that her mom had labeled *Genetics*.

Payton couldn't decipher what she looked at, but she was willing to bet this formula had something to do with the drug. She closed the file and looked through the rest on the drive. She froze as she found a file labeled, *Girls*. She gaped at the file, afraid to open it, but needing to do so. She clicked the file open, and discovered another diary, only this one dealt solely with her and her two sisters.

The file was divided by sub-files labeled, *Victory*, *Payton*, and *Willow*. Her mother had documented every year of their lives and any changes she noticed. She stopped dead when she read how her mom described the individual vitamins she had created for each of the girls and the constant adjustments to each of their formulas.

No, that couldn't be, not their mother. She wouldn't have tampered with their DNA without explaining it to them. She only monitored the changes Dr. Ryker had forced on them before their birth. Yet she read on and on, detail after detail about how her mom implemented small changes in their systems. But why? Were they merely guinea pigs to her?

The devastation of this discovery crashed in on her, and in her mind she screamed, *"Collin!"*

* * * *

Collin unpacked his rucksack, found his sweats and sneakers, and headed out for a short run to clear his head. There hadn't been any texts or phone messages from Payton while he was gone, so he decided she still needed her space. Victory preferred he didn't run without Morgan until she had more time to study his system's reaction to the serum, but he was willing to take the chance. He needed time alone.

He was on his second lap around the lake when he was struck with a crushing pain that tore through him. He doubled over and grabbed his knees for support. He had only felt such pain two other times in his life: when he thought he had lost Emma and when he thought he had lost Payton. He tried to breathe through the excruciating pain and center on the cause. He couldn't pinpoint the origin of the pain, and he lost all focus as he was overcome with another wave of agony.

"Collin!"

As clearly as if Payton were standing next to him, he heard her call his name, only her voice was in his mind.

"Payton, where are you? Are you hurt?" Collin shot back, without even realizing he was communicating with her telepathically. Terror swamped him as the outer edges of his vision dimmed.

"No, dammit." He would not allow the wolf in him to take control. Finally he had learned he had a choice in who would rule his mind, and he decided he would be the one in control. *"Payton, answer me."*

"Collin," she screamed once again in her mind.

He wondered if she was even aware she actually communicated with him. He closed his eyes and centered himself; he inhaled through his nose, and he listened to the sounds around him. He filed through each individual sound one by one as he tried to hone in on something that would help. He snapped his head up and he listened—the dogs. He picked up the slight whimpering of Parker and Kes. He took off full throttle and headed for Payton's office building.

With every step closer to the building, the sounds of the dogs' whines increased. He hoped to God one or both of them weren't hurt. He reached the building, cleared the steps in an easy jump, and placed his hand on the palm reader. He opened the door and was greeted by two highly upset Dobermans.

"Where's Payton?" he asked the dogs.

Instantly they spun around and headed down the hall, Collin a step behind as they turned into Payton's office. He stood in the doorway and saw Payton on her knees behind her desk, sobbing uncontrollably. Both dogs brushed their noses through her hair as they tried to get her to respond.

"It's okay, guys," he said to calm the dogs. "Go lay down; she will be fine."

He could see the contemplation in their eyes as they looked from him to Payton. Eventually Parker backed up a few steps and lay down, and Kes followed his lead.

"Payton," Collin said. She didn't look up or acknowledge his presence. He tried again using their newly found telepathic connection. *"Payton, it's me. What happened, honey?"*

She didn't look up as she said, "My mother used us as human test subjects."

He didn't understand her statement, but he did understand the agony that coursed through her. He crossed the room and knelt down beside her. He gathered her up in his arms and carried her to the sofa, where he sat down and held her tight. He rocked her and kissed her head as she cried in his arms. He was relieved, both that she wasn't physically injured and that she allowed him to hold her.

After she cried herself out, Collin reached out and picked up the glass of water she had left on the side table and offered it to her.

"Drink some water; it will make you feel better," he said.

She took the glass in shaky hands and sipped.

"Can you tell me what happened?"

"My mother experimented on us," she managed through sniffles and hiccups. "I found a USB drive taped to the inside back panel of Victory's antique clock."

"What made you look there?" he asked.

She took another sip of water, cleared her throat, and told him the story.

When she finished he asked, "What makes you think she tampered with your DNA? Sounds to me like she tried to figure out what Ryker did to you."

"I believed that too, until today," she said. "Mom insisted we take these vitamins every day. We started taking them at age four and continued until she died."

"Why is that strange?"

"Because they weren't run-of-the-mill vitamins. Mom developed her own vitamins and gave them to us; she never let us use store-bought."

"You think she attempted to change your genetic makeup using these pills?" Collin asked.

"Yes," Payton said.

"Maybe, like Victory, she was looking for a way to stabilize your systems," he said.

"I never thought of that."

"You sit here. I'm going to get you something a little stronger to drink and phone your sisters."

He returned to the sofa to find his seat taken by Kes. Parker's head lay in Payton's lap, his warm brown eyes staring up into her face.

* * * *

Willow, Victory, and Tristan sat quietly as Payton once again repeated her story.

"I thought the worst, until Collin reminded me about your work, Victory. I believe Mom left you the clock with her research inside because she knew deep down, one day you would return to the company and hopefully pick up where she left off. I don't have any idea what all of her formulas mean. After you decipher them, we should have a better understanding," Payton said.

"All those years Mom drugged us?" Willow asked.

"Don't jump to conclusions," Victory said. "Payton is correct. I will need to study the formulas before we have any idea what she wanted to accomplish."

"But why didn't she tell us?" Willow asked.

"She wanted to protect you. Like any mother, I'm sure she wanted you three to live as normal lives as possible," Tristan said.

"The part I can't figure out," Payton said, "is why the need to hide all her work and to spread her research out in so many different hiding places. You think she knew she was being watched?"

"Like Victory, your mother held the position of a world-renowned scientist. That would lead me to believe she had admirers and even enemies," Tristan said.

"Holy crap," Willow said, nearly leaping up off the sofa. "I gave some of my vitamins to Cassidy."

"Who's Cassidy?" Collin asked.

"She was my roommate through college and graduate school."

"Willow, why would you do such a thing?" Victory asked.

"I thought they were just vitamins. Mom would send me three and four bottles at a time. We were both stressed the first time we had finals. I knew the vitamins helped me, and I offered some to Cassidy. She immediately noticed the difference and even offered to buy them from me."

"How long did she use them?" Victory asked.

"On and off for six years," Willow said.

"Have you kept in touch?" Collin asked.

"Yes, we remained good friends, except she took a new job about a year ago and we kind of lost touch."

"Let's not alarm her yet. I need to review all Mom's research first thing tomorrow. Can you have Jane make four copies of the drive?" Victory said.

"Four?" Payton asked.

"Yes, please. A working copy for me, one to put back in the clock for safekeeping, one for Willow to lock in her safe, and one for my safe. You keep the original up at the house."

Tristan glanced down at his watch. "It's getting late. More than likely none of us have had dinner. Let's head up to the main house."

"Sounds good. You guys go ahead. Can you take the dogs with you? Payton and I will be up shortly," Collin said.

After everyone left the building Collin said, "You probably hate me and you have every reason to."

"What?" Payton asked in surprise. "I don't hate you. I hate myself for what I did to you."

"You did nothing to me. What happened at the ranch was entirely my fault. I knew you were trying to get Dave to drop his gun, and I refocused your energy."

"No, you didn't. It was all me, all my fault."

"Payton, we were connected telepathically. I heard every thought in your mind and I used you to achieve my goals."

"But I thought—" she started.

"You didn't kill Braxton—I did. Until today I thought you had completely closed me out of your life because of the way I used you. Believe me, I didn't blame you one bit. I hoped you would eventually be friendly to me. I didn't know what I would do if you never spoke to me again. Tell me what you remember, and I'll help you fill in the blanks."

Her version of events was exactly as he recalled until the moment Dave put the gun to Emma's head.

"I thought to myself, 'if only I could force Dave to drop the gun, the guys would have a chance to move in.' Then a terrible thought came to me: none of us, including Emma, would really be safe until Braxton was dead. I mentally pushed Dave to shoot him," she said.

"You are correct. Except, the terrible thought you spoke of came from me. I felt a mental conduit emerge between us and used your psychic power for killing. That's who I am, Payton."

"No, that's not who you are. Are you saying you read my mind?"

"Not only read your mind, but sent my thoughts back to you."

"How could that be?"

"We spoke telepathically today, too. I heard you call me and the anguish in your voice. No matter what happens, I will always come when you call me," Collin said.

"I thought my hearing you was merely wishful thinking. I didn't believe you were actually in my mind."

"Will you ever forgive me for what I did to you?" Collin asked.

"Collin, I believe some part of me wanted the same thing, or I would not have let you go through with it. Yes, I forgive you."

"I have to head out again tomorrow. The entire team needs to report to D.C."

"How long will you be gone?"

"It shouldn't be more than a week. I need to know that you will stay on campus while I'm gone. If you must leave, promise me you will have an escort," Collin said.

"I promise."

He pulled her to her feet, dragged her into the warmth of his body, and then kissed her with a passion and longing he had never before felt.

Chapter Thirty

There was a knock on Payton's office door.

"Come in," she said, without a pause in her typing.

"I've made the copies of the flash drive you gave me and I'm walking them over to Victory's lab," Jane said.

"Thanks for getting them done quickly. I'll take them to Victory; I need to speak with her."

Payton peeked into Victory's office and found it empty. She found Victory engrossed and alone in her lab.

"Morning, sis," she said as she entered. "You must have left your house early today. It looks as though you have been at it for a while."

"Yes, Tristan walked me down around seven. He and the guys just left for D.C. Looks as though I have the whole week to myself. I am trying to get a few things cleaned up so I can start on the new information you found," Victory said.

"I have the drives here," Payton said.

"Great. Thanks."

"Can you spare a few minutes for a quick cup of coffee? I have something I want to talk to you about."

"Sure, want to go to the café?" Victory asked.

"No, let's have them deliver. I don't want anyone to overhear."

"I assume you and Collin discussed what happened."

"Yes, we did. He helped me to fit all the pieces together and put the incident to bed once and for all," Payton said.

"I'm happy to hear that. What do you want to talk about?"

"I need to tell you about what happened the day at the helipad and the events yesterday. I can hardly believe I am saying this, but it seems Collin and I have developed a telepathic connection."

"Are you are saying you can actually hear Collin in your mind and he can hear you? You have never had a telepathic connection with anyone else, correct?" Victory asked.

"No, never. I have to say, having someone hear my thoughts is going to take some getting used to."

"Hmm, certainly is an extremely interesting development. Your connection developed under a time of severe stress and emotion, the same way mine and Tristan's developed," Victory said.

"What exactly are you saying?" Payton asked.

"I believe we somehow develop a telepathic connection to the person who is our true soul mate."

"Excuse me?" Payton asked.

"Do you love Collin?"

Payton sat for a moment and thought about her sister's question. Did she love Collin? She couldn't imagine her life without him. He brought her happiness, a feeling of security, passion, and yes…love. Collin had wormed his way into her heart.

"Yes," she finally answered.

"Oh Payton, I'm ecstatic for you," Victory said, as she hugged her sister. She pulled away and looked Payton in the eyes. "You still need to take your relationship slowly. Collin has made great progress, but unfortunately he's not out of the woods yet."

"I don't think any of us are," Payton said. "This leads me to the second reason I am here. Back at the ranch, right after Collin and Tristan found me, we used our abilities to try to locate Emma. I was overcome with psychic power and realized your prediction came true. Not only had my barriers erected themselves without my conscious effort, I also picked up energy coming from the team."

"Nothing unique about that. Since Collin, Morgan, and Tristan all have abilities, I would expect you to register them," Victory said.

"You don't understand what I am saying. Yes, I picked up their abilities, along with Noah and Logan's," Payton said.

"They all have special abilities? Why haven't they said anything? Why didn't General Roberts tell me?" Victory asked.

"Do you think it is possible General Roberts put this team together based solely on their success in the field? Could it be he doesn't actually know the truth regarding them?" Payton asked.

"An interesting thought. I guess we should talk to the team," Victory said.

"Payton, Willow!" Victory screamed, as she ran down the hall. She threw the door to Payton's office wide open, startling the two.

"What in the world?" Willow asked.

"My first real breakthrough. I have deciphered Mom's formula. Collin was right," Victory laughed. "Mom wasn't trying to enhance our abilities, she tried to suppress them."

"Wait. We weren't experiments to her?" Payton asked.

"No. It's what I originally believed. She was trying to curb what Ryker had done to us and stabilize our systems. She wanted us to live full, happy lives and not be burdened by our unnatural attributes. The vitamins she created for us were a DNA suppressant."

"Then why did she keep adjusting them?" Willow asked.

"I'm sure she made slight adjustments each time she saw a change in our behaviors, or if something showed up in our blood work," Victory said.

"And now?" Payton asked.

"Don't you see? It all makes perfect sense now," Victory said.

Payton and Willow looked perplexed.

"The buffers have definitely started wearing off. That's why the sudden changes in Payton's abilities and my abilities. Why our abilities are evolving so rapidly."

"Then why is it I haven't noticed these changes?" Willow asked.

"We will all evolve at different rates. I bet you have experienced small changes; you just haven't noticed them."

"Wonderful," Willow said.

"Can you use Mom's formula to slow down the changes in Collin and Morgan?" Payton asked.

"Mom's formulas were specific to us. Nevertheless, they do have some similarities to the formula that I introduced into Collin's system. With further study and research I should be able to discover the perfect combination," Victory said.

"Victory, will we find ourselves in the same predicament as Collin and Morgan?" Payton asked.

"Not if I can help it. I am counting on the fact that we were born with these abilities and therefore our systems have dealt with them our whole lives, as opposed to Collin and Morgan, who were injected with the DNA and had sudden changes to their systems."

"But, you don't know for sure?" Willow asked.

"No. I will work day and night to find the answers we need," Victory said.

* * * *

Payton looked out her window. The afternoon sun called to her. She could feel fall trying to move into the air. She decided to call it a day and head home to let Parker and Kes enjoy the last rays of the afternoon.

As she walked down the stairs of her building, she felt as though someone was watching her. She looked up and she scanned the campus around her. Up by the tree line, under the identical tree she had found him the first time they had met, sat Collin with Kes and Parker. She smiled and started up the hill toward him.

Collin sat on a blanket between the two dogs. In front of him was a basket, and she could see a bottle of wine poking out of the top.

"We've come a long way. Six months ago you avoided me and took the long way home," Collin said, as he smiled at her.

"Six months ago, I got vertigo just being in your presence," Payton said.

The dogs greeted Payton and then stretched out on the blanket to enjoy the warmth of the sun.

"Sit," Collin said, and patted the spot beside him. "I thought we could enjoy the end of the day with some wine and cheese."

"And what if I didn't leave my office until later?" she asked.

"I gave you a tiny push," Collin said.

"Collin, I didn't even notice. You had better not make a habit of mentally pushing me."

They sipped on the wine, snacked on the goodies in the basket, and soaked up the warm afternoon sun.

"Any other treats in your basket?" she asked.

"One or two," he said. "First I need to ask you a question."

"Sounds serious," she said. She glanced at him and saw a look of conviction on his face. "Collin?"

"I was wondering if you would mind sharing your Dobermans with me?" he asked.

"I would have it no other way." She smiled and hugged him close.

"I hoped you would say that. I need to know one more thing," Collin said.

He pulled the basket closer to him and reached inside, pulling out his hand, palm closed tight. "To make doubly sure we keep your sisters happy, do you like long engagements?"

He opened his hand and she stared at a brilliant square-cut diamond ring with a sapphire-encrusted band.

Her mouth dropped open as she stared at the most spectacular ring she had ever seen.

"I want you to know, Payton Winters, I would pursue you to the end of time, for you are my heart and soul. I know your sisters want us to take it slow—"

"Oh Collin, it's perfect. Yes, I would love a long engagement," Payton said.

Payton finally realized her pursuit had come full circle. This was her time—time to make a mark on the family company and to enjoy her family and her Dobermans. Her time to grab each and every moment and squeeze out every last drop of happiness. Her time for a soul mate and true love. She would not let even one more second pass. She would live, thrive, and love her time. Whatever obstacles still lay ahead, and she knew there would be many, they would face them together.

ABOUT THE AUTHOR

Joanne was born and raised in Sherburne, New York, a quaint village surrounded by dairy farms and rolling hills. From the moment she could read she wanted to explore the world. During her college years she slowly crept across the country, stopping along the way in Oklahoma, California, and finally Washington State, which she now proudly calls home. She lives with her husband and Dobermans, in their home located on the Olympic Peninsula with a panoramic view of the Olympic Mountains.

Joanne writes romantic suspense, paranormal, and contemporary romance. She loves to submerge herself in the world of her characters, to live and breathe their lives and marvel at their decisions and predicaments. She enjoys a wide variety of books including paranormal, suspense, thriller, and of course romance.

Joanne is a PAN member of Romance Writers of America, (RWA), Kiss of Death, (KOD), Greater Seattle Romance Writers Chapter, (GSRWA), Sisters In Crime, and past President of Peninsula Romance Writers, which was Debbie Macomber's home chapter.

MEDIA LINKS~

Email: joannejaytanie@wavecable.com
Website: http://www.joannejaytanie.com/
Blog: http://www.authorjoannejaytanie.blogspot.com/
Facebook: https://www.facebook.com/pages/Joanne-
	Jaytanie-Author/146892025475388
Amazon Author Page:
	http://www.amazon.com/Joanne-
	Jaytanie/e/B00C3458YE/
Twitter: https://twitter.com/joannejaytanie
Pinterest: http://www.pinterest.com/joannejaytanie/
Linkedin: http://www.linkedin.com/pub/joanne-
	jaytanie/61/52b/532/
Goodreads:
https://www.goodreads.com/author/show/7063660.Jo
	anne_Jaytanie
Romance Books 4 Us:
	http://romancebooks4us.com/Joanne_Jaytanie.
html
AUTHORSdb: http://authorsdb.com/authors-
	directory/14114-joanne-jaytanie
Sisters In Crime: http://sistersincrime.site-
	ym.com/members/?id=39477337

OTHER BOOKS BY JOANNE

Chasing Victory ~ Book One of The Winters Sisters
Willow's Discovery ~
     Book Three of The Winters Sisters
Corralling Kenzie ~ Book Four of The Winters Sisters
P.I. ~I Love You
Love's Always Paws-Able
Christmas Reflections
Christmas Ivy
Building Up To Love
Uncharted Love

Made in the USA
Monee, IL
09 January 2021

57030085R00193